Fay Weldon

was born in England and raised i.. ......y or women in
New Zealand. She took degrees in Economics and
Psychology at the University of St Andrews in Scotland and
then, after a decade of odd jobs and hard times, began
writing fiction. She is now well known as novelist,
screenwriter and critic; her work is translated the world
over. Her novels include, most famously, *The Life and Loves
of a She-Devil* (a major movie starring Meryl Streep and
Roseanne Barr), *Puffball*, *The Hearts and Lives of Men*, *The
Cloning of Joanna May*, *Growing Rich* and *Life Force*. She has
four sons, and lives in London.

FAY WELDON

Darcy's Utopia

Flamingo
An Imprint of HarperCollins*Publishers*

Flamingo
An Imprint of HarperCollins*Publishers*
77–85 Fulham Palace Road,
Hammersmith, London W6 8JB

Special overseas edition 1990
This edition published by Flamingo 1991
9 8 7 6 5 4 3 2

First published in Great Britain by
William Collins Sons & Co Ltd 1990

Photograph of Fay Weldon © Mark Gerson FBIPP

ISBN 0 00 654592 0

Set in Baskerville

Printed in Great Britain by
The Guernsey Press Co. Ltd, Guernsey, Channel Islands.

Darcy's Utopia

Eleanor Darcy is interviewed by Hugo Vansitart

A: Well now, you ask, what is this thing called love? To give you a simple answer – love is enough to make you believe in God. It is the evidence you need which proves the benign nature of the universe. Love heightens your perceptions: it makes the air you breathe beautiful. It lets you know you are alive. It makes the news on the radio irrelevant; it turns the television into flickers. Love places you in the very centre of the universe; the knowledge that in your lover's eyes you replace God can only be gratifying. It makes you immortal: love, after all, being for ever. It makes you vulnerable as a kitten in case you're wrong, in case love is not forever. One booted kick from the real world, you fear, and splat will go the kitten's head against the wall, and that's you finished. Yet fate weaves its heady patterns all around, good luck attends you, nobody boots you. That's what I mean by love.

In Darcy's Utopia all men will believe in God and all men will be capable of love.

Q: By men, do you mean women too?

> *The journalist did his best to be cautious in his questions, friendly in his manner. Public interest in Darcian Monetarism remained lively, although Professor Darcy was now perforce silent, being in prison. Eleanor Darcy, his wife, seldom gave interviews. When she did they were expensive; moreover, she had a reputation for taking offence, throwing journalists quite out of the house. Hugo Vansitart did not want this to happen to him.*

A: Of course. As in any legal document, the greater includes the lesser. He incorporates she. Well, that's what love is all about.

Q: I am relieved to hear this, Mrs Darcy. I had feared that, having already banned money in this perfectly wonderful, perfectly nonexistent society you hold in your head, this Darcy's Utopia of yours, you might ban love as well! But you won't, will you?

A: Good heavens, no. The whole place will be riddled with it. Love will serve as our entertainment: it will have to, since there is to be no TV. I do not, by the way, see Darcy's Utopia as a perfectly wonderful place. Let us say, simply, that it is a workable society, as ours, increasingly, is not. But I haven't finished with love. Let me get on. Love flatters women more than it does men. It makes the hair shine and the eyes glow; it cures spots. The woman in love attracts: lovers come in shoals or not at all. The man in love is somehow denatured. He can repel even the woman loved. The smile on the face of the man in love, as he draws near, can disconcert: there can seem something unmanly in such devotion, yet behind that unmanliness is the Devilish intent – and I do not mean that the deed he, and indeed you, intend is Devilish, rather that the sense of his being helpless in the face of carnal desire, driven on by it, seems to come from the Devil, not God – God tending to the hesitant, the tentative, in his works, and that perhaps is why the smile can seem false, soppy and indulgent; but soon the face is too near for you to see the smile, and you and he are one, so who cares? These things flicker on the edge of consciousness, are easily pushed down.

Q: Aren't you talking about yourself, Mrs Darcy?

Outside, above quiet streets, clouds parted and a ray of sunlight pierced the white net curtains to dapple Mrs Darcy's lean and handsome face. How green her eyes were! She moved to be out of the light, towards him rather than away from him. He found himself pleased. He was taking notes, not liking to rely only upon tapes in so important an interview. His writing was a little shaky. Had his hand been trembling?

A: Yes. Of course. But what is true for me is probably true for you, and everyone else. Love gives folk a sense of singularity and a wonderful overflow of benevolence. Quite giddily one skips about. You must have found that?

Q: I'm sorry, no. But then I'm not a particularly giddy person. Shall we get back to the role of money in a perfect society?

A: Not giddy? What, never? Good Lord, we must see to that! Satan, of course, sometimes puts in a literal appearance, just as does the Virgin Mary. My first husband Bernard actually saw the Devil, flesh and blood, bones, horns and claws, hovering outside the window, and a second floor window at that, of one of those concrete blocks for student accommodation they have at polytechnics.

Q: Didn't that give him a nasty turn?

> *When Hugo Vansitart asked this question he bounced a little. He and his subject sat on a shiny sofa, black shantung with great red roses splodged across it. The springs were broken. When she moved, he moved. It was disconcerting.*

A: You are laughing at me. You must try not to. Really, the world is not as you think it is. If these interviews are to be successful, you must try and be more open, less rigid. Giddier, in fact. The Devil did indeed put in an appearance, and very horrible and frightening it was. Bernard was not even in love at the time. But he was between belief structures, and into the vacuum left by both the Catholic and Marxist faiths, had rushed what the Russians used to refer to as 'metaphysical intoxication' – under which heading they would lock up the socially and politically excitable for their own sake and that of society. Thought bounced round the inside of poor Bernard's head like a ball in a squash court. It made him guilty and therefore vulnerable. Reason and ridicule can get rid of faith: but the guilt and the fear of punishment associated with free thinking remain. Besides, a curse had been put on him. Certain people he had offended were trying to frighten him. It was not all that surprising that the Devil materialized in front of his eyes. Yes, indeed, to answer your question, he was not expecting it and it gave him a nasty turn.

> *He noticed that there were grease spots on the sofa. Smeared butter, Hugo thought, left by the children of this household, this hell-hole of suburban domesticity. Already he had jam on his cuff, gained somehow in the walk from front door to sofa. Surely it was possible for Eleanor Darcy to receive him somewhere more suitable. This was not even, it appeared, her own house. It belonged to the mother of the four small children who racketed behind the thin plywood door.*

Q: Your views on love are of course interesting, but not quite pertinent to the series of articles I envisage writing. I wonder if by any chance your husband left any of his unpublished work in your care? If so, could I see it?

A: How you try to divide the world up into sections! It won't work, Mr Vansitart. We must deal with God and the Devil, love and sex, before we get on to economics, party politics, big business, education, crime and the rest. We must establish a framework for our house before we start putting up planks, or they'll only fall down again. I have not yet finished with love. Hyper-inflationary monetarism will come in due course.

Q: But love is the proper province of women's magazines, Mrs Darcy, surely?

A: Do you think so? If you think that, you will most certainly have to have your male consciousness raised!

> *She laughed, but he understood that she was angry. Her face paled. She was beautiful. She enchanted him. He did not know what was happening, what was about to happen. Someone came in with coffee, in mugs. 'Thank you,*

*Brenda,' said Eleanor. He sipped: the coffee
was bad. It had been made from powder and
with tepid water. Dislike of it returned him to
his senses.*

Q: I'm sorry. Won't you please go on?

A: Better to be in love than to be loved, but a state more difficult
to attain. If in the seesaw of affections balance is attained, when
each loves the other equally yet still desperately, why then there
is the presence of God, and paradise: only then what happens is
that we start longing for the snake to arrive and create a diversion,
because we know this intensity of experience cannot be sustained:
because we are, when it comes to it, on earth: and if this pitch of
experience continues too long life itself will be worn away. The
body, however empowered, entranced, in its delightfully sweaty
transports, cannot support for long the trust placed in it by God.
These things are meant for heaven, not earth. Young lovers,
understanding this, will sometimes take themselves off to heaven
by means of suicide pacts to escape the growing past, as much as
a diminishing future. What is the point, having discovered what
life on earth is all about, of going on with it? This world is a
stop-over on the way to heaven: those of us who are in love don't
need Mohammed or Jesus to tell us so, or lay down rules to get
us there – we're on our way and don't mind hurrying up. Or we
wouldn't be so careless of our health and safety. Hi there, darling!
we cry, stepping under a bus in our eagerness to embrace and be
embraced. Hi there!

Failing death, we invoke the snake. How we long for the snake!
Love is like herpes –

Q: Could you repeat that?

A: Love is like genital herpes: once it has infected you it's there
for ever. it stands by, waiting, requiring only certain conditions to
bring it out. Debilitation, for herpes. A surplus of energy, for love.
Forgive me the analogy: I know it is distasteful. But, as you will
see, appropriate.

She was, he thought, poised somewhere between the male and the female: a strong, androgynous, chiselled face. Green witch's eyes. He wanted them to see him, not the journalist; when it came to it, he preferred her talking to him about love, not addressing him as if he were a political meeting. His body stirred, his hand stretched out. Carefully she replaced it, and went on talking.

Q: Perhaps we could continue this interview over dinner? I am supposed to be at a function but I could easily forgo it.

A: I think it would be better not. Let me continue. The tendency of everything in the universe is to even out, seek its own level, as water does: any gross imbalance of good and evil cannot, alas, last. God strikes down into the flat amorality of everyday existence; a bored and irritated power determined to make things Good; the Devil, likeways, elects to make things bad. Look at the way your hand moved just now, following the dictates of your heart, or more precisely, your lust. It is part of the curse placed upon my ex-husband Bernard by the brat Nerina and her cohorts that I arouse these feelings in men. Their power is fading now: so long as they don't start dancing and prancing round their dead goats or whatever and stir the whole thing up again, all may yet be well. Teenagers are hell.

As for me, temporarily out of love, working on my blueprint for the future, and pleased enough to rest from my task for a while, and do this lengthy, all-but exclusive interview with you; let me tell you that, like Bernard, but unlike Julian my second husband, I am not immune to terror.

That is enough for today, Mr Vansitart. Foolish questions, patient answers. Though I daresay you see it the other way round. I must help my friend Brenda put her children to bed.

Valerie Jones is surprised by Joy

Love struck like a whirlwind. I was not expecting it. I did not want it. I, Valerie Jones, a married woman in a good job, with as contented a home life as could reasonably be expected, went in a very ordinary little black dress to a Media Awards Dinner, and was seated next to Hugo Vansitart. I was about to say 'quite by chance' but it was of course our destiny. He arrived late: too late for the prawn pâté – lucky him, I said – but in time for the chicken. There was an instant rapport between us. My husband Lou had not come with me: he hates these affairs: the massing together, as he describes it, of the chattering classes. Or was it because he was in Stuttgart, or Stockholm, or somewhere, playing his violin? I can't remember. It doesn't matter. Nor was Hugo's wife Stef with him. She was in Washington, interviewing the Pope. Or someone, somewhere. I just remember thinking that's the wrong person in the wrong place, how odd. Would it have made a difference if Lou had been there, or Stef had been there? I don't think so.

Of course I knew Hugo Vansitart by his by-line. He is one of our leading political journalists. When I saw his name on the place card I thought, Oh dear, he'll be bored by me. He's much too clever for me. I am features editor of a leading women's magazine – a weekly. *Aura*. We're intelligent enough, I hope, but naturally, considering our market, are more concerned with matters of human interest than anything particularly intellectual. I didn't want Hugo Vansitart to hold my magazine against me: define me by my employers. I had not expected him to be so good-looking. I scarcely liked to look at his face, at first. He just sat down beside me, brooding, dark, vaguely squarish, decidedly male, filling an empty place which had made me feel uneasy. He was late, he said, because he'd done the first of a series of interviews with the Bride of Rasputin out in the suburbs somewhere beside a distant railway line. It had taken him forever to get back to the centre of things. 'Good heavens!' I said. 'Eleanor Darcy! I'm to see her tomorrow. What a coincidence!'

He laid his hand on mine and said oh, dear, he thought he'd had an exclusive: the editor of the *Independent* wasn't going to like this one bit: I said, well, everyone likes to be the only one, in newspapers as in life, but I didn't think he should worry. We might overlap but we would not coincide. He was no doubt doing his pieces on the Bridport Scandal and the phenomena of Darcian Economics: I had been commissioned by my magazine to do a serialized biography of Eleanor Darcy herself. A kind of docudrama for the lay reader.
'Did she approach the magazine, or the magazine approach her?' was the first thing he asked.
'She approached us.'
He did not ask me how much *Aura* was paying, though I knew he badly wanted to. I told him later, in bed. She had asked for a hundred thousand pounds: we were paying half that. Though an interest in Darcian Economics persisted, my editor's opinion, when presented with the demand, was that the public had begun to shift its attention from Eleanor Darcy. Rasputin, Julian Darcy, was famous: the Bride of Rasputin, rightly or wrongly, notorious. Fame is worth twice as much as notoriety. She asked for a hundred thousand pounds, she got fifty thousand pounds. There seemed a kind of journalistic sense in this.
'How do you find Mrs Darcy?' I asked. 'What kind of person is she?'
'Interesting,' he said. 'She talks a lot, not always about what one wants to know. Be sure to ask her about the Devil.'
'Better,' I said, 'that she talks too much than too little. Easier to cut than to pad.'

He said he supposed so. He said how remarkable it was that we should be sitting together. Himself about to write the gospel of Julian Darcy according to Hugo Vansitart, myself the gospel of Eleanor Darcy according to Valerie Jones. Great trust had clearly been put in us. His forefinger moved over mine. It was strange.

So sudden, so unlikely, and yet so right, so fitting. I sat there in my boring little black dress, rather too thin and flat-chested for fashion, too old for comfort – as thirty-nine is – my hair cut too short that very day, in a wrong-headed attempt at sleekness, and felt my whole being lurch out of one state into another. I was all confident spirit – no longer blemished flesh. Then I heard my name being called. I'd actually won Feature Writer of the Year, Women's Media Division. I got to my feet, worked out my route to the top table – I had in no way expected this honour – looked back at Hugo, and we exchanged smiles – or rather committed some kind of Act of Complicity, in which he summonsed and I acquiesced. I had never done such a thing before.

'All treats,' Hugo said, when I returned with my metal statuette – no cheque, alas – 'all treats tonight. Would you like to hear my Eleanor Darcy tapes?'

I said I would and we went to a Holiday Inn together, one of the rather grand, central city ones, which are anonymous as well as luxurious, and hideously expensive, but the beds are huge and the bathrooms good. I listened to Eleanor Darcy's tape and tried to concentrate upon it. 'She should not be so insulting to women's magazines,' I remember saying. Then it was all extraordinary. Why me, I kept thinking, why me, this is so amazing, so out of character, this is not the way I live. One early boyfriend, one husband, now this: myself, surprised by joy.

In the morning he said, 'What will they say at home?'
I said, 'I don't care. What about you?'
He said, 'Neither do I. Shall we stay here? Live here? Together?'
I said, 'Why not? It could hardly be more expensive than living at home.'
And we both knew I lied but who cared?
He said, 'Without home to distract us we could both do our pieces on Eleanor Darcy without others complaining, without children demanding. My tapes will help you, your tapes will help me.'
I said, 'We'll distract each other.'
He said, 'But only in a supportive kind of way. We'll get the balance right. We're both workaholics. We'll fuse.'

They had good office services at the Holiday Inn. They even provided us with word processors, IBM compatible; one each, it being a double room. I went down the road to Marks & Spencer for clothes. Mostly just satin slips and wraps and so on – I didn't see myself going out much. What for? I called my number. Lou had put the answerphone on. The children would have got themselves to school. They were competent enough. My main function in the home, I remarked to Hugo, was as Witness to the Life. I left a message to say I had left home.

I gave my new telephone number to *Aura*, and settled down to love Hugo and prepare to write the life and times of Eleanor Darcy. Hugo went home once to fetch a suitcase, and was back within the hour. We did not wish to lose a minute of each other's bodies, each other's company, if it could possibly be helped. We had each other, we had our work, we had room service – what more did we need? We were well and truly happy. I had never felt the emotion before: nor, he said, had he.

From Valerie Jones' first interview with Eleanor Darcy

A: I will not overburden you with my views on Darcy's Utopia, the multiracial, unicultural, secular society the world must aim for if it is to have any hope of a future. I know you will simply leave it all out when you come to write your history of my life. I know you are concerned with what you call the human-interest angle, how I came to be who and what and where I am. But I have been created by a society interacting with a self: you can't have one without the other. You will hold me up to other women as an example, how to start life in a back street as Apricot Smith, an untidy, misbegotten child; be promoted to Ellen Parkin, working wife of the ordinary down-at-heel hate-the-government kind; and to become the true love and wife of Professor Julian Darcy, Vice Chancellor of the University of Bridport.

You don't care that Darcian Monetarism and the Bridport Scandal changed the thinking of nations: you just want to know how it was that in three decades God and the Devil between them managed to promote me from Apricot to Eleanor, by way of Ellen. And yes, it was promotion. As Eleanor Darcy I can go anywhere: it's like a little black frock: you can dress it up with diamonds, dress it down with a cotton scarf: it always looks right. As Ellen Parkin I was only fit to run down to the corner shop in my slippers, or queue up for family benefit. And who would be interested in Parkin's Utopia? Darcy's Utopia has a much more convincing ring. Parkin smacks of small back streets and long-term illness – what's left when the Devil has flown, sucking love out of you as he goes, leaving a burned-out patch behind. Names are magic, believe me. Better to be out of love as Eleanor Darcy than Ellen Parkin. The Ellen Parkins of the world love only once, and if it goes wrong give up.

Q: But you don't change your nature by changing your name, surely?

A: Oh yes, you do. My advice to everyone is to change their name at once if they're the least unhappy with their lives. In Darcy's Utopia everyone will choose a new name at seven, at eleven, at sixteen and at twenty-four. And naturally women at forty-five, or when the last child has grown up and left home, whichever is the earliest, will rename themselves. Then life will be seen to start over, not finish. It is a perfectly legal thing to do, even in this current fearful and unkind society of ours; no deed poll is required. So long as there is no intent to defraud, anyone can call themselves anything at all. But so many of us, either feeling our identities to be fragile, or out of misplaced loyalty to our parents, feel we must stick with the names we start out with. The given name is a dead giveaway of our parents' ambition for us – whether to diminish or enhance, ignore us as much as possible or control us forever – and the family name betrays our social origins. No, it will not do. It will have to change.

Q: I see. You spoke earlier of the Devil. Our readers are not so domestic as you suppose – any article on Good and Evil enjoys high readership figures. Do you believe in the Devil?

A: Of course. It's unsafe not to. And what a grand creature the Devil is in himself! How he sucks energy even from where he stands! He is all temporary fire and sparks, terror and drama, whisked up out of nowhere: but when he flies off you see the real damage that has been done: something permanently denatured, altogether seedy and totally ignoble. To believe in God is to believe in the Devil. It is quite an insult to God to deny the Devil's existence.

In Darcy's Utopia, men will believe in the Devil in the sense that they will be sensitive to the forces working away within even the best planned of their social structures, bent on their destruction. As it is with people, so it is with these social structures – by which I mean the government, the church, the civil service, educational and caring organizations, lobbies, societies for this and that, quangos and so forth and so on. Wherever, in fact, people are gathered together in the interests of the better and more humane organization of society, there the Devil lurks. The greater the striving for good, the nearer the approach to it, alas, the harder and sharper the fall. In Darcy's Utopia everyone will understand that the more extreme and present the good appears, the more pressing the danger that it will be promptly overthrown. Oh yes, in Darcy's Utopia we will be on our guard. We will be vigilant and, what's more, will understand what we must be vigilant about. We will not hide behind abstract terms such as 'freedom', 'liberty', 'justice', 'dignity'. We will have lesser words, with more meaning.

Q: Talking about words, Mrs Darcy, what a pretty and unusual name Apricot is. How did you come by that? Was your mother particularly fond of fruit?

A: There was not much fruit about when I was a child. Sometimes we had sliced peaches for afters. So far as I'm aware, my mother named me after her brushed nylon nightie.

Q: You have a very soft voice. The tape recorder may not be picking up everything you say. I wouldn't want to lose a word of it. Can you speak more closely into the mike? Her brushed nylon nightie, did you say?

A: That is what I said. There are a number of press cuttings which will help you as to the detail of my early life and times, and here in this folder are a few brief autobiographical sketches I happen to have written over the years. I hope you can read my writing. Do what you can with the material you have, and come back to me with any questions, or just for a chat. I have been rather out of circulation lately, preparing my magnum opus for publication. It's good to be back in the world again.

Q: A magnum opus?

A: A blueprint for Darcy's Utopia.

Q: You've found time for that as well?

A: As well as what?

Q: The court case must have taken up quite a lot of nervous energy.

A: My husband was on trial, not I.

Q: But Darcy's Utopia is a kind of memorial to your husband?

A: He is not dead, Miss Jones, merely in prison. I am sure he would argue very strongly against many of my proposals, were he around to do so. I have borrowed his name because I like it, for no other reason. Besides, it is my name as much as his. After all, we are married.

Q: Of course. I'm sorry.

A: I think it is time to draw this interview to a close. We are going out for a healthy walk. I hear Brenda putting on the children's wellies, against their wishes. Children do so like to go barefooted in the rain. Do you have children, Mrs Jones?

Q: I have two.

A: Lucky old you. I have none. Will you show yourself out? I have been sitting on my leg, and it's gone to sleep.

Valerie gets one or two things wrong

I am not usually nervous about my work. Compared to home, in fact, work is a piece of cake. Many women report the same thing. It is easier to please an employer than a family: a liberation to have a job description, a joy to be free of the burden of peace-keeping. Mediating in the home is like trying to knead a piece of dough the size of a house: get it down here and it surges up there. Compared to all this employment is a piece of cake, yes indeed: or rather a nice firm crisp yeastless biscuit. And I take the view that those who employ me must take some of the blame when things go wrong. I am what I am – I do what I can. If I can't, more fool them for asking me in the first place. And because I am not anxious, I do well. Me, Valerie Jones, Features Writer of the Year! The pleasure which suffuses out from between my agreeably bruised and battered loins is, when I can get round to defining it, the more intense for this unexpected infusion of worldly accomplishment. Valerie Jones, a success!

The trouble is I have committed myself, through my editor, to writing the life of Eleanor Darcy. I can't take on the extra freelance commissions which will now come my way. On the very afternoon of the Media Awards Dinner I signed a contract with *Aura* undertaking to work exclusively on the project until delivery of the ms. Well, I will just have to work hard and get it done quickly. Fortunately, sex with Hugo takes up less time than, to be blunt, not-enough-sex with Lou. There is no time wasted teacup washing, dinner-party chatting, tense family-outering – the things we all do to pretend to ourselves and the world that there is more to marriage than sex. I can simply get into bed with Hugo and out of it to get on with *Lover at the Gate*, as Eleanor Darcy wishes the work to be called. I should feel guilt, remorse, doubt, distress, despair and so forth: I don't. I should be in some kind of shock, but I am not. I should be debating the wisdom of my actions; I do not. I do not look into the future beyond the delivery of the manuscript. Why should I? Let the coins fall as they will: in due course it will become apparent whether they were heads or tails.

So if I get one or two things wrong in my account of Eleanor Darcy's life, I tell myself, it will be her responsibility as much as mine. She chose *Aura*, *Aura* chose me. I repeat – I am what I am, I do what I can. Mrs Darcy does not make matters easier than she can help. I have the feeling she does not like me very much. She threw a few grains of fact at me during the course of the interview, as if she were scattering crumbs for a hopping sparrow. If I were working for the *New Statesman* or the *Economist* I would obviously have more interest in Darcy's Utopia. I have in fact written pieces for both these publications. Because I am currently working for *Aura* does not mean I'm an idiot. I just need to know why her mother called her Apricot, and time is short, because both interviewer and interviewee get tired, and besides, I wanted to get home to Hugo.

Nor did she make things easy for me. Her voice is soft and low and she kept moving out of recording range. She once even said, 'If it's not on the tape, just make it up: it will be more interesting to your readers,' which I thought rather insulting to me: certainly it made me feel diminished in my profession. Journalists are trained to report accurately what they are told, and to come to honest rather than convenient conclusions. We are, as Eleanor made me realize, alarmingly dependent on the veracity of our informants: we come to expect lies or half-lies in some few areas – age, or income, and those in public life will often fail to reveal their true opinions in their attempt to present an acceptable face to the world – but outside these areas the natural inclination of most folk is to speak the truth if they possibly can. They don't speak of themselves and the world as if it were some kind of fictional creation which can be rewritten and subedited at will, as if one version of it were as valid as another. They do not normally pull visions of the Devil, as Mrs Darcy did in her interview with Hugo, out of a hat, to divert and deflect: they do not insist on fusing truth with utopian notions, especially when they have the nerve to charge fifty thousand pounds for the privilege. I daresay Eleanor Darcy thinks money grows out of everyone's ears. It might, for *Aura*, if she were more inclined to talk about the ordinary things of life, such as what she gives her friends for Christmas or what she reads on holiday.

Another thing: Eleanor Darcy is not a *still* person, a *quiet* person, as I am, or try to be. During our interview she quite frankly wriggled. First one leg over the other, then the other over the one: torso first this way then that, sometimes slouching; only once, when talking about her period as Bride of Rasputin, Vice Chancellor's wife at Bridport, did she sit in what I would describe as an ordinary, decorous and ladylike fashion. Although the room was not particularly warm, she wore only a white T-shirt – well, whitish: like so many others nowadays no doubt she uses a phosphate-free environment-friendly washing powder – and jeans. Energetic people, those whose minds and bodies are active, seem, if not to notice the cold, at least to rather enjoy being so. To go about without the vest, without the wellies, without the coat, is to some people as smoking is to others, a celebration of freedom, of coming of age, of an escape from parental control. 'You can't go out like that,' says the mother, 'it's freezing!' And the rest of life is spent without a coat.

Eleanor Darcy said she was thirty: I would give her thirty-four or five. She is good-looking enough but not stunningly beautiful: I am always surprised at the plainness of women for whom men develop irrational and obsessive passions, as Julian Darcy clearly had for Eleanor. How else to explain the events leading up to the Bridport Scandal? Napoleon's Josephine was a little, spotty thing: Nelson's Lady Hamilton a fat and blowsy piece. Eleanor Darcy is intelligent, of course, and intelligence in a woman does turn some men on, though not many. Hugo, thank God, is one of the few.

Intelligence, I have always thought, makes it difficult for a woman to wear make-up: perhaps it's as simple a matter as the mobility of a face making the stuff sink in, vanish, fail to remain the smoothing mask it's meant to be. Eleanor Darcy's skin was *patchy*: she was using too dark a shade of foundation cream. She had smudged a little grey eye shadow around the eye area and lip-lined her mouth rather crudely, failing to fill in with actual colour as most people do: her brown hair frizzed out round her head in a rather uneven halo. I don't think it had been permed, merely squidged and scrunched as it dried. By and large she seemed disinclined to pay her appearance much attention, as if there were other far more urgent things to attend to. The mothers of small children often look like this, as we know, but Eleanor didn't even have this excuse. Her legs were muscular – the jeans were tight: perhaps she had put on weight recently – and she had a strong neck and a firm chin, a shiny nose and bright rather deep-set eyes. People's appearances, of course, add up to more than the sum of their features. A kind of overall impression is delivered, which is sometimes belied by actual detail and is more, I suppose, to do with confidence than anything else. The fact is that Eleanor Darcy looked and acted as if she were Queen of the World, as if to be the one to bring down a government was all in the day's work and she was now turning her attention to the future. I tried not to resent it. I tried to like her, not to be awed by her: to match the power of her vigorous mind with the centring energy I felt in me, by virtue of the fact that Hugo loved me. I did not, as it were, go empty handed into that bargaining chamber, and I was grateful for it.

She spoke, as I would have expected, in mid-English: a kind of neutral middle-classedness which blurred her origins: the kind used by lady news presenters on networked TV. But listen carefully, and occasionally the sloppy vowels of the suburbs would seep through to betray her origins: and even the slight nasal whine of the rather more underprivileged. The child's experience of life comes through in the adult's use of language – whether the desire to escape the original background altogether, or to camouflage, defiantly to accept, or, by denying, to get out into the world and get on. Eleanor Darcy, I had no doubt of it, had been a brave and ambitious child.

She was at home, yet not at home, in her friend Brenda's house. Brenda is a former school friend, who has so definite a 'no comment' policy as to be of very little help to *Aura*'s readership. She is the mother of four children under seven, and I think in the circumstances remarkably loyal to Eleanor, who lounges around

24

her living room, sprawling, filling up time and space, talking about subjects way above Brenda's head, though Brenda told me, as I left – as well as she could for trying to get on the children's boots – that in fact she ran the local branch of the Labour Party and was active in environmental matters. It is always a mistake to suppose people to be *ordinary*, just because they have four children under seven and a low income. Almost no one is ordinary. Dig a little into 'ordinary' lives and you find passion, desperation, amazing acts of self-sacrifice and self-control and often powerful religious belief. It is only when the ordinary are suddenly elevated to the ranks of the un-ordinary that both their virtues and their eccentricities become apparent. Brenda, nevertheless, does still seem rather stubbornly ordinary, as does her house, a new semi-detached on a slip road in an outer suburb. It has the virtuous shabbiness of the home of a good mother of four, whose husband is a mini-cab driver – that is to say is doing the best he can while getting his act together. Brenda brought us, without complaint or comment, many cups of caffeine-free instant coffee during the course of the interview. I can scarcely even remember what she looks like, except that her skirt was too tight and her stomach bulged, as stomachs do when you have had four children in a short time and are too unselfish to take the time to exercise. Her taste in slip covers for her three-piece suite was not good. Red roses on shiny black fabric is out of place in a humble suburban house, when the carpet is rough, serviceable hessian and toys pile up in the corners of rooms, and not even the most dedicated can find the time or energy to move them: if indeed there is anywhere to move them to. Hugo complained that the sofa was greasy and he got jam on his cuff. I did not think he would give much column space to Brenda. Readers do not pay to read about the likes of themselves.

But I may be wrong. One interview with Eleanor Darcy, some nights with Hugo, and I can already see I may be wrong about many things. My mind may, creaking and protesting, have to go into some new gear, as my body has already done, leading the way. I had always assumed that journalists – all professional people, in fact – should keep their work life and their love life apart, were they young and foolish enough to have the latter. I was wrong. I could see lust quite remarkably sharpening the edge of my writing. I had been married to Lou for fifteen years; our children, Sophie and Ben, were now thirteen and twelve. We had led a peaceful organized and unpassionate family life. If I had never been tempted to mix my professional and my personal life, it was because the opportunity to do so, alas, had not arisen. I had seen myself, as I had Lou, as the kind of person who has just about enough sexual energy when young to get it together with a member of the opposite sex and start a family and then leave all that kind of thing to others. I was wrong. All I had done was lower my sights, in the interests of respectability, moderation and a quiet life, and presented myself to the world as someone altogether ladylike, altogether a-sexual. It had worked so far and no further. I had been seated next to Hugo at dinner. Love had struck like lightning, leapt with the whirlwind; I loved, I worked, I thought, I felt, and there was no separating any of them out, or wanting to. Thus prepared, I will insert a new computer disc and begin *Lover at the Gate*.

Eleanor Darcy's birth

'I think I feel a pain,' said Wendy Ellis, Eleanor Darcy's mother. It was the middle of the night, in the summer of a year somewhere between 1959 and 1964. Wendy lay in bed next to her boyfriend Ken. Wendy was twenty-one and wore an apricot-coloured shortie nightie in brushed nylon. Her hair, for all she was eight months and one week pregnant, had that day been coiffeured, lacquered and backcombed until it stuck out all around her head. Wendy lay on her back. No other position was comfortable. Ken lay beside her, stiff and tense, not able to sleep. Her body was warm and relaxed; she had no choice in the matter. The baby dictated things such as maternal temperature and tension. It seemed to have no power to affect the father. Ken had come home late from a gig he had not enjoyed. He played banjo for a living and did a little woodwork on the side: fitting a bathroom here, a kitchen there, anywhere but at home.
'I think he's on the way,' said Wendy.
'She,' said Ken.
'He,' said Wendy. 'I know it's a boy.'
'We only have girls in our family,' said Ken. He had five sisters.

Ken was twenty-eight. He had a round pink face, little bright eyes, a small body, a lot of fair hair, quick fingers, a quick mind, and a great deal of energy. He was no beauty, women agreed, but he had charm. A twinkle from the back of the band and they were his. If he wanted, which he told Wendy he didn't, now he had her. Tonight he was tired and contrary. Anger had tired him. What he described as the class system had rendered him contrary. A private party: mostly Rolls-Royce dealers: five hours' practically non-stop playing: family favourites only: raised eyebrows if the band took a break; stale ham sandwiches and bright yellow orange squash the only meal provided, part of the deal, and ten pounds for the whole band divided by five. Not enough. The guests drank champagne. The men wore dinner jackets: they brayed; the women evening dress and squealed. The band wore dinner jackets too, the girl singer more jewels than the lady guests, but Ken had sussed that one a long time ago. It was a joke played by the haves against the have-nots. You don't work for money, the haves conceded, all you want is to be near us in order to become us. So dress like us for an hour or so: come close, come closer: brush up against us if that's what you want. We'll dance to your tune the happier, syphon off your magic the better. Then take your money and go. Back to your hovels. Now he was back in his hovel and naked, lying next to a girl who was having a baby and had moved in with him on that account.

'If you only have girls in your family,' said Wendy, 'how come you exist?' She was quarrelsome. That too the baby seemed to dictate. She thought perhaps the baby was very clever: her friends remarked upon how sharp she'd got since she became pregnant. It stood to reason, Wendy thought, that the mother–baby connection worked both ways. With every child you had, you'd get infected with that baby's qualities. The 'friends' were mostly girls at work: she had to have those independently of Ken. Ken tended to put people off. He slept when he was sleepy, ate when he was hungry, only talked if he had something to say, whether there were guests in the house or not. Wendy liked him the way he was. He made her feel real. She would rather have him than a hundred friends.

'By mistake,' said Ken sharply. 'Go to sleep.'

'I can't,' said Wendy. 'I keep getting this pain.'

'I didn't hear that,' said Ken. 'I'm so tired I'm deaf,' and he fell asleep. She soothed his brow for a little. He smiled in his sleep. Wendy rang her mother.

'I keep getting this pain,' Wendy whispered. 'Do you think it's the baby?'

'You woke me up,' whispered Rhoda. 'It's only indigestion. You've three weeks to go and first babies are always late.'

'If they're always late,' said Wendy, a little more loudly, 'then they're not late, they're just normal. First babies just take longer to hatch than other babies. So why don't they admit it? Why do they insist all babies take the same time?'

'I don't know what you're talking about,' whispered Rhoda. The phone was by the bed and her husband Bruno slept by her side. Bruno was Wendy's father. He was Italian. He had grey hair and a black moustache which rose and fell as he breathed. Rhoda liked to see it. He stirred and woke and stretched out his hand towards her in an enquiring and generous fashion. Ken, beside Wendy, did not stir.

'I must go now, darling,' said Rhoda.

'But what about this pain?'

'What does Ken say?'

'He didn't seem to think it was anything,' said Wendy. 'He just went to sleep.'

'Then that's all right,' said Rhoda. 'Ken's always right,' and put down the phone. One of Wendy's fears was that if her father died her mother would want to marry Ken. She liked a decisive man, she said. Bruno was not decisive. He was a jobbing gardener by trade. He liked to stand about to see what the weather was going to do next. Wendy took after him, said Rhoda.

Wendy rang her friend Louise but there was no reply. Ken slept on. The pain grew worse. She got out of bed. The waters broke. She mopped the liquid up from the floor with a clean towel, though she knew it meant presently lugging it all the way down to the launderette. Ken didn't like washing machines, or indeed any domestic machinery, in the house. Should it go wrong he would be expected to mend it: he was a musician, not a mechanic. Presently Wendy wrote a note for Ken suggesting he came on down when he'd had breakfast, walked fifteen minutes to the hospital and admitted herself.

The baby was born at 7.20 in the morning, in the labour ward not the delivery room because Wendy failed to persuade any of the nurses that the baby was on the way.

'Nurse,' said Wendy politely, at least once or twice, 'the baby is coming out. I can feel it.'

'Nonsense,' replied the nurses, 'you're not even three fingers dilated,' until one of them, a girl with a lot of red hair, opened Wendy's legs and looked and screeched, 'But I can see the head! Why didn't you tell me?' and ran off for help. The baby was wholly out by the time she got back with Sister, though in a caul, as if giftwrapped in Clingfilm. 'Holy Mary Mother of God!' cried the nurse, crossing herself. Then she fainted, hitting her head on the metal bedstead. Sister attended to the nurse while Wendy attended to the baby, clearing its mouth, nose and eyes. A passing student doctor clipped and tied the umbilical cord for her, and told her the baby was a girl and just fine. These things sometimes happened in even the best run hospitals, he said, and this one was not even particularly well run. By the time Sister returned Wendy had removed the rest of the baby's wrapping, and was reproached for so doing. Heaven knew what harm she had done. But the baby, so far as Wendy could see, was in good order, firm of limb, bright of eye, smooth of skin and, once released from its wrapping, extremely lively.

'Why didn't you wake me?' asked Ken. 'Sounds as if you needed me. You're too independent for your own good.' It was four o'clock in the afternoon. He had wakened at eleven thirty, only just in time for his lunchtime gig. He'd come over as soon as he could. He inspected the baby. 'Are you sure it's mine?' he asked.
'Of course I'm sure,' said Wendy. 'Why do you ask?'
'We're not married,' he said. 'How do I know what you get up to?'
'Perhaps we ought to get married now there's a baby,' said Wendy. The girls at work admired her for living with a man and not being married to him, but she could forgo that pleasure, she thought, for the baby's sake.
'Musicians make rotten husbands,' said Ken. 'When I took up music, it meant giving up all thought of a family. It isn't fair to the kids.'
'I suppose it isn't,' said Wendy.
'I hope this baby doesn't grow up to have your brains and my beauty,' said Ken. 'I hope it's the other way round.'
He'd brought her not flowers, not fruit, but a little orange kitten, which he'd found wandering in the street outside. It dribbled something nasty from its back end on to the white sheet. Ken put it on top of the locker, where it staggered around the perimeter mewing and testing space with its paw.
'You'll just have to take it home,' said Wendy.
'I can't,' said Ken. 'I'm going straight on to a gig.'
He kissed her fondly.

'Rhoda isn't going to like being a grandmother,' he said.

'I know,' said Wendy, happily. Ken went to his gig. Wendy marvelled at her baby. When Rhoda came she brought her daughter a bottle of sherry.

'You're not supposed to drink while you're breastfeeding,' said Wendy.

'Nonsense,' said Rhoda. 'I did.'

Wendy drank half the bottle straight off.

'You're only supposed to have a little at a time,' said Rhoda. 'It's not like orange squash.'

'I was thirsty,' said Wendy.

The baby hiccoughed. Rhoda took the kitten home. Its eyes were gummy. The red-headed nurse said she'd put it in the incinerator herself if nobody took it away, and fast. She said that babies born in a caul were born to great fame or great misfortune, certainly something special. Sister said that was superstition: a caul was just nature's way of giftwrapping.

'Isn't that a sweet idea?' said Wendy.

Rhoda said to Bruno that perhaps all Wendy's brains had gone into the baby. She certainly didn't seem to have any left.

On the day Wendy was to go home a woman came to issue a birth certificate for the baby. She was annoyed to discover that Wendy was not in fact married to Ken: it meant she had to tear up one certificate and start making out another.

'He doesn't believe in marriage,' Wendy explained. 'I'm sorry.'

'I don't take any moral stance on this,' said the woman. 'I just keep the records. If you and the father haven't decided on a Christian name you have just six weeks in which to do it.'

'We decided ages ago,' Wendy said, crossing her fingers. 'Jason for a boy and –' Her eye fell upon her brushed nylon nightie. 'Apricot if it's a girl. Her name is Apricot.'

'You don't have to decide now,' said the woman, quite kindly. 'You might like your thoughts to mature.'

'Oh no,' said Wendy. 'I'm quite sure. Her name's Apricot.' She drank the other half-bottle of sherry: nobody had filled her water jug since she'd been admitted. Apricot!

'But you didn't even consult me,' said Ken reproachfully when presently it occurred to him to ask what she'd called the baby,

our failure, not our success. 'Let them spend more on **health!**' we cry. 'On schools! On happiness!' Spend what? Coins, notes? 'Money' has stopped working. Pour millions upon millions into a nation's health service, it makes no difference: still the people hack and cough and go untended, die for lack of attention, because money no longer represents what it did – labour, skill, concern, capital, organization, involvement. It has become a commodity itself, to be bought and sold by people skilled only in doing just that, and they have taken the guts out of money, weeded it out.

Do you have a mortgage on your house? Have you built up a debt to the bank? If those paper debts were wiped out in the computer that prints your monthly statement, would it make any difference in real terms to anyone else? Would there be less wealth in the world? No! Would it affect the communal resource of food, services, capital? Of course not. Those debts relate to the past, not now. Their wiping out would merely free the individual from anxiety, heal his ulcer, lighten his step, brighten his eye. Money has become a thing of no value: usury, once a sin, is now the faith of nations. Buy on your credit card: buy, buy, buy! What have you got? Nothing that makes you happier than a child's Christmas toy, bought in the land of plenty, broken and forgotten by Christmas night, discarded, swept up, thrown away; some unbiodegradable bit of plastic, moulded into partial or sentimental shape. Transitory, a panacea to stop the wail of the poor muddled infant: one that didn't even work for long. What's it all about? Money! The human race has had enough of it. As a medium of exchange it no longer works, and that's that. We have to face it. Work hard, grow rich? You're joking. Work hard, stay poor; that is the message of money. The brightest are wasted: the cunning triumph: the robber barons are back. Who saves, these days? No one. Who believes that by working now we can store up security for the future? We can't. We know in our hearts money is worthless but how can we escape its tyranny: how begin afresh to judge ourselves and one another?

Q: You have an answer?

A: Wait, wait! For a few to have money in abundance and others too little is the root of all social ills: it is the differential which

34

results in unrest, riot, war, discrimination, class systems, crime, snobbery: the belief that one man is of more intrinsic value than another for reasons other than his temperament, his moral qualities, and his likeability. The only real, the only true wealth lies in friends in abundance, company in plenty, comfort in abandon, love overflowing: what have these things to do with money? – except that we cheat and lie and use money to acquire them; knowing no other way to do it. The man who gives a boat party knows in his heart that his friends like his yacht more than they like him: he is lonely and restless in their company. He picks up his mobile phone, dials his stockbroker in Tokyo. 'More money, more money!' he demands, and clever minds set to work at his behest, the computers shift and change a little all over the world, and presently his bank balance shows another nought; and, so that that nought should be there, somewhere in the undeveloped world another ten backs break needlessly.

Lack of money causes misery, anxiety, early death: the cramping of personality, the limiting of human potential. Lack of money prevents us eating properly when we are children, ruins our health, rots our teeth, makes our parents quarrel and take to drink, stops us having the clothes we want, the friends we like, the parties we long for, stops us having the tuition which would enable us to get an education – makes us end up street sweepers and not doctors; induces women to have babies because there is no money for travel or entertainment, or to leave the parental home any other way: lack of money humiliates us all our lives: lack of money makes us live with husbands or wives we no longer love: lack of money makes us age earlier than we need: makes our hands rough with toil and our brows creased with anxiety: keeps us weeping by day and sleepless by night: the terror in our lives is the bill through the door which can't be paid: our lives close in the knowledge of failure – we failed to make enough money. We never did what we wanted with our lives. How could we? We didn't have the money.

We tell ourselves 'money isn't important', but it is, it is. We couldn't afford this, we couldn't afford that: and our lives and our friendships and our marriages and our children were thereby curtailed, limited.

And we put up with it. We put up with it because we *need* the differential: we like to feel superior to our neighbours, and if the penalty is that the man up the road feels superior to us, we'll put up with it. We like to have kings to worship and admire: we love a bit of gold leaf to ooh and ah at: we don't mind being poor just so long as there's someone poorer than us. Snobbish to our bootstraps. We still believe money equates with worth. That the rich are rich by virtue of being intelligent, bright, strong and powerful. And once at the beginning, when the first few coins were exchanged, the first kings decided to mint the stuff, I daresay that was true. Times change, times change; yet habits hold. Money was handed down from father to son; it lost its merit as a token of worth; the idle and nasty could be a great deal more rich than the hardworking and good. Money and intelligence pretty soon had little connection. Money and privilege, every unnatural link. The rich no longer deserve to be rich, or the poor to be poor: there is no merit in having enough money: there is little pleasure in having too little money. Sex is the source of all pleasure, money is the source of all pain.

Q: You mean lack of money?

A: I do not. It is this assumption that so hampers our thinking. Because lack of money is bad, we assume money itself is good. It is another example of the Trap of the False Polarity. You might in good time like to write a pop-psychology book under that title? Or perhaps not. We'll see.

> *'I most sincerely hope you don't,' said Valerie. 'You are a serious person.' Hugo stroked the back of her neck with his strong fingers, and she quietened and went on listening.*

Q: Perhaps you are not talking about the pursuit of money, but the pursuit of power? Most people equate money with power, power with money.

A: What is power? The desire to make other people do what you want? The power of the parent over the child? The tyrant over his subject? The employer over the employed? Take away money and you deprive the unjust of power. The child can have his football boots because the words 'we can't afford it' will be linked to the long-gone and not-lamented past: the tyrant cannot control against the will of the subject because he cannot frighten his people with notions of helplessness and poverty: the employer will have to charm and wheedle his workers if he wants them to work for him: he will have to sing and dance to entertain them: enthuse them with pleasure for their daily toil: they will be paid with the world's respect, and all around them there will be abundance. We will not be wage slaves any more. We will not need our wages. We may accept them, to oblige: to save another's face. But that's all. In Darcy's Utopia there will be no wages, there will be no money.

Q: Oh come now! Easier said than done.

A: Not at all; it could be done even here – merely increase the supply of money until it becomes something of little value, as plentiful as grass: let it grow on every street corner, pour from the high street banks: see how little by little it is of less and less value: soon it is only stuff fit to engage the attention of those who love to indulge in the act of recycling: we will probably find that, pulped, bank notes are an excellent media for growing acorns into oaks. My husband Julian and I went on our honeymoon to Yugoslavia – annual inflation ran at 350 per cent. A hyper-inflationary economy. Yet people ate, drank, sang, laughed, rejoiced, loved and were happy. Talked – how they talked! The streets were noisy with greetings, chatter and friendship. It was there my husband and I began to develop our theories, Darcian Monetarism as it came to be called: that the answer to our current economic ills is not to control inflation but to encourage it until we cease to be a money economy altogether.

Q: Perhaps, being on honeymoon, you wore rose-tinted spectacles?

A: It is true we had a perfectly wonderful time. As I say, sex is the source of all pleasure, money is the source of all pain.

> *At this point the tape clicked to a stop. Neither Hugo nor Valerie attended to it. It had been running on unheard for some time, in any case.*

Apricot loses one mother
and gains another

'You can't go out like that,' said Wendy to Apricot when she was four, 'it's freezing,' and little Apricot, in nothing but vest and pants, ran straight out into the street and down the long suburban road to the small playground which a benign council had made for the children in the sharp triangle of land where the railway line intersected the water-purifying plant. Wendy ran after her child but her spiked heels slowed her, so she gave up and came back home and made herself a cup of coffee and read the stories in the back of her magazine. Or perhaps she took a swig of sherry.

That was in the sixties, in the years when it was safe for a small girl child to play unsupervised in a public playground, even in her underwear; all anyone had to fear was that she might catch cold. Those were the days: oh yes, those were the days.

When Ken got up that afternoon – he hadn't come home till three in the morning – Wendy said, 'I've really got to go back to work; I'm drinking too much: this life is driving me mad.'
'What's wrong with your life?' he asked. 'You have everything a woman wants. Why don't you change places with me? Me, I'd love to do nothing.' And he thrust his banjo into her hands and little Apricot, watching, winced.
'But I can't play the banjo,' said Wendy, which irritated Ken even more. He made a gesture: she took it literally. But then all his audiences, these days, were unsatisfactory. He had his own band now; he was trying to make a go of it full-time, and it was difficult. No one wanted to pay for music; the general feeling was that it should flow free from the celestial spheres. Now he was off to a nine p.m. to one a.m. British Legion do: they'd hired a Dixie Band but when it came to it would want Country and Western: six in

the band and a twelve pound fee. If you charged Musicians Union rates no one hired you: if you didn't, your fellow musicians hated you: and to stand up there on a platform for four hours disappointing a room full of people was not his idea of living. He'd given up woodwork, having driven a splinter through his thumbnail. It was too dangerous. His main income came through music. He needed his hands.

'I suppose if I had another baby, Ken,' said Wendy, 'that would fill in my days.' He said he couldn't afford it. She said she didn't think money ought to stop people living, actually living: making their lives little when they could be big. But if she couldn't have another baby the newsagent on the corner wanted someone in the mornings. She said Ken could look after Apricot because he was at home when she was out.

'I'd be asleep,' Ken said. 'I don't think I'm the kind of man who ought to have a working wife.'

Wendy said, 'You wouldn't be, because you never actually married me. We were going to once but when it came to it you didn't have the money for the licence. You said you'd spent it on a new banjo.'

Ken said, 'I had to have a new banjo. Some fool backed over mine in a car park. It was a wonderful instrument. I'll never get another one like it.'

She said, 'More fool you for leaving it in a car park,' and little Apricot said, 'Yes, that's right, Mum. That's what I think!'

Ken said, 'I had to put it down while I put the amp into the van. I forgot it. By the time I went back for it, it was too late. If you'd come out on the gig with me you could have held it for me. But you're not interested in my work at all. All you want to do is sit home and drink gin.'

'I have Apricot to look after,' said Wendy. 'You forget that. You forget everything important, that's the trouble with you.' She'd put her finger on it. Sometimes it takes people years.

'Well,' said Ken, 'don't expect me to look after Apricot while you're at work. I'm a musician, not a father.'

'Oh well,' said Wendy, 'that's that,' and poured herself some sherry.

Rhoda said when she came to tea at the weekend, 'You only remember what you want to remember, Ken; serve you right. How many gigs have you missed in the last few months?'

'Only one,' said Ken, 'and that wasn't because I forgot it: it was because they'd given me bad directions.' But he smiled sheepishly and cheered up. Rhoda always cheered him up.

Rhoda said, 'What's that you're pouring into your cup, Wendy?'

'Whisky,' said Wendy.

'You have a real drink problem there,' said Rhoda.

Wendy sat at home and polished her nails. She listened to the Beatles on the radio; it could only be to annoy Ken. He was out every night and most weekends and if he wasn't out he was asleep. She told Deval the newsagent all about her problem. His wife had died suddenly a couple of years back. He needed cheering up too. Dev said to Wendy, 'You don't need Ken, he'll never amount to anything: he treats you like shit: what you need is a man like me,' and Wendy believed him.

'Can I bring Apricot with me?' she asked.

'No,' said Dev, 'a woman shouldn't start a new relationship with a child hanging around. It isn't fair to the child.'

'I expect you're right,' said Wendy, and left Apricot with Ken.

Rhoda said to Ken, 'If you ask me, the girl's in love with love, not Dev, and she'll come back. She was like this as a little girl. Looking after stray kittens and then getting bored.'

Ken took Apricot with him on gigs for a time and quite enjoyed it, but found getting her to school and organizing her clothes and meals onerous. When Wendy's father died of lung cancer, he asked Rhoda to move in and presently got it together to marry her, thus putting a stop to Wendy's sudden plan to abandon Dev and move back in with Ken.

'She's just jealous,' said Rhoda, comfortably. 'Take no notice. Older women with younger men never goes down well, except with the parties involved.'

Wendy and Dev presently parted; Wendy, who by then had a real drink problem, was hired to do a milk delivery round which took her to her own doorstep, and daily contact with Apricot, until Ken put a stop to it. If Rhoda put out a note for half-cream milk, Wendy would deliver full-cream. Ken complained to her employers, and she was put on another round, but kept forgetting the orders and was presently let go.

And that was how, in a gradual and non-sensational manner, Apricot's mother became her sister, and her grandmother her mother. Her father at least remained her father.

Valerie leaps to conclusions

There is no getting away from it. A study of life, death and marriage certificates show Apricot as the daughter of a certain Wendy Ellis and Wendy herself the legitimate daughter of Bruno and Rhoda Ellis. Ken Smith is named as Apricot's father and Rhoda Ellis married a Ken Smith in June 1965, Bruno Ellis having died in March of that year. The ages tally. It puts perhaps a kind face on things: but sometimes families do just get into dreadful muddles, with no one doing anything particularly awful. In 1973 Wendy Ellis, poor Wendy, a spinster, died aged thirty-five of liver failure. Livers fail because of cancer, or hepatitis, or drug overdose, but mostly I suppose because they are assailed by alcohol and just can't cope. And no woman, I daresay, can settle easily to the knowledge that her child's father has married her own mother: and drink, while ruining livers, certainly eases pain. But I don't think the readers of *Aura* will want me to dwell too much on the pain. I try to be unemotional, without much success. Sex renders one tearful, I find.

A love song on the crackly Holiday Inn radio which the maid always switches on as her final flourish after she's done the room (Hugo and I go down to the pool and swim and use the sauna while we wait for her to finish) or a pop song on the telly as Hugo and I eat our continental breakfast (orange juice, coffee, a croissant and a Danish each), too languid even to stretch out for the remote control and switch it off – will make tears come to my eyes: move me with the desire to say, You *do* love me, don't you! This love will last for ever. This love, lasting forever, makes me immortal. This love replaces death. I don't say it, of course. I have read too many surveys in *Aura* – written them indeed – which prove that men feel trapped and uneasy if the word 'love' is mentioned, especially in proximity to any other word suggesting permanence.

I just roll the phrases round inside my head, smoothing them out, absorbing them back into me, until they're gone.

When I heard Eleanor Darcy's eulogy on Hugo's tape, I was much moved. Her soft determined voice inspired me: any doubts that remained evaporated: guilt and fear were dispelled, embarrassment fled: my body led me, not my mind. Eleanor Darcy spoke and I left home and hearth to follow my lover.

'Look here,' Hugo said, 'surely I had something to do with it?' and I laughed and said, 'How could you not? You too heard the tape!'

Lou has never seen love as a sufficient motive for anyone doing anything, which, when it comes to it, I daresay is why I left. I can trust Hugo not to treat me as I have Ken treat Wendy in *Lover at the Gate* and, if he did, I would never indulge him as Wendy did Ken. Look where it led! Women do have to fight back. Apart from anything else, I can't help feeling that if women let men get away with too much bad behaviour, men do not forgive them for the burden of guilt they then have to bear. They feel their shoulders breaking beneath the load. They get out from under.

I am a self-contained person: neat and elegant: or was until I met Eleanor, who, disgraced, childless, alone, sprawled and wriggled against the shiny black sofa with the big red flowers, and I knew I would rather be her, her life out of control, than me as I was with Lou; a woman whom an editor could describe as 'the mistress of controlled reportage'.

'Valerie,' the editor of the *Mail on Sunday* said to me once, after I had filed a neat and convincing piece on an earthquake – the ground had trembled beneath me in Rome, where Lou was playing with the London Symphonic and a wall had fallen on top of me and trapped me for two hours – 'you are the mistress of controlled reportage. We can't run the piece, as it happens. The stock market has collapsed. I hope you didn't get your hair mussed.'

I just smiled and said 'a little' – but I was hurt. I thought he was laughing at me. I joined the staff of *Aura* shortly afterwards. 'Mussed' is a word so outmoded I'm surprised the God of Media didn't strike him down on the instant with a thunderbolt. Pre-

Hugo, come to think of it, my hair never got mussed. Now I can scarcely get a comb through it in the morning. To each their own earthquake.

Valerie Jones returns to ask further questions of Eleanor Darcy

Q: Tell me about your educational background. Were there books in your house? Did your parents encourage you to read?

A: What you want me to tell you is how I, victim of a class-ridden society, managed to escape the long side streets of the outer suburbs and reach the shores of academia. Well, a few of us manage it. It helps to have a high IQ, though I suspect a talent for mimicry is more useful; being able to adopt at will the tones and attitudes of the educated middle classes. That I have.

> *Valerie sat on the sofa. Eleanor sat in a chair. Why, Valerie wondered, did Eleanor share the sofa with Hugo, but not with her?*

First, of course, you have to know what you are: that there is another life, another set of attitudes, other responses out there in the world, which prevent most of us from aspiring to better things. We know what we like, like what we know, unless something quite powerfully intervenes to shake us out of it. The child from the fish and chip shop can only end up running Liberty's if he has some idea of what Liberty's *is*. How very snobbish of you, you will say; why should Liberty's be seen as superior to a fish and chip shop?

Q: I wasn't conscious of accusing you. Aren't you being a little defensive?

A: I daresay. I was married to Bernard Parkin for fifteen years, a man who came from the lower middle class, but identified quite violently, for a number of years, with the workers. He would never set foot in Liberty's, let alone Harrods – those haunts of the rich

45

and the would-be rich represented for him the scornful laughter of the haves towards the have-nots. While some downright starve, and others scrimp and save to afford the large cod and chips, not the small, a few spend thousands on sunken baths and antique rugs. Poor Bernard. He was a good man.

Q: Was?

A: One speaks of ex-spouses in the past tense. Don't you do the same?

Q: I don't have an ex-spouse.

A: No? Well, I daresay you will, from what Mr Vansitart tells me.

> *To cover her discomposure, Valerie readjusted the microphone. She was flattered and excited that Hugo had talked of their relationship to Eleanor: offended that her privacy had been thus violated. The pleasurable feeling won.*

You have pushed the microphone out of range. Shall I adjust it? We live in a world of surplus but can't bring ourselves to believe that we do. We go on behaving and thinking as if there would never, never be enough. Gimme, gimme, gimme! Before someone else gets it. My sunken plastic bath better than your old cast-iron tub. If the poor have their faces ground into a mud made sharp and painful by slivers of diamond and chunks of ruby, whose fault is that? Those who shove their faces into it? – Bernard's view. The consistency of the mud? – my view. Or that of the poor themselves, for daring to bend their heads and stare?

Q: You went first to the Faraday Junior School, I believe, an ordinary state school. What were your experiences there?

A: I understand what you are saying. Badly born, poorly educated as I am, how do I have the nerve to pass comment on the society I live in – let alone marry a professor of economics and co-author with him – the publisher's term, not mine – a book on Darcian Monetarism?

46

She rose from the chair. She paced. Today she wore a tan silk shirt and tight dun-coloured trousers. She had the air of a female terrorist: someone who might take it into her head to shoot at any moment. Valerie thought, Good heavens, it was safer, after all, on the Mail on Sunday *than on* Aura, *earthquakes notwithstanding. This may yet be the end of me.*

Q: No. I was not saying any of that. I was asking how you enjoyed school.

Eleanor calmed, sat down again.

A: Yes, I believe you were. I had a bad time at the hands of male journalists during Julian's trial and in the period leading up to it: some residual paranoia sticks. They look for a *femme fatale*, a Mata Hari of world finance, a seductress. If a woman is to be taken seriously she must either be past the menopause or very plain, preferably both.

Let us return to the Faraday Junior School. Fresh-faced and bright-eyed, we five-year-olds trooped off to school: troubled and sophisticated we returned, the stuffing all knocked out of us. Schools are a strange contrivance; they do not occur in nature, yet somehow we suppose they do. Because a woman, by virtue of giving birth to a succession of children, is then landed with the task of bringing them up, is no cause to suppose children are best taught by the handful, the dozen, the score. Nature, as ever, provided a minimum, not a maximum, for our survival. Any mother knows that it takes more than one adult to cope properly with even a single child. The child has more energy and more passion than the adult. To make it sit still, sit up and oblige, because it is smaller than you and you can compel it, is unkind. To make it do so in company is bizarre.

In Darcy's Utopia the first rule of education will be that in any school the teachers shall outnumber the pupils, and no pupil need attend who does not wish to do so. I suspect budding essayists and technicians will continue to turn up to be educated; those

47

others, who find lessons a humiliation because they are daily exposed and defined as dullards, will not. Much will be gained by the individual and very little lost to society. Teachers, teaching only those who wish to learn, will regain their self-respect and that of their pupils. They will stay even-tempered from morning to night. In Darcy's Utopia you will not see the eyes of the child dulling, the brow furrowing, as puberty arrives.

Children do quite like to gather together, in fits and starts, to enjoy one another's company, to find out how others live. It is natural enough for them to want to acquire knowledge from their elders. But it is unreasonable from this to extrapolate 'the school' as one of the cornerstones of society – for what are schools but institutions in which, in the name of knowledge, we ghettoize the young, and keep them from adult company, coop up the violent with the meek, those who like learning with those who don't, and in general fit them for the modern world, which one quick glimpse of the television will show them to be a violent, murderous, greedy, vulgar and horrid place, in which people in a good mood throw custard pies at one another and in a bad mood chop each other to pieces?

Q: I take it you did not like school?

A: I liked it very much. I was sorry for those who didn't, who by far outnumbered those of us who did. I daresay the Faraday Junior was no worse than any other school: indeed even a little better. No one was moved to burn the place down and the teachers were not encouraged to beat the children: though I had my knuckles painfully rapped on various occasions when I had apparently failed to decode some mysterious message or other. Teachers get irritated, of course they do, their elaborate and expensive training courses notwithstanding. Why? Because they are doing the most unnatural thing in the world, which everyone tells them is perfectly natural, in order that little children should all sit down quiet and good in one place and learn to take the world for granted, and not attempt to change it.

Q: But you tried to escape? You did want to change your situation?

A: When you ask that you betray your belief that one class is indeed superior to another: that to be born to the uneducated lower classes is a singular life-problem: though I'm sure if I asked you straight you would, in your gentle, blind, liberal way, deny it. The class distinctions we employ, you would maintain, are descriptive not pejorative. The person with, say, the pinched and nasal accents of the English Midlands is no worse than the one whose language has the rounded and lordly ring of London's Knightsbridge, merely different. Tell that to employers, boy-friends, doctors, the dinner party hostess. Second-class citizen! goes up in neon lights when those who use the pronunciation of the streets and not of the written word open their mouths. Rightly they are discriminated against! Woe unto them, say I, who do not seek to improve themselves but cling with misplaced loyalty to the speech of their parents, as they do to the homes they were born into.

In Darcy's Utopia it will be as normal to practise elocution as to brush your teeth. If more than lip service is to be paid to the notion that we are all equal, then it must be first acknowledged that we are born unequal, and that some of us have to work harder than others to make up for it. We must be prepared to make value judgements – allow Milton to be better than Michael Jackson in absolute terms, not just because that one's your cup of tea and that one's mine. The politeness of the cultured towards the uncultured, the hurt defiance of the latter to the former, compound one another. With misplaced kindness, the best of us refuse to discriminate against the worst. All things are equal, we say, and we lie, and know we lie.

Q: You seem very conscious of class discrimination. Were you much aware of it as a child?

A: Yes, but I can't say I suffered from it. To have hurt feelings is not a particularly painful kind of hurt. Toothache is much worse. I was certainly made very aware, as a child, of the strange and complex attitudes people had towards my father, the entertainer. They depended upon him for their pleasure, they admired him because he had a skill they did not, they liked him because he was charming and energetic, but they did not treat him as their equal.

49

The best were patronizing; the worst could not help but insult him. The band would be required to eat, in the kitchen, cheaper food than that offered the guests: be offered beer if the guests had wine, wine if they had champagne. Should that have upset him? It always did. Jazz was popular in all circles during my childhood – the demand now is for more structured music or the cold beat of the synthesizer – but through the sixties the music of Black Africa in distress appealed to softened hearts. We went everywhere: from garden parties in the grounds of castles, wedding receptions in marquees, hunt balls in assembly rooms, university teas on graduation day, garden fêtes in the bishop's palace, to the annual parties of car salesmen, the golden weddings of simple folk – once I even remember a gypsy funeral – ladies' night at the masonic lodge, and the British Legion get-together. I went to them all and watched and listened and made my own judgements. To be the hired help is to be helpless in the face of taunts and insults. Just as the waitress gets blamed for the quality of the soup, so will the band get blamed for the non-vitality of the guests. If the guests won't dance when the host expects them to, has depended on them to, that's the band's fault and they don't get paid, or only after an argument. As the wine waiter trots back and forth to establish the status of the customer as connoisseur, so the band will be required to play the most tricky musical number – 'Maryland' for example – to prove the musical expertise of one or other of the revellers.

If I, the child groupie, was noticed – and I tried to make myself invisible – I would be treated in kindly enough fashion, but as something of a curiosity. Also, I used to think, as an embarrassment, as if the presence of children put a damp blanket on everything; made flirtation self-conscious, drunkenness difficult, dancing almost disgraceful. If the English do not like children, it is because they think they ought to behave properly, responsibly and quietly in their presence and can never riot or have a good time when they're around. Children are real party-poopers. Ask Brenda. I learned a good deal about the role of food and drink as a socio-economic indicator. In the palace, the castle, the country house, the wine would be good but the food tasteless, and the band given beer and sandwiches on the assumption that this would be their preference. The middle classes would serve sour cheap wine but exotic foods and the band would eat whatever the guests ate, but not for long: the hosts having paid for the band to play, not to eat. The lower classes – if we talk about upper and middle how can we not talk about lower? – served tea, beer, gin and stodgy food, cut as often as not into hamfisted wedges, fit to fill the belly not the hand, and, understanding that the band was working for a living, treated it with respect and decorum. Everyone got happily drunk together and a good time was had by all; so long as the band kept the beat, what they played was immaterial. I was given, in all circles, a great deal of orange squash, then as now considered the drink most fit for children, though only loosely connected to the orange. I can tell you that the further down the social scale we went the brighter and sweeter and richer the orange squash, and the more I loved it.

In the palace, in the castle, at the hunt ball and the country house men brayed like donkeys and women shrieked and swooped like owls: the middle classes made me fidgety with their concern – was I not out too late? Was my father being nice to me? Not *too* nice? Wouldn't I fall asleep in class tomorrow? Wouldn't I like to curl up on the sofa? – and mostly I enjoyed the sweaty heaving pleasures of the British Legion do, where the guests galumphed and the men got drunk and waved bottles around – and one thing I noticed through all the ranks of society, no matter what the background, or the income, or the form the party took, was that as the evening wore on women would begin to look pained and patient and longed to get home, but didn't like to say so for fear of being accused of ruining the evening's fun. Men do so dislike women who stand between them and drink.

In Darcy's Utopia there will be no drinking before six in the evening and no one will mind, because life will be okay without it. It will be the custom rather than the law. We will have as few laws as possible. Persuasion will replace compulsion. To be drunk will be recognized as a symptom not of manliness but of extreme unhappiness, and since only on rare occasion do we want to broadcast the fact of our unhappiness to the world, the lager lout, the whisky soak, the sherry drunk will become a rarer and rarer phenomenon, until finally withering away.

Q: Were you brought up in any particular religious or political persuasion?

A: My father was converted to Communism when I was eight. I would stand on street corners with him while he sold copies of the *Morning Star*. He would instruct me in the history of the world while the people of the world walked by, ignoring the salvation we offered them, and the icy wind blew around our ankles. In the evenings we would have readings from *Das Kapital*. Yes, we did what we could to save the world, my father and I.

Q: You were very fond of your father?

A: I adored him. There was no denying he was forgetful. He forgot to hand in such little money as he collected from sales of the *Morning Star*; they prosecuted and he was put on probation for two years. That upset him very much. He felt keenly the ingratitude of the Party and lost his faith. During those difficult years, when he drank rather more than he should, he would sometimes even forget on the way home from gigs I was his daughter and not just an ordinary groupie.

Q: You mean you were a victim of child abuse?

A: How simply you put it. Never quite. Often nearly. But who isn't, at least in their own minds? That is all for today. It is tiring to think about the past. How are you getting on with *Lover at the Gate*?

Q: I am not sure that it's an appropriate title. Why are you so keen on it?

A: Because of the way life changes when the lover at last appears. Haven't you found it to be so? In most people's lives the lover stands there, at the gate, faithful, waiting, unnoticed. All we need do is ask him in. Not all of us have the courage, of course.

Q: But you had, Mrs Darcy?

A: Oh yes, and still have. So have you, Mrs Jones. One little push and the whole world's one, no woman's better than the next! Here's Brenda with more coffee. Or is Jones your maiden name? Many women choose to work under their maiden names.

Q: Jones is my married name, as it happens.

A: I can see that might in the end cause some complications.

> *Valerie Jones made her excuses and left – she had had more than enough coffee. She felt sleepy rather than tired, as a result, she told herself, of having had so little sleep of late. She felt rather superior to Eleanor Darcy on this account and left Brenda's house in good humour.*

Valerie and Lou manage
a conversation

Eleanor Darcy told me I was welcome to call her if necessary; if I needed any further factual details for my *Lover at the Gate*. She didn't go so far as to give me her telephone number, but I prudently copied it from the instrument at a point during the interview when she was distracted: when one of Brenda's children had somehow slipped into the room to find a drum stacked halfway down a pile of similar toys. My own children, Sophie and Ben, managed their early childhood well enough without the help of noisy, let alone musical, toys. My husband Lou was musical – a professional musician, in fact – and, I suppose understandably, couldn't endure the sound of good instruments badly played, or bad instruments played at all. I notice I refer to him in the past tense. *One speaks of ex-spouses in the past tense. Don't you do the same?* But Lou is still legally my husband: Sophie and Ben are certainly my children, not my ex-children. The title outruns even death. I suppose if a court denied me access to them, I might speak of them as ex-children. But that kind of thing doesn't happen now. It used to, of course. Adulterous mothers would be prevented from ever seeing their children again, lest they spread the contamination of sin. Then I suppose they did turn into ex-children.

Lou is a kind, understanding and reasonable man: friend as well as spouse. All that has happened is that I met Hugo at a party and came to understand that, as well as having friend and spouse, a woman needs the excitement of a lover from time to time: a re-basing, as it were, in the physical: the reincarnation of the carnal self in a body which gets, over the years, far too controlled by spirit and mind. The customary sex of the marriage bed does so little to stop the mind working, and the mind must stop working

54

if the flesh is to have its due gratification; the acknowledgement of its glory.

I called Lou. It seemed to me I owed him some explanation. Besides, he might be worrying about me. It was 10.23 according to the Holiday Inn's radio alarm clock, which flashed on and off on the bedside panel, redly. I wished it would just steadily and quietly glow. My nerves were a little on edge. Shortage of sleep was beginning to tell. Lou would be in the middle of practice. He was – is – a man of regular habits: up at seven thirty, breakfast at eight, mail at eight thirty, and so on. Even his phone calls were planned and made on the half-hour. I should have postponed the call for seven minutes. It might have gone better.

'Lou,' I said, when I heard his quiet, familiar voice on the phone. 'I think I'm possessed by the Devil.' It wasn't what I meant to say, but that's the way it came out.

'General belief is,' he said, 'that you've gone mad. My advice to you is to see a psychiatrist. I'm in the middle of practice, as you surely know. Have you anything important to say?'

'How are the children?'

'As well as children are when their mother fails to come home from a party because she's shacked up with some gorilla in a cheap hotel. The children have rather a low opinion of you, I imagine.'

Lou is a slight, controlled man with a sensitive face: Hugo large, grizzly and loose-limbed.

'Lou, you haven't *told* them?'

'We agreed to be honest with the children, I seem to recall.'

I could have taken him to task about how he was defining 'agree' and 'honest', but just somehow didn't.

'The Holiday Inn is far from being a cheap hotel,' was all I could think of to say. 'On the contrary, it's rather expensive. They've taken a print of Hugo's Amex, but I don't somehow think he's on good personal terms with them, and you know how tight everyone is on expenses, these days.'

'You just stay in the media world you know and love,' he said. 'It's all you're fit for. Leave me and the children in our little patch of civilization. Roll round in the gutter as much as you like, but don't call me to tell me all about it. We're doing just fine without you.' And he put down the phone. No, it was not a good phone call. It brought back to me the reality of the life I had so abruptly left behind: I had somehow assumed it would fade out of existence when I wanted, fade back in when convenient, unchanged. That that was what years of impeccable behaviour earned you. A holiday. Apparently not! The clock flashed 10.27, 10.27, 10.27. I wondered if Lou would take up his bow and play until ten thirty, or whether he would extend his practice time for four minutes. He would probably do the latter, and hurry through the change of clothes which would prepare him for the half-hour's weight-training which he did between ten forty-five and eleven fifteen every Tuesday and Friday. Today was Tuesday. I had not seen Hugo for three hours. Already my body was beginning to feel restless: demanding reunification with the object of its yearning. I could feel Hugo's body similarly missing mine. What confidence, what pleasure this physical certainty of need and equal need begat. I felt my breath come short, my eyes seemed to roll in my head: I wore no clothes. I stalked the room naked. I, Valerie Jones, ex-wife of Lou; poor Valerie, uptight Valerie, Valerie of mind triumphant; ex-mother of Sophie and Ben: the phone rang: it was Hugo, of course it was.

'Darling.'

'Darling. Christ I miss you. I can get there at one. Only for half an hour.'

'Make it thirty-three minutes.'

'Why thirty-three?'

'Any time without a nought on the end.'

'You are all mystery. Stef was never a mystery.'

Stef was his wife. He'd used the past tense.

The phone call eased the torment of desire a little. I found that if I settled down to the tape and the life of Apricot Smith, I became quite comfortable.

Presently I remembered that it was when I had been about to call Eleanor Darcy and confirm the year of her marriage to Bernard Parkin, when I had found myself calling Lou instead, on impulse. I called the number. Brenda answered. Eleanor Darcy was out. No, she could not confirm the year of Eleanor Darcy's marriage to Bernard.

'But you were Mrs Darcy's school friend.'

'I can't remember; I'm sorry.'

56

'When will Mrs Darcy be back?'

'I don't know: I'm sorry.'

'I wonder whether you could help me a little, Brenda. I'm writing a pen picture of Eleanor Darcy's father Ken.'

'I'm not able to help you in that area. I'm sorry.'

So much for leading questions. I wondered where Eleanor Darcy *went*. I had somehow supposed her to sit in that room for ever, real only when Hugo or I were with her. I could see that writing *Lover at the Gate* had implications more profound than I had supposed. The boundaries between the real world and its imaginary reconstruction became stretched thin, almost invisible. Already I had ceased to be sure which side I was on. Even Lou's piranha snapping now began to seem like something read rather than experienced.

I put my conversations with Lou and Brenda from my mind, at least for the time being, and had switched on the WP and was enjoying the little moans and buzzes of its warming up, when there was a mighty banging on the door and there stood Hugo.

'Why weren't you in the corridor with the door open, waiting?' he asked.

I scarcely had time to close it before he was upon me. For some reason I thought of President Kennedy, bounding down the corridors of power, forever chasing the flick of a skirt, the back of a knee, the glorious in pursuit of the grateful. It was a couple of hours before I could get back to Eleanor Darcy.

Apricot Smith marries
Bernard Parkin

Apricot was in the sixth form doing her A levels. Rhoda had a nasty pain in her stomach but refused to see a doctor. A faith healer, Ernie Rowse, moved in to No. 93 Mafeking Street, two doors down from Ken, Rhoda and Apricot. On Sundays men, women and children would collect in Mr Rowse's back garden, dressed in white robes, singing strange hymns and raising their hands to heaven. They were collecting, they claimed, divine energies for Mr Rowse to dispense during the coming week. They would shake their empty hands over a barrel lined with tinfoil, from which he could at a later date draw out benison. They saw gold and silver dust drift downward from their hands, they told Rhoda. Rhoda was forty-eight, blonde, buxom and so cheerful Ken said she ought to be a barmaid. Rhoda could not see the heavenly dust, but liked the idea of it. Mr Rowse's followers said when she was whole she would see it. During the week supplicants, bent, bowed, ill or in pain, fell in line down the path between the narrow rosebeds and out into the street, in search of a miracle cure. Every ten minutes, when Mr Rowse was working, the line would shuffle forward one place. When Mr Rowse took a rest, the line stayed as it was, sometimes for hours. Occasionally, in the evenings, Mr Rowse would catch up with himself and the line would clear altogether. But it wasn't uncommon for clients to stand waiting all night.

'Just like Harrods' sale,' said Rhoda.

'Not in the least like Harrods' sale,' said Ken. 'These people are destroyed by the system, not those who lick its arse.'

'Neither of you have ever been to Harrods' sale,' said Apricot.

'Oh-ah,' groaned Rhoda this Thursday morning in November, holding her stomach. It was a warm day for the season, though damp. The roses had given up their annual struggle to keep things cheerful and now hemmed in Mr Rowse's path with thorns.

'You'd better go to the doctor,' said Apricot.

'And sit in his waiting room and catch God knows what? I'd rather die.'

'Then why don't you go to Mr Rowse?' said Apricot. 'The line's only as far as the gate.'

'Ken wouldn't like it,' said Rhoda.

Mr Rowse's patients, forever winding down the path, oppressed Ken with the sense of his own age and mortality.

'Ken won't know,' said Apricot. So Rhoda went.

Rhoda came home without a pain, besotted by Mr Rowse.

'When he touches you his hands strike fire into you,' she said. 'I'm still tingling from head to toe.'

'Did he say what caused the pain?' asked Apricot, who, perforce, spoke and behaved pretty much like Rhoda's mother, rather than her granddaughter.

'He said I'd done something bad to deserve it,' said Rhoda. 'And he's quite right, I have.'

'What was it?' asked Apricot, interested. Burned Ken's sheet music by mistake or on purpose, argued with him, failed to stay up till he got home, and/or have his supper waiting in the oven? Those were the normal and acceptable patterns of Rhoda's crimes. Apricot's were to spend too much time on homework, not to have a boyfriend, not play an instrument, talk too much and be too big for her boots.

'You remember your sister Wendy,' said Rhoda, 'the one who died of drink so young? Actually she was your mother. I should never have married your father. I told myself it didn't matter because they weren't husband and wife but Mr Rowse said the ceremony made no difference. Sin's eaten a hole in the lining of my gut. Now I've got that off my chest I feel much better. Make me some cheese on toast, there's a dear. It will give me a pain but it's worth it.'

Apricot made Rhoda some cheese on toast, overcooked it and shrivelled the cheese.

'Poor me,' said Rhoda, 'poor me,' and she poured herself another cup of sweet strong tea, which burned all the way down. She wasn't looking well. Her eyes were huge, her hair grey and her skin papery, but her heart remained childlike. The longer she lived with Ken the more like Wendy she became.

'Poor you,' said Apricot, agreeably. There was little point in taking offence, and no time to do so in any case. She had to pass her exams.

Rhoda's pain and Mr Rowse battled it out for well over a year. Rhoda took to table-tapping and seances and reported seeing the ghost of Wendy hovering over her bed at night. Ken was always asleep when Wendy appeared.

'I'm surprised she bothers,' said Ken. 'I'm surprised she isn't too busy delivering milk bottles in the sky.'

'She's like she was the day she had Apricot,' said Rhoda. 'Her hair all frizzed out like a black halo and ever so sweet. One thing you could say for my daughter, she never let herself go. Even when she'd had a drink or so too many she still had her stocking seams straight.' Since Wendy had taken to hovering over the bed, Rhoda had reclaimed her as a daughter and now spoke freely of the past. 'She should have consulted me about Apricot's name,' said Ken. 'She had no business not doing that.' Some things out-rankle death.

'Are you sure you shouldn't see a doctor?' asked Apricot, as Rhoda's cough grew nastier. She smoked sixty cigarettes a day. The white paint on the window frames was encrusted with black. 'What can a doctor do for her?' said Ken. 'When your number's up your number's up.'

Money was tight. Ken found it hard to adapt to the new age. Music was now for the young, not the middle aged: folk had taken over from jazz as the language of the radical and the sentimental. Ken's band dissolved and reformed under a succession of names. The Dixie Syncopaters, Jazzorola, Folkwise, Folkways, the Red Resolution, and back to Dixie Railroad; too many musicians chased too few gigs: that's the way it was. Rhoda had to give up work, and no sickness benefit was available since Ken had never let her succumb to the system and pay national insurance. Not that she'd ever wanted to, as she told Apricot.

'Better to live in the present, dear,' she said, 'while you can. That's your father's motto and he's right, as usual.'

Apricot sometimes wished she lived in as ordinary a household as did her neighbours; though the more she considered the neighbours the less ordinary they seemed. Mr Rowse the healer at 93 Mafeking Street, a Miss Potter and sixteen cats at No. 95, themselves at No. 97, a Mr Hill in a *ménage à trois* at No. 90 – perhaps all the normal people lived down another street? She had good friends at school: Brenda, Belinda and Liese. Brenda and Belinda, like herself, were scholarship girls, in a school where the others paid. Their names went up on a list on the school board as being entitled to free lunches. Liese's father owned a chain of garages: he'd been a prisoner of war, had married an English girl. Liese was a vague, sweet girl who had all the pocket money she needed and kept Apricot, Brenda and Belinda in clothes and shoes. Belinda, short and fat, knew most of Keats by heart, and large chunks of Shelley. Brenda, tall and languid, was captain of the netball team. Apricot came top of everything. But they were still the scholarship girls, objects of envy because they were not ordinary, objects of pity because they were poor, their accomplishments scarcely the point. 'You are all outsiders,' said Liese's father. 'That's why you stick together.'

'Liese isn't an outsider,' said all but Liese. 'She doesn't have free dinners.'

'She's half-German,' he said. 'That's more than enough.'

'How do you win?' asked Apricot.

'Men never do,' he said. 'Once an outsider, always an outsider. But girls can marry in.'

His wife was Jewish, he had converted to Judaism. There'd be soft tomato sandwiches for tea, and chicken soup and dumplings for supper. The lights were soft, the carpets thick, hot water flowed from taps; everyone liked to be comfortable.

'You English,' he said, 'hate to be comfortable. You think it will stop you getting to heaven. You would rather stand in the rain any day than in a bus shelter.'

'Bloody foreigners,' said Ken, though he mellowed when he heard Liese's family was Jewish. Blacks, musicians and Jews, all victims of an oppressive society, were of the same family of misfortunates as himself. There were eleven taps in Liese's house – Apricot had counted – including the garden tap. Taps, she reckoned, were the real symbol of wealth and success. At 97 Mafeking Street there were four; and think yourself lucky. Many of the houses had no bathrooms. Ken kept his sheet music in the one he had constructed in the small back bedroom, so fear of splashing kept it on the whole unused. There was carpet in the living room, lino elsewhere; gas fires downstairs and no heating in the bedrooms. The beds were damp and the floor cold when you put your bare feet out in the morning.

'What do we want money for?' asked Rhoda. Now she smoked eighty cigarettes a day. 'You, your dad and me!'
'So I can turn on the gas,' said Apricot.
Gas flowed to cooker and fires when coins were put in the meter, not otherwise.
'Put on your coat,' said Rhoda, 'if you feel the cold,' but Apricot never would. She went round to Liese's instead, where there was central heating. Brenda and Belinda went too. Belinda sucked sweets and read Tennyson aloud. Brenda talked about boys and Liese's mother provided food.
'That girl's an opportunist,' said Ken.
'I don't know what that means,' whispered Rhoda, 'but I'm sure you're right.' She lost her voice quite often. Mr Rowse said he was helpless in the face of the extravagance of her sin.

It was unusual for anything in particular to happen in Mafeking Street. The residents now took for granted the shuffling queue outside Mr Rowse's surgery, or temple. Someone would get a new car, or a new cat: a tree would be lopped: the milkman's horse bolt. A baby would get born and an upstairs window be lit at night: an old man would die and the hearse arrive, and a gap be felt for a while, but the very pressure of ordinariness, or whatever it was, soon healed it up. Ken would annoy the same neighbours by slamming the same van door twice a week in the same early hour. Now Rhoda had stopped work she would go down to the newsagent on the corner for her cigarettes at the same time every morning, each day a little lighter on her feet. She was now scarcely seven stone.
'At least I don't have to watch my weight now,' she'd say. 'Not like you, Ken.'
In the afternoons she would go and see Mr Rowse. She was allowed in by the back door. She didn't have to queue.
'I'm a priority case,' Rhoda said. 'He's wrestling with my sin.'

'He doesn't want the others to catch sight of you,' said Ken. 'They'd all be off home!'

Rhoda looked at herself in the mirror and said, 'I don't see much wrong with me. Nice big eyes at last!'

When Apricot was three weeks away from the examinations which were, in theory, to get herself, Belinda and Brenda out of school, away from home and into a preferable social and intellectual environment – Liese was happy enough to fail hers, and be allowed to stay cosily at home and be married off to someone suitable – there was an unusual uproar in Mafeking Street. A group of students, chanting and carrying placards, milled round in the road outside Mr Rowse's house, accosting his patients, pleading with them to go home, abjure the Devil and seek proper medical attention. Their placards announced them as 'Catholic Youth Against Witchcraft'.

Rhoda went out to give them a piece of her mind.

'Mr Rowse is a saint,' Rhoda told them.

'He's an agent of the Devil,' they assured her. Apricot followed Rhoda out to see what was happening. The young man whom she was to marry approached her. He was tall, he stooped, he wore a pale blue anorak and sturdy brown shoes. His eyes were bright and intelligent. He had a little beard, neatly and tidily cut. He was sincere. He explained to Rhoda and Apricot at some length the difference between religion and superstition. He said his name was Bernard Parkin, and that he was studying theology. His group were worried about the rise of superstition worldwide, and took positive action when circumstances warranted. He himself was destined for the priesthood.

Rhoda nudged Apricot.

'There's a challenge,' she said. 'Nice young man like that wasted.'

'Oh shut up, Rhoda,' said Apricot, embarrassed, but she could see what Rhoda meant.

The police were called and required the protesters to go home, in the name of religious freedom. This caused further argument and noise. Police reinforcements arrived. Bernard took refuge in Rhoda's house. Fortunately Ken was out.

'Is it superstition to believe in ghosts?' Apricot asked. Rhoda tactfully left them alone. She could be heard hawking and coughing in the upstairs bedroom.

'There's no such thing as ghosts,' he said.

'What about Jesus appearing to the apostles?'

'That was a miracle,' said Bernard. 'But I'm glad to have this discussion with you. Perhaps God has sent me to help you.'

He ate all the biscuits on the plate. He said he didn't mean to worry her but her mother did look as if she needed to see a doctor. Faith healers gained their power – if power they had – from the Devil, not God: they worked more mischief than anyone knew. Apricot explained that her mother was a ghost and Rhoda her grandmother. Bernard settled down to re-educate her. She liked his mind: she liked the quality of his convictions, although, as she explained to Brenda, Belinda and Liese, she could not agree with those convictions.

Bernard told Apricot that to believe in ghosts was to insult God: the souls of the dead went to heaven, purgatory or hell, depending, but did not hang around afflicting the living. Bernard and Apricot, at his suggestion, sat up all one night together when Ken was away to prove that the apparition of Wendy appeared in Rhoda's head, and nowhere else. Apricot sat closer and closer to Bernard on the stairs, and he edged further away, distancing himself from temptation.

'Sex before marriage is a sin,' he'd already told her, 'and if I read the Gospels right, sex after as well, unless for the procreation of children.' He failed to quote chapter and verse when Apricot asked him to, and then said it was a personal matter, in any case: if he was going into the priesthood he'd rather do it celibate.

'Look, look, my mother's ghost!' cried Apricot, pointing, though there was nothing there, or hardly anything, just a warning shimmer in the air outside Rhoda's bedroom. Bernard looked up and Apricot made a dive to undo his zip. He shook her off and made his way, groping through a dark lit only by the red light of the fish-tank heater, to the front door and out into the street and away. 'I didn't think you were that kind of girl,' he said, 'and I shan't see you again. But do please get Rhoda to a doctor.'

Apricot persuaded Rhoda to go to the hospital.

'What I don't understand is this,' said Apricot to Brenda, Belinda and Liese, 'why was Bernard Parkin sitting next to me on the stairs in the dark if he didn't want sex!'

They searched for an answer but couldn't find one. They were full of complaints. They compared notes. What was it men wanted? They asked around. Liese's father replied, 'True love.' They thought this was very continental of him. Ken, when they put the question, replied, 'A quiet life,' but they didn't believe that either.

Exams were approaching; and, with them, trouble on all fronts. Mr Rowse refused to see Rhoda any more because she'd been seen talking to Young Catholics Against Witchcraft. Ken chatted Belinda up so she said she wouldn't come round any more, or so Brenda reported. Apricot had a row with Belinda. Brenda sided with Belinda, Liese with Apricot. Rhoda vomited blood over the breakfast table. The hospital said she had cancer of the stomach, the throat, the liver, the bladder and everything. Ken, upset, tried to drive his van through the line of Mr Rowse's patients: he broke the ankle of an elderly man too feeble to jump out of the way. The police were called: arrest narrowly averted. Mr Rowse's Sunday Angels, or someone, put a dog turd through Ken's letter box. The council tried to take Mr Rowse to court for fraud and deception, and asked Rhoda to be the star witness for the prosecution but she refused, and had a startling remission, as Mr Rowse had promised her she would if she were only loyal. Mr Rowse left the area and set up elsewhere. He had millions in the bank, rumour went, and had never in all his life paid any tax at all. He went without even paying the cleaner.

Apricot waited until her exams were over and then went down to the Catholic church and hung about until she met Bernard coming out of confession.
'What were you confessing?' she asked, bold as brass, walking up to him in her everyday short skirt and torn black stockings, as if the terrible incident on the stairs had not happened at all.
'Sins of the flesh,' he said, 'committed in the head with you.'
That quite compensated for the insult he had offered her on the stairs.
'Please marry me,' she said. 'It's no fun any more at home. If I don't get out I might go under.'

He understood her predicament, or seemed to, and, much to Brenda, Belinda and Liese's disgust, married Apricot in a registrar's office, in a civil ceremony. She was seventeen. This would do, he told her, until such time as she became converted to Catholicism and they could marry properly. Or not, as the case might be. They set up house in No. 93, which was now to let. She would have to go out to work, it appeared, to see him through college. But at least it was no longer theological college. He could not marry and be a priest. He would be a social worker instead.

'Like mother, like daughter,' said Ken, who had given his consent without argument. He had started a new career as a singer. 'Let's hope she won't have to do a milk round.'

When Rhoda died, a month or so later, Ken married his ex-saxophonist's widow, who understood the rigours and demands of the musician's life, and who had a teenage daughter. It was the kind of household he understood. Nevertheless, he felt abandoned and betrayed by the women in his life.

Eleanor Darcy speaks to Hugo, and Valerie listens

A: Why are you so buttoned up, Mr Vansitart? So singularly ungiddy? You have a love bite on your neck, yet you go on asking me for my views on the multicultural society, on secularism, on Darcian Monetarism. What you really want to know is what men always want to know about women, namely would she, if asked, and if not, why not. And would they want to, if she would.

> *'I meant to start the tape a little further on,' said Hugo to Valerie. 'However, let me assure you that the thought hadn't even crossed my mind.' 'I should hope not,' said Valerie, but the thought was now in her mind. They sat up side by side in the bed, naked, listening, but Valerie no longer felt safe.*

But your training is at stake, your professionalism: you cannot ask the question: so few can. Like everyone else you must have your face-saver; yours in particular being that, in the quality newspapers at least, the mind is interesting, the body is not. Well, keep your face saver; stay buttoned up. Don't ask; I won't answer. So many things you refrain from asking that you'd love to know. For example, how does it happen that I married a good Catholic at seventeen and here I am at thirty-something, childless? Is it because I am a bad woman, a selfish woman, the kind who chooses to stay childless: or am I an unhappy woman, an unfortunate woman, and can't have them? Barren! Or just an unlucky woman because it just so happened my Catholic husband was infertile? Let me answer, at least this one unasked question.

Certainly it was Bernard's initial belief, in the early days of our marriage, that contraception was a sin: Papal authority held it to be so, and Bernard's allegiance was to the Pope. Because the Pope, according to Bernard and his friends, alone among all men had the ear of God, and God, it seems, thinks the more people down here on earth the better. God is the Great Factory Farmer in the Sky; closer and closer we are crammed together, the Pope our Bailiff, hatching our young for his profit, for, as the Bishop said to Marie Stopes, the purpose of man is to increase the flow of souls to God and to stand between God and his purpose is surely sin. And men like my husband Bernard, full of love and trust, look up to heaven with adoring eyes, victims of the phenomena of positive transference which the tortured so easily develops for his torturer, and plunge about in female flesh crying, 'Only procreate and all will be well.' Men do so long for someone to be *in charge*. In Darcy's Utopia each man will attempt to read the mind of God and not rely on others to do it for him.

Q: Are you telling me that Darcy's Utopia will be a secular society?

A: Yes, Darcy's Utopia will be a secular society. Men and women can believe whatever they like about the nature of God, and worship whomsoever they like, from trees to cows to Mohammed, but in the privacy of their own homes.

Q: As in the Soviet Union in the heyday of religious persecution?

A: No. As in Darcy's Utopia, in the future we aspire to. There are few lessons to be learned from history. Because things went wrong in the past does that mean they will necessarily go wrong again? Of course not! Because *we* are different! Do we not know more than we ever did about crowds, power, group behaviour, motivation, national and religious hysteria and so forth? We know ourselves, as once we did not. I promise you, we have progressed! Had those early Communists received their education in a contemporary society, understood themselves and others better, they would have laid down a rather different and more workable framework for the new society. We contemplate past failures of humankind in its search for the perfect society and become depressed. It will never work, we say! But it will, it will! What did we expect? That we'd

68

get it right first time round? How could we? It may take a couple more hundred years, a thousand, but we will get there. Let me repeat, in Darcy's Utopia Church and State will be firmly separated: religious broadcasting will be forbidden on the grounds that it is divisive, racist, sexist, and an incitement to violence as belief structure clashes with belief structure – Christian at the hands of the Jew, Hindu the Muslim, Protestant the Catholic, Sikh of Buddhist, Capitalist of Communist, and of course vice versa – and no doubt the Moonies and the EST-ites will soon be kneecapping one another with a clear conscience. Incitement to non-thought, conversion to blind belief, will be considered the most antisocial of all crimes. It is from closed minds that so many social evils flow.

Q: I thought you said money was the worst thing?

A: You try and catch me out, Mr Vansitart. The streams of evil flow and merge: their source is myriad. Are you hot? Why don't you take off your jacket? Here . . .

> *Valerie listened for suspicious sounds on the tape, and despised herself for so doing. But only the occasional innocent – so far as she could tell – twang of the springs of the hideous black and red sofa punctuated the interview.*

A: Mr Vansitart, what courage it takes to think! To acknowledge that we stand alone on this whirling ball of rock which we call earth, hurtling God knows where through space, and that there is no God to hold our hand! God not so much the Prime Mover – we can do without him – but the God who understands *what's going on*. There must be some really nice, other, stationary, less-inconceivable place, we think, than the world; some permanent non-whirling static heaven somewhere where fairness and justice triumph. Surely! If we can conceive of it, it must exist. And it would be really nice to think that the ones who keep the rules are going to get there. So we dream up sets of rules, we try and live by Holy Books, from the Ramayana to the Koran to *Das Kapital* by way of the Bible. Words are magic, words are power.

Don't you think, Mr Vansitart, that the really nice thing about human beings is the notion we do have that things ought to be somehow *fair* – though nowhere in nature do we have evidence that God understands the concept at all. Justice simply does not seem to be built into the system. All I can conclude is that the human race, at its best, is really very much pleasanter and kinder than this God it invents to hold its hand. The closer men get to God the nastier they get: the more judgemental, the more punitive, the more murderous in their determination to have got God right, and everyone else to have got God wrong. The Pope says that since God initially made us multiply, as is obvious from looking around even the famine fields of Ethiopia, we'd better do as much of it as we can. God needs his nourishment, his daily fix of souls as by the million every day we drop off the perch, and so Bernard and Apricot – renamed Ellen as a condition of marriage – if they're to do God's will, must reproduce till the cows come home, though nowadays of course the cows never leave home in the first place, they're linked up permanently to milking machines. So how can they come home? In and out, in and out, him into her, after the pub – drunkenness is encouraged in Catholic societies: another incitement to non-thought – bang, bang, whoosh, and bingo, there's another one. If you don't look out.

Q: I take it you wouldn't describe yourself as having a maternal nature?

A: How right you are. Congratulations on a comparatively giddy question. Fortunately during the first few months of our marriage Bernard, how shall I put it, practised asceticism – I had no chance of getting pregnant, or very little, and after that he was converted to Marxism, and though we were at it all the time for years, he stood over me daily to make sure I ingested a contraceptive chemical. 'Ellen! Time to get up! Time to take the pill!' It was our duty, he felt at that stage, to desist from overpopulating the planet. And what sort of world would we be bringing children into? It wasn't fair on them to give them life. Better not to exist at all. Spared the curse of life! With Bernard, if it wasn't one thing it was another. In Darcy's Utopia the paradox of procreation is dealt with very simply. But I think you're still much too stiff and male and professional: I will talk about that with Valerie, when she can be bothered to come along. What I do so like about Valerie is how relaxed she is! I have talked more than enough for today. Shall we ask Brenda for a cup of coffee? Or I have some vodka in the fridge.

Q: Vodka? What a brilliant idea.

Here the tape ran out. Hugo told Valerie that nothing else of import had been said. 'What did she mean by relaxed?' demanded Valerie. 'I'm not in the least relaxed.' He did not reply, merely smoothed her lips closed with his fingers, only to part them again with his tongue. 'Incitement to non-thought!' ran through her head as she went under, into the soft seas of non-self.

Valerie suffers from emotion

I've never felt sexual jealousy before. I have seen it in others, and despised it. What a lack of self-belief is here displayed, I have thought; what lamentable failure of nerve. I have noticed women at parties distracted and uneasy, seen them leave the group they're in to join another, where their partner, they fear, is having too good a time, his attention too focused for comfort on another woman. Men do it too, of course, but I think women do it more often. Perhaps they are just more practised in forethought, especially if they have children. Act now, save trouble later! But this particular act is counterproductive: it brings trouble nearer. The man knows quite well what's going on, sees his freedom restricted, his dignity insulted, his lust observed, if lust it is, and is angry and resentful either way. And how *public* –

Jealousy – destructive, pointless, pitiful, pathetic! Or so I thought, in the good days, the wonderful days, before I felt it. Now I see it's the energy that makes the world go round. Mine, mine, you can't have it! Hugo is mine, not Eleanor's. Hugo is visiting Stef, his wife; I don't mind that so much, not quite so much. Perhaps I acknowledge some former claim. Wives are boring things. How I must have bored Lou. Always there, never jealous. Never valuing him enough to be jealous, never arriving suddenly to catch him out, never finding his mail interesting enough to steam open! Nothing more insulting than a non-jealous partner.

'So there you go, Lou, off to Amsterdam with the Philharmonic! Have a nice time. See you Wednesday.' Never even thinking what sort of nice time. Isn't she rather attractive, the girl harpist: has he noticed the bend of her white swan neck, the discreet flicker of her fingers; wondered how the neck would seem, the fingers flicker, in more intimate a situation? Or Lou, jealous of me? Is he jealous now? Does he suffer? I think not. This is what irks, what irritates. I have gone, and Lou doesn't mind, hardly notices.

Lou and I have always presented a good public face: we make a happily married couple, a busy professional pair; she in the media – seen as a little suspect, a little too clever for her own good – he in the interpretive arts: sensitive, hard-working, dedicated: often away. Just as well, they say, that Valerie has the children and her work to keep her occupied. Perhaps, in retrospect, rather a dull pair to have at a dinner party. Lou and Valerie. Most of the friends are from the music world, not the media: they don't mix easily. Orchestra talk is very different from newspaper talk, and, as so often, the husband's occupation wins. Musicians are by their very naming *good* – media folk are noisy, rackety, flip.

Lou, Valerie, Sophie, Ben. One of the strangest things is how little I think of Sophie and Ben. As if I were not one person as I had always thought, but divide very simply and cleanly into two – the erotic and the maternal. The erotic has swept in and taken over: split the maternal off, like a tree split by lightning – one half stands and grows, the other simply falls and dies.

I say I do not mind Hugo visiting Stef but why is he so long away? It's time he came home to me. I do not like the thoughts in my head. I need his presence to drive them away. He said it was to discuss the children but what was there to discuss? She will look after them, no doubt, as Lou will look after Sophie and Ben. Let him communicate with her by letter, if he must: let solicitors arrange money matters. Stef has a good job: she can support herself. She is a financial journalist with her own by-line. She is a cold, unfeeling and unresponsive woman: she must be, or Hugo would not have left her for me. She was his youthful mistake: she is in the past tense. She lives in time: Hugo and myself out of it. I wonder if I were to kill her, if she were dead, if she were knocked over by a car, would that make the jealousy, that mixture of anxiety, grief and fear of exclusion, simply stop? Is it Eleanor's notion or mine that sex in itself is a drug: that its effects are like heroin? In which case I can see jealousy as one of the nastier withdrawal symptoms. Only Hugo, once again in me, part of me, driving in like a needle into flesh, will stop this particular distress.

I look Stef and Hugo up in the telephone book. I punch out the numbers. The hotel phone sings its special little sickly Stef-and-Hugo tune. A child's voice answers. No doubt Peter, aged eight. The eldest. The other two are twins; aged four, I seem to remember Hugo saying. Peter ought to be in bed. What kind of a mother is she? I find I am lost for words: put down the telephone, but not before a woman snatches the phone and says, 'Who's that? I know who that is! Bitch!' before I cut her off. She shouldn't speak like that, behave like that, in front of her own children. No wonder Hugo prefers Valerie the Comparatively Well Behaved.

Presently the phone beside the bed goes. It is Hugo. He can come for an hour. Why only for an hour? Isn't he living here with me? Never mind, never mind.

I hear his step; I open the door into the hotel corridor. It has a timeless, placeless look: it could be anywhere in the world. There is not enough air on earth for me to breathe: my love is consuming all the oxygen in heaven. We are on the floor together: the door has to swing to on its own, as it is designed to do, though more for the sake of security than lovers. Oh, the fix, the fix!

Now I am myself again I can get on with *Lover at the Gate*.

Bernard and Ellen's
Catholic months

'You're absolutely right,' said Ellen to Bernard on the first night of their wedded life. 'Sex is not only sinful, it's disgusting.'
'You shouldn't not do it because it's disgusting,' said Bernard, 'but because it's carnal.'
'Absolutely,' she said. 'The more you pay attention to the body, the less attention you've got left to pay the soul. I really do understand that.'

She agreed with him whenever possible. That way, she imagined, domestic harmony would lie. They took the little house two doors away from Ken and Rhoda; her own to play with, to sweep and dust and arrange as she liked, and meals for two to cook at her discretion, and her father and grandmother just down the road so she had both a respite from them and could keep an eye on them, not too close but not too far. Though what the eye saw was increasingly dismal. Then one day Rhoda went off like a damp squib into eternity: and after that it went into a sort of *déjà vu* double vision, watching Ken and his ex-saxophonist's widow get together. She slept a good deal.

'But, Apricot,' protested Brenda and Belinda, 'you can't just give up and do nothing. Not after all that.'
Brenda was going to a college where there was an excellent women's hockey team, and Belinda to university to read English literature. Liese was doing a secretarial course, but they'd all rather expected that.
'I'm not doing nothing,' said Apricot 'I'm getting used to a new life. And I have a really nice little part-time job at an optician's. Goodness knows where it might not lead.'

75

'You're the receptionist,' observed Brenda. 'It will lead precisely nowhere except sitting around will give you a fat arse.'

'She'll never have a fat arse,' said Belinda. 'Not like me.'

Bernard came in and they moderated their language. He had that effect on people.

For their parting present, before they went off into their futures, they gave Apricot six months' supply of contraceptive pills. Brenda's brother was a certified drug addict and stole more prescriptions from doctors than he ever needed to use.

'I don't need them for the moment,' said Apricot, 'because Bernard and I don't do it. He says we can't until we're properly married in the eyes of God as well as man; he says it's worth waiting for. I certainly hope he's right.'

Belinda said it was and Brenda said it wasn't. Liese said she was not in a position to say. Bernard said, 'Ellen, the sooner your friends stop coming round and chattering the happier I will be.'

Brenda said, 'Apricot, how can you *do* it? He won't even let you have your own name!'

Ellen said, 'I prefer Ellen to Apricot. Apricot was my mother's fantasy and my mother was an alcoholic who deserted me. She had no sense of responsibility, no vision of the future. She was even worse than Rhoda.'

Liese said, 'But, Apricot, you can't speak like that about your mother. Anyway she didn't desert you. She came back as a ghost.'

'I'll have no talk of ghosts in this house,' said Bernard, 'that's for sure.'

She liked him to be masterful. She liked to be frugal: to have money and carefully dole it out. She would never be feckless; not like Wendy, not like Rhoda, not like Ken. She listened to Bernard's account of his faith with increasing mystification. She liked Bernard. She liked the way his mind went back and back in layers: how he tried to justify emotion with reason. She enjoyed figuring it out. She liked his torments, his inability to be happy, his sense that he must be busy saving the world. Where Ken wanted to jolly the world along, Bernard wanted to push it and shove it for its own good. He knew, or thought he did, what was right and what was wrong, and she was glad he did, or thought he did. She knew otherwise. He was taking a degree in sociology. He had a government grant to do so. As a married student he received extra money. She wondered if he had married her to get the better grant. As she had married him to get away from home, she could scarcely complain if he had. She thought his Catholicism, the emotion he mistook for faith, was a pity. As soon as she had recovered from the months of Rhoda's illness, and come to terms with her death, and adjusted to the sudden change in her circumstances, she would do something about it.

They slept in twin beds in the front bedroom of 93 Mafeking Street. There was lino on the floor and lace curtains at the window. There was no bathroom, but a bath in the kitchen covered by a shelf. Bernard would lie awake for hours waging his nightly battle with carnality, slapping it down, groaning. Ellen just went to sleep.

'You're unnatural,' he would complain.

'I expect I am,' she would say. Then one day she said, 'Please, Bernard, I want to become a Catholic.'

'It's not possible. You have no religious instincts. I'm not blaming you. You were brought up in a hotbed of superstition and anarchy: you can't help it but it's hopeless.'

'But I do believe; I do have faith: I have recovered from my childhood. Honestly, Bernard. I believe what you believe, that God came down to Mary, who was a virgin, in the form of a dove – or was that to her mother, so that Mary could get pregnant and be an immaculate conception, which had to happen on account of how sex is so polluting, and give birth to Jesus? That way everyone born after that particular time would have their sins forgiven so long as they believed in Jesus. I don't want to go to hell because I don't believe in Jesus. I wouldn't even go to limbo, Bernard, because I know about Him and haven't converted: I'll have to go to *hell*. Please, Bernard, let me be converted or we'll be separated after death and I couldn't bear that.'

'You're not sincere!'

'I am, I am! I'm your wife. If you don't let me be converted, then you're sinning. You're depriving God of a soul.'

Night after night she'd nag, and in the morning would peck his cheek affectionately if he walked by the cooker where she was frying up his bacon and eggs for breakfast. She dressed trimly for work; neat white blouse, tight black skirt, bright seventeen-year-old eyes: no ladders in her tights now she was settled and happy. He didn't like her going out looking so smart and cheerful. Who might she not meet? He didn't trust her. 'You aren't serious,' was all he could say.

'But I am, I am. Isn't this what you believe? Haven't I got it right? Well, I believe it too.'

'Not put the way you put it.'

'That's why I have to have instruction, Bernard. So I'll put it properly. And then He cursed the fig tree because it was barren: I don't want to be cursed, Bernard. So I suppose one day sooner or later we'll have to do this disgusting thing in order for me not to be barren, but I don't look forward to it. Do you? And then He was crucified and three days later rose from the dead, and at Mass the bread and wine actually turn into flesh and blood, so you shouldn't have breakfast that morning but take it on an empty stomach. And when the Virgin Mary died she rose from the dead too; not just her soul went up to heaven, but her body too.'

'No, Ellen, that is not the case.'

'It is, Bernard. The Pope declared it in 1954. Transubstantiation of the Virgin Mary. And it hasn't been rescinded. It took them nineteen hundred years to decide, but then God dwells in eternity, and the Church too, so there's no hurry. Fancy that, Bernard! Isn't that somehow just *neat*? Do you think she went up with her arms raised; I kind of see her that way. And were they old arms or young arms? Would they change on the way, or before her body began to rise? I wouldn't like to rise to heaven except in my prime. Would her wishes be taken into account? I *do* need instruction, Bernard. Where *is* heaven, anyway, for her to go to in the flesh? I'd always seen it as in some other dimension. Can flesh move from one dimension to another? I am so ignorant I can't bear it!'

He locked away his books on Catholic theology but she took the bus to the Westminster Cathedral and bought more from the bookshop there. When he came home from college she'd be reading *The Catholic Mind*. She read the Catechism in bed at night, occasionally sighing; she would turn towards Bernard and her long hair – she wore it up for work, half-down in the home, fully down in bed – would fall over her face, over her white shoulder.

'We're not going to succumb, Bernard,' she would say if he made a move towards her, and she'd toss her head back in a swift, moving, golden curtain. 'You and I are going to be strong against temptation. We are going to nurture our souls, not give in to lust. We aren't animals – God has blessed us with free will. By sacrifice and submission and by the Grace of God I mean to become a truly serious person, fit to make a new beginning and become a Catholic and a proper wife to you. We'll be married in the Catholic Church, and I'll teach all our children to be good Catholics. I'll have eight, I think. After that we'll stop having sex.'

Bernard's mother sent a Christmas card and in the name of Catholic family unity Ellen invited her to stay. Bernard cringed. Mrs Parkin smoked. Bernard, who neither smoked nor drank, had to keep opening the windows. She was a widow, fleshy, piggy-eyed, slack-mouthed, with a taste for sweet sherry. She wore a cross around her reddened crinkly neck, wore black as befitted her widowed state, and her hair in tight grey curls between which lines of white, stretched skin showed. She brought as a present a portrait of Mother Mary as she appeared to the children at Fatima, executed by someone of sentimental disposition, and a statue of the Virgin Mary, the mould fashioned by someone of a melancholy and austere frame of mind. Ellen put them in pride of place above the fireplace in the front room downstairs. The fireplace held a gas fire; the walls were a figured cream paper: the three-piece suite of maroon uncut moquette. There was a glass-fronted mahogany cupboard where Ellen insisted on keeping Bernard's family photographs, which she had found at the bottom of a suitcase. The Parkins had migrated from Dublin when Bernard was eight, young enough to take advantage of an educational system which allowed bright children to climb up and out of their allotted place in society. Bernard's father had been a builder, his two elder brothers were house painters; his older sister was married to a carpenter: another just left nursing to be married; his two younger sisters were still at school and planned to go to college against their mother's wishes.

'They'll never find husbands,' complained Mary Parkin, 'if they've too much knowledge in them. It's unsettling for a girl.' And she crossed herself. A touch to the forehead, a touch to the left of the chest, the right, and the solar plexus: rapid, never quite touching self: Jesus crucified an inch before the body, forever.

'It certainly is!' agreed Ellen. 'Look how I gave all that up for

79

Bernard! It's so important for a wife to be able to look up to her husband. It's because she can't we get all these divorces.' And she too crossed herself.

Mrs Parkin would take quick sidelong looks at her new daughter-in-law, hoping to catch her out, but there she'd always be, merry as a chicken, tra-la-lahing amongst the pots and pans in the kitchen, or lipsticking her lips in the frameless octagonal mirror in the parlour, or telling her rosary in front of the Virgin, apparently more devout even than Bernard, the most devout of all her sons. She'd hoped Bernard would grow up to be a priest: now he'd taken up with a woman. She didn't trust Ellen one bit.

'You mustn't worry about my not being Catholic,' said Ellen. 'I'm going to convert the minute Bernard thinks I'm serious enough. Do you think being serious is the same as being unhappy, Ma?'

Bernard's mother was not accustomed to such questions: she shook her head and took another fag and another cup of tea and longed to be off to stay with her eldest son. She felt uneasy amongst non-smokers and a home without children didn't feel right, and Bernard didn't look happy.

'Your mother's bound to go to heaven,' said Ellen to Bernard on the afternoon of the morning his mother left. It was teatime. She had made scones. 'She never misses Mass. Lucky her, a proper Catholic! And I expect if your father hadn't died she'd have had at least twenty children! The salt of the earth, your mother.' She stirred four spoons of sugar into her cup. 'What a pity cirrhosis got to him so early!'

'Don't do that,' he begged. 'You'll get fat.'

'I'm not vain,' she said. 'You wouldn't want me to be vain. Vanity is a sin.'

'You'll get just like my mother.' In the past, he had only ever spoken well of his mother, when he spoke of her at all.

'I'd be proud to be like your mother,' said Ellen, and she glanced towards Mary smiling on the mantelpiece and crossed herself.

Bernard put down his scone. He had lost his appetite.

'My mother,' said Bernard, suddenly, talkative at last, 'is a mean-spirited, disgusting bitch; a big fat mammy, and to think that I was born from between her legs makes me want to vomit. She made my life hell. She sneered and bullied and slobbered: she nagged my father to death, and when she wasn't nagging she was muttering. I hate her. Why did you ask her here? What are you trying to do to me, Ellen?'

And he got to his feet, skin white beneath his little beard and his brown eyes desperate, and swept the Virgin Mary to the ground, where she failed to break.

'Just as well she's plastic,' said Ellen placidly. 'It must be very unlucky to break the Virgin. More bad luck years even than breaking a mirror. But that's superstition, isn't it? I hope it isn't a mortal sin, for your sake.'

Bernard jumped upon the Virgin and she cracked and flattened.

'I don't think you should,' said Ellen doubtfully. 'You weren't like this when I married you. Jumping on poor Mother Mary. It won't diminish her powers one bit!'

He wept, his head upon her knee, and presently his hand crept up between her knees and she didn't even pull away with a 'Sweet Jesus, what do you think you're doing?' but drew the curtains to and lit the gas fire to warm them both. She had an approved menstrual calendar and knew it was more or less – or at least with an acceptable risk factor – her safe time of the month.

'It was worth waiting for,' she told Brenda. 'You were wrong and Belinda was right.'

The next day Bernard went to talk to Father William, and came home to say yes, it was okay, Ellen could take instruction and, if all went well, could become a convert to Catholicism. They would be properly married in church: they'd discuss the question of children later. Ellen undressed for bed and fell on her knees and prayed, instead of getting into it.

'Now what?' he demanded. 'Are you thanking God?'

'I'm praying to Mary to restore my virginity,' said Ellen. 'Don't interrupt.'

'What are you talking about, Ellen?' he demanded, grabbing her by the hair. 'Are you insane?'

'She can do it, honestly,' said Ellen. 'It says so in a little book I got from Our Lady's Bookshop. She can restore virginity not just in the soul – well, anyone could do that – but in the body, if you pray enough and feel sufficiently remorseful. Actually in the flesh, the way she went up to heaven. I simply adore Mother Mary. I wish I could make an unconditional "yes" to God the way she did. I do so want to be pure in body and mind. She had a head

81

start, of course, what with her mother being immaculate too. I don't somehow see Wendy as having me that way. We succumbed to temptation once, Bernard, but I'm sure Mary will forgive just so long as we never, ever do it again.'

Bernard let her hair go.

'You win,' he said. 'I'll become an atheist.'

'That's going too far too fast,' said Ellen, getting into bed. 'The position mightn't hold. How about an agnostic?'

But he felt that position to be untenable. It was cowardly. If you lost your faith you lost your faith, and that was that. He understood the absurdity of his beliefs. He regarded them now as he regarded other ordinary but embarrassing habits of youth: odd hair styles, a passion for cheap cologne, eccentric dressing, strange obsessions – all things to be grown out of. He even thanked Ellen for this new, sudden, unexpected leap into maturity. But some few weeks later she happened to bring home from the library a volume of Marx's early writings.

'It was a conversion experience,' said Ellen to Liese. 'His hand shook, his mouth fell open. He believed.'

'Well,' said Liese, who was now engaged to a nice young architect called Leonard, and who was proud and plump and stuffed as full of delight as a feather cushion – over-stuffed, Brenda remarked – 'I suppose it's better to believe in something than nothing. Leonard isn't orthodox, thank goodness, or I'd have to shave off all my hair. He worships me, I'm glad to say.'

A bust of Lenin stood on the mantelpiece where once the Virgin smiled. The theological books went to the jumble sale; political science took their place. Friends no longer came to gather in prayer, but to further the revolution. Bernard believed. He understood that heaven and hell were here on earth, and that little by little heaven would drive out hell, and that the efforts of men of intelligence and goodwill should be dedicated to hastening that process; and that even the word 'should', with its implication of duty and overtones of guilt, was in this brave and newly discovered world, inappropriate.

'"The abolition of religion as the 'illusory' happiness of men is a demand for their 'real happiness',"' he read aloud to Ellen. '"The call to abandon their illusions about their condition is a call to abandon a condition which requires illusions."' How bright his eyes were. His shoulders squared and straightened. He no longer walked in guilt, but in hope.

The twin beds went. The saxophonist's widow refused to lie in Ken and Rhoda's bed, so Ken offered it to Bernard and Ellen: they took the offer, rightly, as a gesture of approval, and the four of them carried it one very early morning from No. 97 to No. 93.

'You can't lie in that bed,' said Brenda, 'it isn't decent. It's the bed your mother and your grandmother slept in with your father.' She was engaged to a lecturer in economics: a straightforward young man. They were saving to get married. They would have everything new.

'I like the idea of it,' said Ellen. 'It gives me a sense of continuation.'

The bed was old, soft and lumpy. She felt she would draw strength from it. She needed strength: her and Bernard's nightly love play would go on for hours, limbs lurching and surging in some kind of gladiatorial combat as if the one who weakened first lost. Oddly, she felt less happy, less content, less well able to go about her daily business than she had in the three painful months of her sexual abstinence. Perhaps sex was a drug. The more you had the more you needed. First the relief, then the surge of pleasure, then the peace: then the niggle of dissatisfaction growing into active discontent, into a sense of loss, of desperation, of craving – and then the fix. People would do anything to others in order to get the fix. But perhaps she was just short of sleep: there were other ways of looking at it.

'Marxism is to Catholicism as methadone is to heroin,' said Ellen to Belinda, 'but enough of an improvement to count.'

Belinda said she didn't have a boyfriend, but Brenda, Liese and Ellen knew she was having an affair with a married man.

'She has low self-esteem,' said Brenda, 'from being so fat, and a romantic nature. That's how it ends up.'

Ellen said, 'Then why doesn't she go on a diet?'

The remark got back to Belinda, who didn't speak to her for years thereafter.

'Apricot was one thing,' said Belinda, 'but Ellen is just too ruthless for comfort. Ellen and Lady Macbeth? Nothing in it!'

Valerie's garden interview with Eleanor Darcy

Q: So you stayed happily married to Bernard for fifteen years?

A: Journalists always make the assumption that to be married for a number of years is to be happily married for those years. What has the length of time to do with it? Couples stay together for any number of reasons other than happiness: questions of money, children, accommodation or idleness, depression, habit, fears above all: fear of what the neighbours will say, fear of loss of status – fear of going without sex being chief amongst them. And I daresay the worry about what to do with the cat or the problem of finding spare time in the executive diary keeps other unhappy couples together. But yes, as it happens, Bernard and I were happily married for fifteen years, in the face of all likelihood, and against the prognostications of our friends.

Q: To what do you attribute this success?

A: Success? Why do you equate being happily married with success? However, we'll let that pass. I attribute it to frequent and energetic sex, to our not having children, to my habit of deferring to him, and lying about my actions, my whereabouts, my politics, my emotions and my orgasms.

> *The day was bright. They sat in the back garden at Eleanor Darcy's insistence. Trains passing the other side of the wooden fence interfered with the recording. Brenda's children played in the paddling pool. Valerie faced into the sun. Eleanor wore a pretty straw hat. Valerie wore a little scarf around her neck to hide Hugo's love*

bites. She could not see the state of Eleanor's neck because Eleanor wore the collar of her crisp white blouse up. Why, on so hot a day?

Q: But isn't this dishonest?

A: Of course. You asked me how I stayed happily married and I replied. The reply is honest; you just don't like it.

Q: But isn't marriage about partnership, trust?

A: Yours may be. Mine are not.

Q: But surely women have a right to sexual fulfilment? Men should work to achieve it. The woman ought not to lie about these things, or how will men ever learn?

A: There is no such thing as a 'right' to anything: Right to Life, Right to Choose, Right to Housing, Right to Orgasm – all it means is 'it would be nice if only'. Of course it would be nice. It is just that so many desirable ends are incompatible. Or, if interests overlap, they do not necessarily coincide. What is good for the child is often not good for the parent, and vice versa. What is best for father and child may be perfectly horrible for the mother. And where sex is concerned it is perilous to talk about shoulds and oughts. Shoulds and oughts end in far too many impotent and guilty middle-class men writhing around hopelessly in the beds of friends and strangers. The upper and working classes, being less verbal, less given to talk of shoulds and oughts between the sheets, have less trouble, if you'll forgive me, simply getting it up and putting it in, to the relief and satisfaction of everyone concerned. In Darcy's Utopia there will in general be little talk of 'rights'. And in sexual matters men and women will aspire to individual pleasure not proper behaviour, and go about it however they see fit, and with any luck without too much talk about it.

Q: I am interested in this Utopia of yours. I am sure our readers would like to hear more about it.

A: Then bully for you and bully for them, though I suspect you're lying. Now I know Utopianism has recently had a bad press. Unrealistic, naïve, elitist to envisage a better society, a perfect state, and work towards it. We have decided human nature is bad, that people only work for money, respond only to the profit principle, and must be controlled by threats and punishments. They forget that it is 'we' – or ourselves on a good day, 'society' as we call it – who understand that punishment is appropriate. In other words, that we are *good*. When we get it together to be so. And what else are we to do, not just as individuals, but as a society, but plan some kind of future for ourselves? Drift on as we have been: in our sour, brutish, dangerous cities, in our pesticide-soaked countryside: the will of the people increasingly triumphant, and not its best will, likely as not its worst will? One day the electorate chooses a government to exterminate the Jews: the next day decides on one to take it down the Marxist–Leninist road: the next that all it wants is dishwashers and CD players. Who wants the people's will to prevail? Not the people. They've too much sense. Democracy is a dicey business: it must be seen to work, but not actually to apply, or else we're all in the soup.

Q: The readers of *Aura* might find that rather hypocritical. Dangerously so.

A: Better a government that pays lip service to democracy than one which doesn't even do that. Political parties have somehow got it into their heads that voters want to agree with them, so put up policies with which voters will agree. But voters merely want to elect representatives who have the time and wit to run the country so they can get on with their lives in peace. 'Democracy', rule by the people, did not always have the good press it enjoys today. It was seen as something to be avoided at all costs. It was the demagogues of Ancient Rome who first made proper government impossible. Citizens, whipped up into a fervour of indignation, simply stopped doing as they were told: started bringing horses noisily in by night for deliveries, not washing the sidewalks and so forth, just for the hell of it. Just to show they *could*. How the senators, the patricians, fumed!

Pure democracy has never worked: it works in a moderated form where there is a literacy qualification, or a property-owning qualification – which usually amounts to the same thing – and the voter is capable of making an informed judgement. But life has got too complicated to understand: the vote is no longer sufficient protection for the working man. In Darcy's Utopia there will be elections, but people will be expected merely to vote for people they personally like. It will be a popularity contest. An annual 'boy or girl most likely to run the country' jamboree. And annual; by the time they've got themselves together it will be practically time for them to disperse. The civil service, again composed of volunteers on Community Tax Service, will spend time un-making regulations and shortening forms. Most legal documents will merely state, 'common sense will prevail'.

Q: So all the work in Darcy's Utopia will, as it were, be a tax paid to the community. An ability tax, not an income tax?

A: Exactly. Good for you! Though workaholics will be free to work as long as they please, if they can find something to do machines can't. You're a workaholic; you'll have a brilliant time.

Q: Thank you. Now a question our readers always want to ask. Is it possible to love two men at once?

A: Why do you ask? Is it you who are interested, or your readers? Shall we go inside? The wasps are beginning to annoy me, and I see they quite frighten you. And it's such a busy day for trains. All those people, off to work, off shopping, off somewhere. Do you think we have a group soul? A group identity, the way they say black beetles do? You seem quite tired and nervy; not at all the way you were last time: very trim and self-contained. I hope nothing bad has happened? As I said before – was it to Hugo, or to you, Mrs Jones? – curses have a peculiar knock-on effect. I was never the focus of an actual focused ill-wishing, merely a bit part player in Bernard's drama, but look what happened to me!

> *They were inside, in the kitchen. Brenda washed up mugs at the sink. Eleanor Darcy made coffee, using a frugal quantity of powder and low-fat milk, too late for Valerie to murmur that she*

took hers black. She took the opportunity to check
the tape was running. It was not. She would
have to rely upon her notes.

Q: How could you tell if a misfortune was the result of a curse, or
just ordinary bad luck? A simple matter of cause and effect?

A: Ah. Your wife leaves you, you lose your job, your friends quarrel
with you. In themselves these are not misfortunes. It is in your
reaction to them that misfortune lies. You are *humiliated* by your
wife leaving you. You *hate* being on social benefits. You are *lonely*
without your friends. Indeed, the expectation of such misfortunes
quickly brings them about. You may indeed deserve to lose your
wife, your job, your friends – naturally it is easier to accept the
power of the curse than the fact of your own selfishness, unlike-
ability, destructive bad temper and so forth. Just as it is easier to
blame witches, agents of the Devil, for male impotence, famine,
drought, war, plague and so forth than it is to blame God whom,
in spite of all evidence to the contrary, we insist on regarding as
a benign and even moral being.

Q: You keep coming back to God and the Devil. Why?

A: So would you if you'd seen the Devil, snarling and slavering
and trying to get in a window of the second floor of a students'
residence. Even through the double glazing the glass was beginning
to melt and you could hear this horrible panting sound.

Q: I thought you said your husband had seen the Dark Thing?

A: I saw him in Bernard's face. If you believe in the Devil you
had better believe in God, or else what a fix you're in! If you have
finished your coffee I think it is time you went. I find myself very
tired today, I don't know why. There is very little to do here;
idleness quickly makes one tired. At least I expect that's it. I never
answered your question about loving two men at once. Isn't it
strange that men never seem to wonder whether it's possible to
love two women at once? They usually say to the old love about
the new, 'I love you but am in love with her,' meaning that their
nature is divided: their protective and uxorious souls reach out for

the old love: their sexuality towards the new. I should consider that a little, if I were you.

> *And, as if she were the therapist and the journalist the patient, Eleanor ushered Valerie from the door. When Hugo, later that day, tested Valerie's recorder he could find no fault with it. 'You just forgot to switch it on,' he said. Such as had been recorded was all but inaudible; though the sound of trains, children and wasps was clear enough. 'I have never in all my professional life forgotten to switch the tape on,' she said. 'Darling,' he said, 'you have never in all your life been in love with a man as you are with me, yet it happened.' And she was obliged to admit he was right.*

Valerie ventures out of
the Holiday Inn

I was trying to make sense of my notes, and dabbing lotion on a nasty wasp sting on my finger, when Hugo turned up with the twins, two untidy little girls with red noses and pale wispy hair. They were, fortunately, not identical, though why I should be pleased they were unidentical I don't know, as identical twins are conceived of the same coupling; unidentical very often of two separate couplings, and so far as I was concerned the less sexual congress Hugo and his Stephanie had the better. Stef was turning out to be very trying; she seemed unable to accept that one love can finish just like that – poof! – and a new one begin. She believed, wrongly of course, that Hugo was infatuated by Eleanor Darcy. The timing of his leaving would naturally suggest just such a conclusion.

'Valerie,' he said to me, 'I'll have to take these two to my mother again,' at which the little ones set up an ungrateful wail, 'but I'll be back as soon as possible. I'm sorry but Stef is really behaving in an impossible way. The children were her idea, not mine.'

I set aside *Lover at the Gate* to attend to the children's needs – Coke and hamburgers from room service soon quietened them. Stef, Hugo pointed out, was dead set against junk food. It is unwise for mothers to be too ideologically sound in matter of diet – it makes it so easy for rivals to the children's hearts to worm their way therein, and win.

A taxi was called and Hugo and the children left for Liverpool Street and I was left alone with my own thoughts, in a state of mind I could only describe as lustless. It occurred to me that I should perhaps wait for my daughter Sophie outside her school, to make sure she understood that I had not abandoned her, had merely left Lou for a man who loved me and would make me happy; that things would presently calm down, and as soon as Hugo and I had sorted things out a little and established our new home she could join us. In the meantime she was more than welcome to share the facilities of the Holiday Inn – room service and swimming pool and sauna. Sophie was after all thirteen, and it's a rare contemporary child – especially born to parents in the communicative arts, that being the only umbrella heading under which both Lou and myself could suitably cluster: though he saw, probably rightly, greater sensibility and sensitivity in a Bloch quartet than he did in a *Sunday Times* editorial – who can expect both parents to live permanently and companionably together.

I left the hotel, feeling rather like the Lady of Shalott, breaking the spell, leaving her room, her castle, going only to the river's edge, there to drown herself, and made my way to the Navimore School for Girls. One by one they sauntered out, or clustered together for safety in great rushes: all in theoretical navy and white, but with such imaginative variation in those two colours and where and how placed, and in what fabric, as to make their apparel singularly unalike. The girls were, however, very much alike: wide-eyed, glossy-haired, with a hunch of shoulder and ease of hip that made them all the sisters they longed to be. And there, yes, that *was* Sophie. She had a little mole above her pretty upper lip, so I knew it was she. I approached.
'Sophie –' I said.
And she cut me dead. My own child looked through me with her wide, hazel, dark-fringed eyes and cut me dead. *Was* it Sophie? She swung round and I recognized the broken metal heel guard on her right shoe. Yes, it was Sophie. She would not part with her shoes for long enough for me to have them properly repaired.
'Sophie,' I begged, but she walked on, with a flick of a navy pleated skirt on which I recognized a cigarette burn. Lou smoked three cigarettes a day: it was his one bad habit – and on one occasion Sophie's skirt and a stub had somehow come into contact.

What had Lou told Sophie? What had he said to her? How had he betrayed me? Poor child, she must be suffering. What had I done? I saw Sophie swing lithely on to a bus before it stopped moving. How many times had I told her not to do it? – to *wait*.

But she was right: if you didn't get on the bus while it moved, you didn't get on it at all. The driver seemed to be playing some kind of survival game with the girls of the Navimore School: he slowed down out of courtesy to the bus stop sign, but took it no further than that. He drove, they leapt, all survived.

I stood, shaken, watching after the departing bus. A dog, some kind of uneasy black and white mixture between collie and labrador, trotted happily towards me. It looked at me in the kind of easy, assessing way dogs on their peculiar errands do look at strangers – and then looked again, and stopped dead: his hackles rose: he backed, he made a kind of howling noise, turned tail, and fled.

Abashed, I made my way back to the Holiday Inn. I passed a church on the way and really believe I would have gone in to sprinkle myself with holy water – but it was locked, as churches are, these days, against vandals. It was left to the glass, chrome and carpets of the Holiday Inn, the sense of un-exotic, common-sensical luxury, to sustain me. The third floor was a no-smoking floor or I think I might have started smoking again after six years' abstinence. The ambience presently calmed me. The sense of order, of human needs being comprehensible, in fact meetable, was reassuring. Plentiful towels, hair dryer, little bottles of everyday necessities – shampoos, conditioners, shoe horns – whoever uses shoe horns? – our one suitcase each, the few clothes neatly hung: our personal computers, reference books – the tools of our trade. What else could a man and a woman need, I repeated to myself, except each other?

Poor little Sophie would by now be suffering pangs of guilt for her behaviour towards me. I wondered whether to call and say I understood, I forgave her; we'd meet next week some time. I decided I would. I called home. Lou answered. On hearing my voice he put down the phone. I was devastated. Forget Sophie, who was given to drama and tantrum anyway, what about Ben, my little boy? Apple of my eye? Perhaps Lou had told him the monstrous lie that I didn't love him any more? Of course I loved him. It was just that I loved Hugo more. I had met Hugo at a party and unforeseen and overwhelming emotions had consumed me. That was all. The love of man and the love of children are different things: the one does not exclude the other. Surely Ben would understand that, if Lou explained it properly? Ben spent so much time playing computer games, barely pausing to eat, that lately I'd sometimes wondered if he knew I existed at all. He seemed scarcely even to register the changing faces of au pair girls.

I looked at myself in the mirror. I am not bad-looking, but no beauty: too thin, too earnest, too practical, I had always thought, to inspire sudden, romantic love. And yet I had! When the two halves, separated by that terrifying law which parts the two who were never meant to be divided, defy that law and meet, there can be no gainsaying them. Hugo and Valerie.

There was something wrong here, something I didn't understand. I wanted Hugo to return at once, at once, to keep the niggling doubts down where they belonged: what was going on? I noticed I had my pen in my hand again. When I wrote a line or two of *Lover at the Gate* I felt at ease, buoyantly happy, confident. Put down my pen and I heard in my ears the howl of the fleeing dog, saw the metal flash of Sophie's shoe – I could not bear it. I picked up the pen. Anxiety dispersed.

The phone rang. I ran to it but it wasn't Hugo. It was Eleanor Darcy.
'How did you know I was at the Holiday Inn?' I was puzzled.
'Is that where you are? What a strange place to *be*! Do you really like hotels? I hate them. I just called the number Brenda gave me. She's good at names and addresses and details. I'm hopeless. I think we've got an arrangement to meet tomorrow. I'm sorry, I can't make it. It's visiting day for Julian tomorrow, in prison. It quite went out of my head. I know what you're thinking: fancy forgetting a thing like that! The trouble is, it's quite easy. Out of sight is out of mind, when it comes to people as curse objects.'
'Curse objects?'
'Well, that's what Julian is, I'm sorry to say, in relation to me. My falling in love with Julian was nothing to do with me, nothing to do with Julian, but part of the curse put on Bernard that his wife would become the love object of a man more attractive, more wealthy, more intelligent and of a higher status than he, so he

93

didn't stand an earthly. What chance did I have, fond of Bernard as I was, but also, as I daresay you have concluded, and like so many, including I daresay yourself, bored? How is *Lover at the Gate* coming on?'

'I keep getting interrupted. Personal matters intervene.'

'I expect they will. It's hot stuff you're dealing with. Is Julian standing at the gate yet, knocking?'

'Not quite. Just about. I have to get Bernard into Marxism and out the other side. I'm still not sure what you mean by a curse object. Sex objects, love objects – but *curse* objects?'

'It was none of our faults. Though I do blame Bernard, for getting himself mixed up with ethnic minorities. After he gave up Marxism, and was out there all on his mental own, as it were, without fear of hell or counter-revolutionary thought, it went to his head. He became irresponsible –'

'Would you mind if I taped this conversation, Mrs Darcy?'

'Look, I'm not giving an interview. All this is off the record. I thought that would be understood. I called merely to say I couldn't meet up with you tomorrow. I'm sorry. But if you'd like to come over this evening – ?'

But I couldn't. I was waiting for Hugo.

'Oh well,' she said, 'Hugo's coming over tomorrow anyway.'

Hugo had left a full packet of cigarettes by the bed. He left them around to prove to himself that he really didn't smoke. I broke my faith and smoked one. Just one.

Ellen's Marxist years
with Bernard

'I'm so proud of you,' said Ellen, and meant it. Bernard hammered and puttied, putting their home to rights, at one with the worker, his brother; no longer above manual toil but now rejoicing in it. He who had palely loitered, fearful of moral contamination, now boisterously stamped through practicalities.

'Man's self-consciousness is the highest divinity,' he said. 'There shall be no other Gods beside it.' He had shaved off his beard. His chin jutted sexily forward.

'The criticism of religion leads naturally to the criticism of social relations,' observed Ellen. 'How wise Marx is: how everything applies: as true now as then!'

They rivalled each other in anti-deist sentiment. She worshipped him for worshipping Marx, or appeared to.

He had torn the little gold cross from around her neck, during love, with such force she was left with a welt which never ever seemed to vanish. She didn't mind one bit, she said. She was proud of it: proud of his masterful nature – or appeared to be.

'The social principles of Christianity preach cowardice, self-contempt, abasement, submissiveness, meekness –' she read aloud from the early works of Marx, which she had never returned to the library, property being theft, and knowledge free for everyone.

Bernard looked robust rather than pale: had lost his translucency along with his soul. He looked others straight in the eye, he shouted their arguments down. 'Religion is the sigh of the oppressed creature, the sentiment of a heathen world; it is the very soul of soulless conditions,' he harangued his erstwhile comrades in the streets, the vestries. They crossed themselves and prayed for him. This was what happened when you married a non-Catholic.

'Accumulate, accumulate! This is Moses and the prophets to the capitalists!' he declaimed to his fellow students in the college library. Unlike Ellen, though, he always returned his books on time, so the librarians put up with him.

Bernard now argued with his teachers about his grades. Faint-hearted, they took his essays back for remarking and upgraded them, as an airline always will a seat for a vociferous passenger. He plotted to overthrow the senior lecturer in psychology who was fifty-two and had not rewritten his lecture on Piaget for fifteen years. He worked up a cabal against poor old Professor Litmus, who taught statistics and never did anyone any harm, but droned on, and on, and at least never minded when his students slept. If Bernard could change, the world could change: and the sooner the better. He sat in smoky rooms like like-minded friends, talking late into the night. Wives and girlfriends made coffee. They rooted out revisionists, pilloried Trotskyists, jeered at the Anarchists, and even burned the works of Kropotkin in public. They chose Guy Fawkes' night to do it and the gesture went unnoticed – he found a lesson even in this.

Brenda and Belinda were both by now feminists.
'You shouldn't make those men cups of coffee,' they told Ellen. 'Let them do it themselves.' Belinda had lost two stone, given up her married man and was speaking to Ellen again.

Ellen put the point to Bernard.
'As Jenny Marx said in 1872,' she observed, '"in all these struggles the harder because the pettier part falls to women. While the men are invigorated by the fight in the world outside, strengthened by coming face to face with the enemy, we women sit at home and darn." What do you say to that, Bernard? Or do we have to stay fixed in 1872? Is it revisionism to see some improvement in the human consciousness since then?'
'I doubt it was 1872,' Bernard said tenderly. 'You're just making that up, the way you make so much up. And I certainly don't expect you to darn my socks. I have other things to worry about besides socks. Coffee's different. Someone has to make it, and the women just sit smiling and nodding so it might as well be them. Just remember that as the State withers away, so will the many

96

evils which accompany the capitalist state. Sexism included. Only work for the socialist revolution and you work for justice for everyone; blacks, women, oppressed minorities everywhere. Even musicians like your father. What did Marx say in his letter to Kugelmann? "Everyone who knows anything about history also knows that great historical revolutions are impossible without female ferment. Social progress can be measured precisely by the social position of the fair sex – the ugly ones included. Why don't you ask Brenda and Belinda to come along to Friday meetings? I don't think Liese would get much benefit from them.'

'Brenda and Belinda are separatists,' said Ellen, 'and don't go to meetings attended by men.'

'You mean they're lesbians?'

'I do not,' said Ellen. 'Was that Marx's joke about the fair sex, the ugly ones included, or yours?' asked Ellen.

'Marx said it,' Bernard said. 'Why?'

There was a feeling at the Friday meetings – more men than women attended – that sexual possessiveness between men and women was out of order. It was said that there ought to be more sharing and swapping, in the name of change, equality and the exploration of the self. Men and women, everyone agreed, were after all free and equal; marriage was a symbol of bourgeois oppression. One evening a row broke out when Jed Mantree slipped a beery hand into Ellen's dress. Jed was a post-graduate student in psychology. His wife Prunella was present. She was pregnant and poorly.

'Bastard!' cried Bernard, belabouring Jed with his fists, splattering cheap red wine over books and walls. Ellen had to take Jed to casualty to have a cut above his eye stitched, as poor Prune was too upset to do it. They were away for hours. Bernard was in a torment of perplexity. Prune said dismally that she didn't think it was right to stand between a man and his freedom. She went home to lie down.

'See it in its historical perspective,' Ellen comforted her husband when she returned in the small hours. '"Men make their own history," to quote the master, "but they do not make it under circumstances chosen by themselves, but under circumstances directly encountered, given and transmitted from the past. The tradition of all the dead generations weighs like a nightmare on the minds of the living. And just when they seem engaged in revolutionizing themselves and things, in creating something that has never yet existed, precisely in such periods of revolutionary crisis they anxiously conjure up the spirits of the past to their service and borrow from them names and little cries in order to present the new scene of world history in this time-honoured disguise and this borrowed language." Let me put it another way, Bernard, when you uttered your little cry "Bastard!" Ireland spoke through you, and your mother, and a whole history of sexual repression; the knee-jerk of an oppressed peasantry rose up in you when Jed's fingers tweaked my nipples and you hit him, comrade in Marx though he was. You should have let him finger on. You should have been above it. All I had to do was step backwards. I didn't mind. Neither did Prune. But how could you help it? Marx acknowledges the inevitability of your protest. Understands and forgives it, just like Jesus. I really do believe sexual possessiveness is something we should struggle against, no matter how difficult we find it. Of course Jed should not have tried to come between us; it was a counter-revolutionary act on his part, Trotskyite even, when you think about it, but in that act was Praxis, the moment when theory becomes practice, and you should not have interfered.'

Ellen had long ago given up her part-time work at the optician. She too was taking her degree in the social sciences. Bernard was by now a junior lecturer in the same college where he had taken his degree. He was in a permanent state of outrage.

'You are quite right,' Ellen reaffirmed. 'What are your employers but State parasites? As Marx so aptly put it, "men richly paid by sycophants and sinecurists in the higher posts, absorbing the intelligence of the masses, turning it against themselves." Nothing changes!'

'Let it work its way through him,' said Ellen to Brenda, 'let it work its way through and out; the harder I put it the faster it will happen.'

'You want him to worship you,' said Brenda, 'the way Leonard worships Liese.'

Liese and Leonard had a wonderful wedding; now they lived with central heating and embroidered sheets.

'I just want him to be rational,' said Ellen.

'I want, I want,' said Ellen, pinning up above their bed her favourite William Blake print. It was of a man reaching out for the moon, crying 'I want, I want.'

'Not babies, I hope?' asked Bernard. 'What sort of world is this to bring babies into? Nuclear war is inevitable.'

'Not babies,' said Ellen. 'According to Marx, you are quite right, war is inevitable.' And she got out of bed, looked up the page, and read, '"A reduction in international armaments is impossible; by virtue of any number of fears and jealousies. The burden grows worse as science advances, for the improvements in the art of destruction will keep pace with its advance and every year more and more will have to be devoted to costly engines of war. It is a vicious circle. There is no escape from it – that Damocles sword of a war on the first day of which all the chartered covenants of princes will be scattered like chaff: a race war which will subject the whole of Europe to devastation by fifteen or twenty million, and which is not raging already because even the strongest of the great military states shrinks before the absolute incalculability of its final result. And failing that, the class war as interpreted by Engels, a war of which nothing is certain but the absolute uncertainty of its outcome."'

'Do come to bed,' said Bernard.

'Marx and Engels, messengers of God,' murmured Ellen. 'I believe. Help thou my unbelief,' and she got back into bed. Bernard and she had discovered a whole new range of fashionable sexual positions. Their minds raged free: they talked, they shared. Nothing was shameful.

She watched a vase move of its own accord along the bedroom shelf and fall off and break.

'Subsidence,' said Bernard. 'It's been a hot summer. The ground beneath the house has shifted.'

'More like poltergeist activity,' said Ellen. 'Perhaps the ghost of my mother came with the bed.'

'I am sure Marx did not recognize the existence of ghosts,' said Bernard, 'but please don't go looking for the reference; not now!'

Ellen waited for something to happen, something to change, but nothing happened, nothing changed. A little struggling lilac tree in the back yard died, because, Belinda said, too many men had pissed on it, out the window, not bothering to wait for the lavatory to be free. 'Men talk,' said Brenda, 'and it's all piss and wind and ends in death.' Ellen would lie in bed at night watching the objects on the mantelpiece in the glow from the street light, hoping they would move again: that something from another world would intervene, give her a clue as to the nature of her existence. The curtains were too thin and let the light through. But books, papers, cigarettes and matches – they both smoked now – stayed where they were. Nothing moved. She read some more books, wrote some more essays, passed some exams. Drank more coffee, poured more wine, sidestepped Jed's hand, sometimes didn't. Nothing changed.

A stray, dingy orange kitten came yowling up to the back door one night. 'Don't feed it,' said Bernard, 'or it will never go home,' but she did, and the next night there it was again. She opened the back door; it rubbed up against her leg. She let it in, fed it well, took it to the vet: the animal plumped up and out: it lost its dinginess, it all but glowed orange in the dark. It lived with them. They called it Windscale, after the power station. Windscale slept on the bed, moving over reluctantly as warm comfortable pockets changed shape and form while Bernard and Ellen made love.

Ken said – he came for Sunday lunch now, often with his step-daughter but without his wife, who felt awkward in Ellen's presence – that it reminded him of a kitten he'd given Wendy on the day she gave birth to Apricot. Perhaps it was a descendant of that same animal. Why not? Ellen was pleased to think it might be so. It gave her a sense of history. But still she wasn't happy. She didn't understand it.

'I believe,' said Bernard, in and out of the classrooms, cafés, kitchens, street corners, pubs, while Ellen nodded and agreed, 'I believe. That the aim and purpose is to bring about the fall of the bourgeoisie and the rule of the proletariat, to abolish the old society based on class differences and to found a new society without classes and without private property. There is no such thing, mind you, as private property for nine tenths of the popu-lation: its existence for the few is solely due to its non-existence for those nine tenths. I believe that the revolution cannot just come and go but must be permanent, and it is our duty to further it. I believe!'

'Holy Mary Mother of God,' said Ellen, sitting upright in bed in the middle of the night. 'I know what the matter is. I'm bored. This can't go on!'

Valerie receives a letter from Eleanor Darcy

Jack, the Holiday Inn bellboy, came up to Room 301 with a letter for Valerie. She put aside her manuscript, opened it, and read. It took some courage to do so. Missives from the outside world had begun to make her uneasy. She, who usually looked forward to the telephone ringing, had become nervous even of that. Safety lay in words on the page. Outside, all was danger and sudden, nasty surprises.

Dear Mrs Jones,

I drew our phone call to a rather abrupt end and I am sorry. I felt we were perhaps rather straying from the point. Let me give you the text of a talk I gave to the Bridport Women's Institute, before the Scandal, and when Julian and I were still developing our blueprint for the world of the future. They were attentive listeners. Housewives, like the readers of *Aura*, are not idiots! Here goes –

'The rich have got to come to some accommodation with the poor. The poor are winning; they are all around, making themselves felt. They are victims, which means that though not necessarily good, or pleasant, they have a moral ascendancy over the rich. Those who are in the right tend in the end to win: those who are in the wrong to let them win. The war is hotting up. The poor creep out of alleyways while the rich put the BMW in for the night and hit the rich over the head and steal the tyres. The rich do not dare to be alone at night in their grand houses: who lurks to rape around the panelled corners, swings to attack from the ropes in the work-out room? Their talk is of property prices, hired body-guards and stun guns, because the poor are at the gate, inside the gate in the form of the Mexican nurse, the Filipino maid, the Irish girl, the Yugoslav lass; the ones who stand while others sit, and wash the dishes while others eat. The ring on your finger is their dinner for a year. The homeless sleep up against the air vents of the great hotels, supping on the scent of hot fudge sundae and clam chowder.

'Do not suppose the rich have taste: they spend for the sake of spending, to spite the poor, to say "see what I have that you don't". The poor have standards, dignity, taste, conviction: they live honestly, full of hate, shitting in the houses of the rich if they get a chance to break and enter. And why should they not? For the rich get richer and the poor get poorer, and no one troubles to hide it any more; to shut the poor away in poorhouses, the old in almshouses, the mad in madhouses, the orphans in orphanages. They are all out in the street now, in every city in the world, and their eyes follow the rich and plan their revenge. And why not? The rich live as fearful princes: the poor live as angry beggars. And there is no pleasure left in the life of the rich: for who can tell lumpfish from caviare any more, and caviare is cholesterol-rich anyway, and forbidden: and when the rich grow old and hired nurses dab away the dribble, can you trust the nurse to love you, or does she hate you? She hates you. She will twist your poor rich senile arm to pay you out, because you have an airy house on the hill, and she goes home to a room in the damp and humid valley. No, the rich must come to some accommodation with the poor: must acknowledge their existence: must open their houses and their fridges and their bank accounts and let the poor in. And there will be no poor.

'In Darcy's Utopia this lesson will have been learned. That if the poor are hungry they will eat your food, and why should they not?: that if they are dirty they will infest you with disease, and so they should: that if you ignore them they will mug you and steal what you have, which is no more than you deserve: that if they sit barefoot at your door they will hurt your conscience and you will have to let them in. That therefore there must be no poor, and for there to be no poor there must be no rich.'

So you see, Mrs Jones, something has to be done. The proportion of the underclass to the rest rises yearly, both nationally and internationally. We have grown too good, kind and sensitive to mow them down with machine guns, starve them out of existence. We must incorporate them, or die ourselves. They'll see to that. We must build our Darcy's Utopia before it is too late. Our systems, our structures, have to change. I do not expect you to agree with me on everything. I do not maintain I am even necessarily right. I just want you to think about it, and the readers of *Aura* too. Okay? I'm lunching with Hugo tomorrow. Isn't that exciting!

With all good wishes,

ED

Ellen's Marxist life with Bernard comes to an end

'Perhaps we should go on holiday?' Bernard suggested to Ellen. Perhaps that was what she wanted: a holiday abroad might make her eyes look at him and not beyond him.

'Oh I don't think so,' she said. 'I think going on holiday is a very bourgeois sort of thing to do.'

'How do you know? You've never been on one.'

'Neither have you,' she said. It was true. He longed to go. His elder brother had been to Yugoslavia, one of his sisters to Greece.

'In Russia,' he said, 'workers most definitely go on holiday. They even get sent to health farms, to relax.'

'The Soviet Union,' said Ellen, 'and herein lies the tragedy, has become a revisionist state. We can take no lessons whatsoever from the Soviet Union.'

If he lingered in front of travel agents, she hurried him on. 'Poor exploited things,' she'd say of the couples who entered, hand in hand, full of pleasurable anticipation. 'How they fall for it! The sop from the bosses: the holiday abroad!' And she'd take him off to the second-hand bookstall which specialized in the politics of the left, or to attend a useful meeting, and stand around with banners.

'All the same,' he said, when the spring buds burst on the seven trees that grew in Mafeking Street, along which Wendy had once half-run, half-walked, on her way to give birth to Apricot, 'it would be nice to be somewhere different, just for a time, just for a couple of weeks.'

'You will see the same pattern everywhere you go in the world,' Ellen said briskly. 'The exploitation of workers; the disruption of native cultures; evidence of the military-industrial ethos, you will walk like a fool amongst other fools: a tourist, staring at the remnants of the past, memorials to worn-out cultures, galleries dedicated to the ostentation and decadence of slave-masters. Bernard, if we have any time to spare, better to stand and gaze at the name of the very street we live in, "Mafeking", and contemplate its significance. How many died, how many wretches suffered and starved in that particular disgraceful military episode, so that the workers should be duped yet again in the name of the Empire? Worker set against worker, race against race.'

'You're quite right, of course,' he said. What else could he say?

He wanted to buy a car, but she said that was a waste of money and anyway what was the matter with buses, why should they ride, filling the air with fumes, while others walked? She put all spare money into her bank account. 'You'll only waste it,' she said, and she was right and he knew it.

At the beginning of every term he filled in a form habitually distributed to all teaching staff, requiring details of authorized absences from college; for sabbaticals, or the marking of outside examinations, or simply because contractual staff—student contract hours had been fulfilled.

'You shouldn't complete that form,' she said. 'What are you thinking of, Bernard? This is nothing more or less than an abuse of your professional integrity.'

The degree of his paranoia rose and fell, easily and rhythmically, like some distant lake she had once heard of, which locals claimed breathed in, then out, as if a living thing, among pleasant groves: if she dropped in notions, like stones, when the lake was at its fullest with what power did the ripples surge and spread. Bernard took the matter of the offending questionnaire to the union forthwith: the local dispute quickly turned national: Bernard spoke to the press, rallied his colleagues; but alas, all too many wanted no more than a quiet life: Bernard confided that sometimes he had to eat alone in the staff dining room.

'The point is not to be liked,' said Ellen. 'The point is to seize the day! There were times when even Lenin stood alone! If we stand firm, the bosses will collapse. All the same, Bernard, I suppose you could sometimes talk about other things.'

Ellen now worked at an adventure playground – the Christabel Focus – for underprivileged girls in an ethnically mixed section of the city. It was a wasteland of sour earth waiting development: wooden structures had been hastily erected: old tyres swung from ropes: a lean-to hut provided shelter. The Focus, as it was called, had been organized by separatist feminists. Muslim parents favoured it for their daughters because men were barred the premises. Ellen was no longer a student – she had been asked to leave, having flung a pot of paint at a visiting Minister of Education. She had planned both the paint-throwing and the expulsion. She really could not bear to sit and listen for a minute longer, as she explained to Bernard, to the lies of the imperialist lackeys. Besides, she wanted to give more time to the Focus.

'But Ellen,' said Bernard, 'if you'd only stuck it another month, you'd have got your degree and we could have begun to live quite comfortably.'

'I don't work to be comfortable,' said Ellen. 'Why should we be comfortable when all around us are living in poverty?' On Friday nights, when Bernard thought she was supervising Karate for Girls at the Christabel Focus, she met Jed in a motel. He fumbled and humped and heaved and never mastered the art of supporting himself on his elbows so she would arrive home quite squashed and breathless; which was only appropriate.

Bernard's second sister went to Corfu for a holiday and came back with holiday snaps.

'Sometimes,' said Bernard, 'I too feel like going to a hotel somewhere and looking out over a blue Mediterranean sea. You and I could have breakfast in bed, Ellen. Wouldn't you like that?'

'And who would bring us our breakfast, wash our dishes?' she asked briskly. 'The underpaid, the overworked, the exploited? How about us going to the study group on Marx and the Hegelian Fallacy next month in Blackpool? That's by the sea.'

They went. Bernard fell asleep mid-seminar, and Ellen wept, or was seen to weep, from the shame of it.

There was an unfortunate incident at the Christabel Focus: two young girls, aged six and eight respectively, hitched up their trousers to better climb a rope ladder in the presence of a visiting male observer from a possible funding body. Flesh had been exposed. The elders of the local Muslim community objected: the girls were withdrawn from the playgroup. Bernard, by now spokesman for the local race relations committee, accused the Christabel Focus of racism: of wilfully offending the religious sensibilities of a minority group. Then a group called 'Mothers in the Majority' accused the Christabel Focus of lesbian activity – not without some justification – in front of the children; Ellen accused Bernard of being anti-feminist, and attempting to ghetto-ize ethnic minorities; he accused her of racism and white elitism. Bernard slapped Ellen. Ellen slapped Bernard back, and the next day, after a meeting of all parties at which the local Director of Social Services tried to please everyone and offended everybody, lingered after the meeting, provocative and yawning amongst the filing cabinets, until he caught on, locked the door, and embraced her thankfully. That affair continued for some months. She felt the balance of her marriage with Bernard was thereby restored.

Bernard and Ellen went to visit Belinda, who had renounced her separatist tendencies sufficiently to marry a graphics designer. He was poor when she married him. Now he was rich. They had an expensive apartment of minimalist decor: spindly lamps, metal and glass furniture, real paintings on the wall and not a pot plant in sight. Bernard loved it, and said so, as they returned to the dingy familiarity of Mafeking Street.
'Bourgeois decadence,' sneered Ellen, and he shut up.

They went to visit Liese. Liese's father had died. She had inherited a chain of garages. Leonard had given up architecture to help with the business. It flourished. There wasn't a book in the house, but there was an indoor fountain.
'Inherited wealth!' said Ellen when they got home, before Bernard could say a word. 'The very prop of capitalism.'

They went to visit Brenda and Peter. Brenda was teaching PT in a secondary school. Peter was now a colleague of Bernard's at the poly. They had a new car, and went to the cinema and ate out.
'These days it takes two people's wages to keep one household going,' observed Bernard.
'We'll manage on one wage,' said Ellen. 'That is to say, yours. I have no time to work, I'm far too busy.' Ellen had retired from the Christabel Focus over a question of principle. The polytechnic staff were now on a work to rule, though only at local level – a

vote or so at national level having gone against them in spite of a good deal of cooking of the agenda – and she was, as she said, too busy getting a strike fund to so much as think of earning, let alone working; let alone getting to bed before Bernard had long since fallen asleep. They had no television, of course: Ellen scorned it. The new opiate of the people, she jeered; now that religion had failed, TV had taken its place: the gods and goddesses of the new world were the stars and staresses of soap: the bosses' latest plot to keep the minds of the proletariat addled. Bread and circuses! Holidays and TV! There was enough political theory for Bernard to read, God knew, without turning on the box. Let him get on with *Das Kapital*! 'Praise Marx,' Ellen was fond of saying, eyeing Bernard, 'and pass the ammunition.'

One day Bernard sat up in bed and noticed the bruises on his wife's neck. He didn't think he had put them there but couldn't quite be sure. He shook her awake.
'Ellen,' he said.
'I have to sleep,' she said. 'So do you. We have an important meeting in the morning. If we're clever we can win a procedural point on the Matters Arising Item 4 (2).'
'Ellen,' he said. 'You win. I don't think I can describe myself as a Marxist any more. I am resigning from the strike committee. I want a proper life the way other people have it. I want a car, a nice home, a working wife, a child, and to go on holiday.'
'Capitalist swine,' she murmured, and sank back into a sleep in which she tossed and stretched and he was sure muttered someone else's name, but in the morning went with him to a garage and they actually bought a car, albeit second hand, and she let herself be dragged into a travel agency and they booked a holiday to Spain just like anyone else. And for some time after that they went to bed at the same time and Ellen gave up both Jed and the Director of Social Services; and when both threatened, in grief, spite and unreason, to report her infidelity to Bernard, said, 'Tell away!' and neither of them did, which rather disappointed her.

She felt no particular guilt: merely that marriage was a kind of old-fashioned scale: a tray on either side in which the fors and againsts had somehow to be kept in balance, and that extramarital sex had sometimes to be heaped on one side just to keep it steady

109

because indefinable things were piling on the other. Were Bernard to be unfaithful to her, she was convinced, she would leave him at once. But she did not think he ever would be. Now he could see the world ranging round him, as it were, free, exciting and full of possibilities, neither limited by the encircling arms of Jesus, nor somehow squared off in a kind of boxing ring, with Marx, Engels, Lenin and Hegel fierce at every corner, barring all the exits. Now he could go inward, freely, into his own mind, Ellen had great hopes for him. She thought they could even be happy.

She thought she could in the end be legitimized, be more than just the girl who had married the first man who came along in order to get away from home: daughter of a mother who'd shacked up with her own mother's boyfriend at that own mother's unconscious behest – and had thereby had her life negated forever. Wendy betrayed by Rhoda's desire for Ken: betrayed by the author of her own being: no wonder she had faded out of the world so quietly and gently and quickly, as if understanding it were better she had never been born. Apricot the accidental: Ken the instrument: Rhoda the foolish but all-powerful. Apricot, who, like Wendy, should never have been born. Apricot, now Ellen, reborn. Windscale the cat stopped coming into the bedroom: lay on one of the new chairs in the living room instead. At least that didn't keep moving all night.

Hugo's restaurant interview with Eleanor Darcy

Q: Would you say that feminism played an important part in your life, Mrs Darcy?

A: As I have already explained to your colleague from *Aura*, Mr Vansitart, I was a feminist of the socialist variety. Don't the two of you discuss me? I have a feeling you have become quite close. Giddy, even. Perhaps too close, too giddy, to allow much time for discussion? Let me say I believed that the wrongs of women were interconnected with and subsidiary to the wrongs of man; that to work for the revolution was to work, indirectly, for women. That as the State withered away, so would sexism, racism and all other unpleasant social evils. Our agitations were of course not so much for ourselves, for we were all comfortably enough off – that is to say we could afford a bottle of wine every now and then and very few of us rose with the dawn and laboured until nightfall – but sprang from a burning sense of general injustice or a generalized sense of burning injustice, whichever quote's the best or whichever your readers prefer. Gladly we gave our hearts and minds to others. We were the intellectuals of the revolution: our function to rally and inspire the workers. At my suggestion Bernard tried rallying and inspiring the college support staff – the groundsmen and the cleaners and the canteen ladies – but they weren't interested. They wanted to get home to watch telly. In Darcy's Utopia there will be no television.

Q: In that case I imagine people will flee Darcy's Utopia in droves. Don't you?

A: No, actually, I don't. I believe if you took a referendum today a majority would agree that television should be stopped forthwith.

Present them with a vision of a world in which meals were eaten at a table instead of on the knees before the flickering screen; in which conversation was commonplace; political and social ideas worked out by individuals, not spoon-fed into the mind by paid commentators; a TV-less world in which we danced and sang and played charades to entertain ourselves or even popped round to the neighbours; in which our children were not fed visions of death and dead bodies on the daily news, their infant imaginations no longer turned feverish and fearful by the sobs and sorrows of the bereaved; nor subject to the cruel, disagreeable and frequently morbid fictional fantasies of others – would we not really vote for this? Are we not well enough aware that on the screen, as on the page, good news is no news? Where is the drama in easy times, good times? Where is the benefit in *not* raping when rape is on the cards, *not* killing when killing can be done? Inasmuch as "good" television is confrontational, violent, full of event – why then, I think most people would agree, on reflection, yes, communally, we could do very well without TV. We certainly don't want to do without it if others have it, for fear of what we might be missing, but if we *all* gave it up – Mr Vansitart, because the human race has invented TV doesn't mean we have to put up with it.

Q: But surely people need to know what's going on?

A: I suppose we could have one news bulletin a month, by which time what was important and what was not would have become apparent. And the occasional newsflash, I daresay, should a swarm of killer bees approach, or a hurricane, or a radioactive cloud, might well be useful. But the race to be first with the news which so obsesses journalists is quite pointless – a childish game they play at the behest of their capitalist masters: to be there first! Why? Who cares? In Darcy's Utopia we will make do with listening to the radio. Hearing voices in our heads, we must work to make our own pictures. Hereby our imaginations will be educated and stimulated, not grievously curtailed and made afraid.

> *They sat in a fashionable Italian restaurant in the city. At nearby tables people nudged one another and whispered 'Eleanor Darcy'. There had been a month or so where her face had been*

seen almost daily on TV: they had not yet quite
forgotten. She changed seats with Hugo so that
she sat with her back to the other diners. She had
told him that Brenda was obsessively vegetarian,
and that she longed for red meat: would he take
her out? It was her idea, in other words, not his.

Q: You don't imagine the TV industry would take kindly to its abolition?

A: Oh, we don't have to be quite so drastic. Let them make programmes for each other. They do it anyway. Just let them not transmit them. I'll have the lemon sole.

Q: But I thought you wanted meat?

A: Only in theory; when it comes to it. Faced with the actuality of change, one avoids it. One likes what one knows, and knows what one likes. Now when I was with Julian, my second husband, I was a great meat eater. Julian was fond of steaks: we got through jars of mustard. While I was with him I even developed a liking for steak tartar. Bernard was a pork and beans man, with a weakness for the occasional Irish stew, on the greasy side. Rhoda and my father lived on sausages and mash, and little crisp frozen chicken pies.

She wore a dress of fine and flowing black fabric
and many long strings of blue crystal beads and
a rather affected little red hat. Her hands were
small, long-fingered and strong. The tape re-
corder sat on the table between a fluted glass
containing an artificial rose and the giant black
pepper grinder the waiter had inadvertently left
behind. The more he required her to talk about
herself the more he longed for her to ask him
about himself.

Q: But what are people going to do all day in this TV-less world? Can you give me some idea as to their sexual and marital mores? I take it second husbands are allowed?

A: There, you see! Trying to catch me out again! The fear of governments always is that if people are not occupied playing competitive sports or watching TV they will be *at it* all the time. That there will be copulating and fornicating wherever you look – beneath the counter of the wool shop, behind the grille at the bank, in the schools' staff rooms – everywhere you look there will be limbs writhing in ecstasy: only look upwards and you will see the mighty outspread wings of the Devil casting their reddish glow over all the land, and from the black and foaming pit of his fanged mouth the dreadful word will issue: 'Fuck, fuck, fuck!'

> *Diners glanced surreptitiously over their shoulders. Eleanor's voice rose. 'Hush,' he implored her. She apologized at once and moderated her voice. He thought she was glorious, glorious. Her green eyes glowed.*

But no. It will not be like that. The inhabitants of Darcy's Utopia will have as much or as little difficulty getting together as anyone else. Fear of rejection will inhibit many, others will cringe before fear of complications, responsibility, hurting others, failing to perform adequately, or having to reveal physical imperfections. Cellulite of the thighs keeps many a woman chaste: a potbelly keeps a man on the straight and narrow like nothing else. Most will stick to a partner chosen in the madness and self-confidence of youth, as they do outside Darcy's Utopia. Women will continue to choose men – or men women; each sex always believes it is the other which does the choosing – the man being a little older, a little richer, a little more decisive than the woman, for this is how the majority of the human race pairs itself off, and why the myth of female inferiority is so prevalent throughout the world – it being the direct experience of so many children in so many households that Daddy knows best and Mummy's a fool. The woman searches – though these days she doesn't know it, matters of procreation being so far from anyone's thoughts – for a good father for her young, adequate in looks, more than adequate as a provider; the man searches for a good, kind and competent mother for his children, not such a dog as to make copulation a problem – both settle for the best he or she can do. We rank ourselves amongst our peers very early on, so far as our physical attractiveness is concerned: we make our sexual moves within the group appropriate to our vision of ourselves. In Darcy's Utopia people will make up and change their minds, try something new, retreat to the familiar, suffer from requited and unrequited love as much there as anywhere else: how can it be otherwise? But what they will be is discreet about it all. 'What the mind doesn't know the heart can't suffer' will be inscribed above every double bed in the land. No man will publicly humiliate a woman because she is 'old' or he finds her sexually unattractive: no woman will deride a man for his sexual insufficiency or because he is 'weak' or 'wet' or a 'wimp'. It will simply be unthinkable so to do. Thus happiness and self-esteem will be maximized. Did you know, by the way, that statistically a woman tries out a new partner once in every two thousand copulations?

> *She ordered her fish unfilleted. Delicately and discreetly she parted flesh from bone. Her nail varnish was pearly pink. He thought of Valerie waiting for him. He did not think of Stef at all. His children were safely in Norfolk, with his mother, so why should he?*

Q: Really? What is the figure for men?

A: I don't know. I'm sorry. In Darcy's Utopia, however, though love will flourish, and pleasure abound, furtive alliances be formal and reformed, and sexual excitements be breathless and secret and glorious, marriage will be beset around with difficulties and obstacles and deep seriousness: only the very determined will marry. Livings together will happen in abundance, of course; but marriage will be another matter: marriage will imply intent to procreate. Of all matters in Darcy's Utopia only procreation will be subject to rules and regulations. It will be a most serious matter. You cannot have women popping new people out of themselves just at random, when and where they want. In Darcy's Utopia there are bound to be children, but their parents will be carefully selected, and being in short supply they will grow up in a world which loves and admires children and finds them interesting, and doesn't herd them together in schools to get them out of the way, dunk them in front of obscene videos to keep them quiet, and slap them about and threaten them in the streets, which is what happens in this society of ours which you seem to find both perfectly ordinary, and, worse, inevitable. Well, I don't. How many children do you have, Mr Vansitart?

Q: Three. A little boy of eight and four-year-old-twins, girls. Loved and wanted children all of them. I find what you say monstrous. I cannot believe you mean it. You're joking.

> *Hugo looked up in alarm as a woman in a black belted mackintosh and beret pushed her way through the restaurant towards him. He got to his feet. 'Stef!' he pleaded, but she slapped his face, there and then, in front of everyone. 'Your mother brought the twins back. I'm taking Peter with me on holiday. The twins are in the buggy outside,' she said. 'You'd better bring them inside before someone steals them.' And she left. Eleanor Darcy said, 'Don't bother about me. I'll find my own way home.'*

Valerie meets her lover's wife

Reception rang through and said there was a lady waiting to see me in the foyer. I was in the bath. In the better hotels there is always a telephone by the bath – the sense of importance of those who soak in the provided scented foam being thereby increased. 'Look, I am the sort of person who is always in demand – always! Why, I can't even take a bath without being pestered for my time and attention. I'll come to your hotel again, and tell all my friends.' And I said, 'Ask her to come up,' without thinking too much about it. It might have been my colleague Ann – who knew my whereabouts – or even my editor, come to congratulate me on the first pages of *Lover at the Gate* which I had faxed through from the hotel's secretariat – or even Sophie, come to apologize, though I hardly imagined she had been promoted from child to lady in the few weeks of my absence.

And I stepped out of the bath and wrapped myself in one of the big white towels in which these places specialize, and, with an innocence born no doubt of the habit of the past, opened the door.

A small indeterminate woman in a lightly belted black raincoat slipped in past me: she had wispy fair hair and I could see at once from whence the twins had inherited what I can only describe as their nebulousness – a sense of the nebulae or star cluster that is better seen out of the corner of the eye. If you look too hard it disappears altogether into a kind of wistful, disappointed light in the night sky. Yet she managed to be a rather successful financial journalist. Perhaps all the figures permuting in her head had somehow sapped her reality
'Can I help?' I asked, rather wishing I had more clothes on.
'I am your lover's wife,' she said, and then I was glad I had so little on. I felt like flinging aside the towel. Hugo kept telling me

117

my body was glorious and I had come to believe him. Lou never even looked, on Tuesday and Friday nights, any more than he looked at the instrument he played. He knew it too well. Just as he practised the violin every morning between nine thirty and ten thirty, so I always had the sense he practised his lovemaking on me, getting ready for the real thing, only this with me was not it: I was not it. With Hugo, I was quite definitely the performance: Stef, the more I looked at her, obviously a mere rehearsal. I was surprised when she said:

'Eleanor Darcy I could understand. But *you*! What goes on here?'

'I didn't ask you here and I don't want to see you and I have nothing to say to you,' I said, showing her the door but, alas, she seemed to have no intention of going through it, so I capitulated rather too easily and offered her a drink from the mini bar. She said she'd have a sherry, a nebulous drink itself, so I poured her as dark and sweet a one as I could find in the little tight tiny rows of sinister bottles, and while she drank it I put on trousers and sweater.

'Hugo likes really thin women,' she said, 'when he likes women at all. My own opinion, for what it's worth, is that he's a closet gay.' I said I didn't think her opinion was worth very much: if that was the opinion she had of her husband then naturally he preferred someone who admired, loved, trusted and desired him, and why didn't she just go away?

'I've been to see your husband,' she said – I didn't like that at all – 'and he asked me to tell you that if you don't return home by the end of the week he is going to join forces with Kirsty Bull: she's coming to live in and look after your children.'

Kirsty Bull is a friend of mine whose husband left her six months back. I know Lou admires her. She plays double bass, and I reckon Lou is quite stirred by the sight of the hefty instrument so sturdily placed between, let's face it, equally hefty legs. She tends to wear full denim skirts with lace borders and her hair falls over her face while she plays. Not a style I wish to emulate; I prefer a kind of brisk straight-lined tidiness; but of all the women in the world Kirsty Bull is the one I would prefer not to move in to babysit. It is one thing to move out – not to be able to move back in because one's place has been usurped is quite another. I didn't like that one bit.

'And Hugo will come back to me because he always does,' she

said, 'when the guilt gets too much. So I've just come out of the goodness of my heart to warn you to save yourself while you can: you'll lose Hugo – where is he, by the way? Not here? No. I can tell you where he is. Chatting up Eleanor Darcy in a flash restaurant. She's next. Not only will you lose Hugo you will lose your home, husband and children as well.'

She was trying to frighten me off, of course. I didn't believe a word she was saying. The phone went. It was Hugo.

'Your wife's here,' I said.

'The bitch,' he said. 'Don't believe a word she says. She said the twins were outside in their buggy and she was lying. By the time I got back inside Eleanor Darcy was gone.'

So I didn't believe a word Stef said. She went, and I got on with the life of Ellen Parkin, about to emerge from her chrysalis, to spread her wings as Eleanor Darcy.

Bernard's encounters with Nerina

'Ellen,' said Bernard one morning at breakfast, 'I have made a breakthrough. Nerina is going to stay on to take her degree.'
'Nerina?'
'I've told you about Nerina. Her family is from Pakistan. But her father's a lawyer and her mother does part-time filing work in the college office.'
'What does she look like?'
'The mother?'
'No. Nerina.'
'Stunning.'
'So she's not covered up with bits of black in case she turns you on?'
'Ellen, she wears bits of jeans and bits of T-shirts like the rest of the group. There is more than a touch of racism in your assumption.'
'Yes, well you're liberal-racist. Why don't you say right out "this middle-class westernized Pakistani girl called Nerina"? You can't bring yourself to do it. It's the little "but" gives you away. "But" her father is a lawyer.'
They were both trying to give up smoking.

Presently Ellen said:
'What sort of stunning?'
'A perfectly oval face: large almond eyes: rather like one of those plaster Madonnas made in India.'
'Like the one you jumped on?'
'No. That was Italian.'
'You're just saying that. You've no idea where it was made. I expect you'd just rather it was Mediterranean because it would feel less racist.'
'Perhaps you'd better have a cigarette, Ellen.'

'Yes, I will.'
They both did.

Ellen finally said:
'Okay, what sort of breakthrough?'
Bernard told Ellen that Nerina had come to him in tears. Her
brother had joined the fundamentalists, and was putting pressure
on the family to withdraw her from college and marry his friend
Sharif.
'What's Sharif like?'
'Ellen, I have no idea. It is hardly the point.'
'If I was one of your students and you lot were counting up your
staff–student contact hours, working to rule and refusing to mark
exam papers, I might well prefer to give up the course and marry
my brother's friend Sharif. If he was halfway good-looking.'

Bernard left for college early and said no more about Nerina.
Christmas was coming and Ellen took a part-time job in the college
office to meet the extra costs of the season, and there met Nerina's
mother, a pleasant woman wearing a serviceable sari and black
lace-up shoes.
'I believe you have a daughter in the college, Mrs Khalid,' said
Ellen. Both women were transferring confidential student records
from file cards on to computer. Occasionally, on whim, they would
allow a finger to slip and up-grade exam results. 'I'm just about
coming to the Ks.'
'Her name's Nerina,' said Mrs Khalid. 'N. S. Khalid.'
Nerina's card showed two years of B pluses and A minuses in
communication studies and sociology, and then a term of Cs and
Ds, and then back up to straight As.
Ellen turned the Cs and Ds into Bs. The girl might yet come out
with a first.
'She went through a bad patch,' said Mrs Khalid. 'She fell in love
with her brother's friend and wanted to leave college but we made
her stay on. I think she's over it now.'

'Nerina's always on at me to wear western clothes,' confided Mrs
Khalid, 'but I like to be comfortable. I feel happier wrapped, and
able to eat as many buttered tea cakes as I like. And of course it
keeps her brother Fariq quiet. He's eighteen; he's turned funda-

mental at the moment. But I expect it's no worse than being a punk. He's at us all the time, but boys of that age do so like to be morally superior, don't they?'

'I wouldn't know,' said Ellen. 'I don't have children, or mean to.'

'You're very young,' said Mrs Khalid comfortingly. 'You'll change your mind.'

Mrs Khalid had a soft expression and lively eyes but a never-say-die-ishness that quite reminded Ellen of Rhoda. She wondered whether, if Mrs Khalid were in love with her son's friend Sharif, would she do as Rhoda had done, try to marry off her daughter to Sharif just to keep him in the family? And thought no, probably not. Sometimes Ellen felt the need for some understanding older woman in whom to confide. Her mother Wendy hovered round the house in too petty and ethereal a form to be much use: the occasional glimmer of light where no light should be, an object in motion which by rights should be still. And Rhoda, dead and buried, stayed firmly silent, finished and underground. Perhaps the reward of the wronged was to have eternal life? Perhaps the punishment of the wrong-doers was just to be finished, kaput, over? Though to think in terms of rewards and punishments was childish. Story book notions. Nothing to do with real life.

'I might not change my mind,' said Ellen.

'A woman without children might as well not be born,' said Mrs Khalid. 'It was to have children that Allah put her on this earth. Can you think of any other reason?'

'No,' said Ellen. 'Not really. Unless we lateral think and it wasn't him put us here.'

'I wouldn't want my son to hear a thing like that,' said Mrs Khalid. 'Especially not as you're wife to a member of staff. It might be dangerous.'

'Tell me more about Nerina,' said Ellen to Bernard, over breakfast. They had both settled down to non-smoking. He put down a volume of Hume – he no longer read the daily papers, but was working through the world's philosophers, from Plato onwards, and had now reached the Scottish humanists.

'What about Nerina?'

'Why did she go from As and Bs and then down to Cs and Ds and then to steady As.'

'I'm not having a relationship with her,' he said, 'if that's what you think.'

'That is not what I thought,' said Ellen, 'but it must have crossed your mind or you wouldn't have brought it up.'

'It is not possible,' he said, 'to move amongst these nubile girls and have no reaction whatsoever.'

'I absolutely understand,' said Ellen. 'Any more than it's possible for me to work up at the college with all those strapping lads running round in jockey shorts and have no reaction whatsoever.'

'All brawn and no brain,' he said. 'Of no possible interest to you. Even Nerina worries about the sudden jump to straight As. It's happened since she joined the black magic course. She finds it disconcerting.'

'Black magic? The poly now teaches black magic? It is that desperate for students?' Under the new educational regulations any increase in students meant a concomitant increase in funding. 'Of course we don't teach black magic. Jed is running a course in the psychology of group reaction. Mass hypnosis, mass psychosis, as related to auto-suggestion. That kind of thing. It is the students who refer to it as the black magic course. Please, Ellen, I'm reading.'

'And they stand around in pentacles trying to raise the Devil?'

'I really don't know what they do. Please, Ellen, I'm trying to ascertain the nature of reality.'

'Bully for you. And all of a sudden she got straight As? Does she have a thing for Jed, or Jed for her? That would be a more likely explanation.'

Bernard put Hume down. He had been paying more attention than she thought. He had shaved off his beard again. She liked the tender line of his lip: she could see now what he was thinking. 'Jed is a married man,' said Bernard, 'of considerable integrity. He does not have affairs with students and if he did it would certainly not affect their grading.'

Windscale the cat jumped off his lap and sat on Ellen's. It had never properly mastered the art of sitting on humans. It faced outward, not inward, and kept its claws out to keep itself locked on. 'Ellen,' as Bernard sometimes observed, 'puts up with more from cats than she does from humans.'

Bernard, Ellen observed, had become rather thin. He ate as much as usual, but gesticulated more. He waved his hands around a lot. She hoped that when he stopped smoking he would fill out a little and his knees would be less likely to bruise hers in bed, but no. He went to bed late and rose early, and the space in between was lively with frequent, prolonged and energetic sex.

'Sometimes,' she said to Brenda, 'I wish he'd just stop.'

'I always wish Peter wouldn't begin,' said Brenda.

Belinda said, 'I told you so. Now he's not a Catholic, now he's not a Marxist, there's no control at all. Why do you think he had those belief structures in the first place?'

Liese said, 'Len and I are totally happy.'

The springs in Ken and Rhoda's bed twanged apart and jutted sharply through the mattress. Ellen wondered if she should perhaps look for a replacement, but put it off. Money was tight, and the Christmas season approaching. She thought they might have a Christmas tree; for the first non-ideological season for many years.

Nerina called in at the office to see her mother. Mrs Khalid introduced her to Ellen. Nerina was beautiful, in a languid kind of way. Her palely dark skin glowed with the light of youth. She was serene. Perhaps too serene, Ellen thought: there was something static in her expression, as if the skin had been plumped out by a layer of silicone wax beneath, and made her doll-like. Her bottom lip pouted. She moved slowly and gracefully, conscious of a femaleness it would, Ellen could see, be quite natural to want to drape with fabric rather than exhibit. Her bosom was too large, too suddenly plump, to fit neatly inside its T-shirt. Her jeans were very tight, her feet tiny and her heels high.

'Thank you,' said Nerina, 'for what you did with my records. My mum told me.'

'Don't mention it,' said Ellen. 'In fact don't ever mention it.'

'Okay,' said Nerina, 'but I guess I owe you a favour, all the same. A lot of us do.'

'Nerina,' said Mrs Khalid, 'supposing your brother saw you wearing that T-shirt.'

'My brother,' said Nerina, 'can go to Saudi Arabia for all I care.'

'Or Sharif?' her mother pleaded. 'You know you like Sharif. What would Sharif say?'

'He won't see me to say anything,' said Nerina, 'will he? I hope you don't suppose I'm insane!'

'Since she started at the poly she's been very difficult,' said Mrs Khalid. 'I'm not sure about education for girls.'

'My mother's quite right,' said Nerina. 'I used to have a head quite full of interesting things. Now I'm at college there's only a kind of vacuum. I fill it up with facts and theories, but it's going to take for ever: it's a deep, deep well.'

'Nature abhors a vacuum,' said Ellen. 'You'd better be careful. All kinds of things can come rushing in to fill it up.'

'So I'd noticed,' said Nerina. 'Well, I'll be off,' and she swayed away, leaving a drift of rather heavy scent behind her.

'You're in her good books,' said Mrs Khalid, 'that's the main thing. She can be quite tiresome when crossed. I wish she'd wear trainers. Those shoes are so bad for her feet.'

Now that Bernard left industrial action to others, the heart had quite gone out of the staff's work-to-rule and normal relations were resumed. Neither side won. A draw was declared. But now both the academic board and the management team viewed Bernard with some apprehension, fearing where his energies would next take him. It was with some relief that they assented to his desire to take over outreach work in the local community. It was on his prompting that ethnic drop-out youths were now accepted onto college courses without formal qualifications; it was on his urging that examinations were now being set and marked in Urdu and other minority languages, the faculties shamed at last out of their insistence that English was the only language in the world that counted. Bernard was triumphant. The college was at last loosening up. The Faculty of Art and Design now ran courses on graffiti in conjunction with the Faculty of Social Sciences. 'The Role of the Magic Mushroom in Primitive Cave and Contemporary Wall Art' won its author a first. When Bernard went to the canteen there was a stir, a breath of recognition. The young, the bold, the lowly paid and overworked, acknowledged him as their spiritual leader. The few, the old guard, who could see what generations of scholars had endured for, struggled for, thus lightly swept away, were not so happy. Notions of excellence, of the primacy of scholarship, the victory of steady thought over wild opinion, the sense of generation building upon generation, all thus abandoned in the craven desire to please the student, entertain the student, keep the college in funds. The few were shrewd, powerful, influential and dined in high political places; Bernard knew it, and did not care. Indeed, he found it energizing. 'No one worth their salt,' he said, 'but does not have enemies. Once the mind is free from its self-imposed shackles anything is possible. Even changing the world.'

Mrs Parkin came to stay for a week and went after a day. Bernard would not let her set up Jesus, Mary and Joseph on the mantelpiece even though Christmas was coming.
'Look, Mum,' he said, 'I can just about stand Christmas dinner as a family get-together. But I will not have idols in the house.'
Mrs Parkin left, blaming Ellen for having turned her son from a faith that had sustained her family through death, famine, hardship, war, bereavement. Ellen said it was nothing to do with her, but she was lying, and Mrs Parkin knew it. Once she was gone Bernard and Ellen were able to ask Jed and Prune round for Christmas dinner. Prune was pregnant again and wore a murky green long woollen smock. Ellen wore a skin-tight gold dress with black glittery trimmings.
'Isn't that dress rather low cut,' asked Bernard, 'for a simple Christmas dinner with friends?'
'I bought it at Oxfam,' said Ellen, as if that excused everything. But Bernard paid the matter little attention. There was a kind of dance of thought going through his head: he had to keep in step. He couldn't stop it.
'The synapses are twanging,' he complained, on occasion to Ellen. 'They get out of step. The rules are gone: the safety nets. Everything links, from cosmology to microbiology. When it finally does link up the computer will explode.'
'I hope you don't talk like that at college,' she said.
'Of course I don't,' he said. 'I'm not mad.'

Sometimes his eyes would glaze over for a second or two as if he were out of their world altogether. Ellen wondered if he had petit mal and looked it up in a medical dictionary – neither of them went to doctors if they could help it – but the entry was not very helpful, and it seemed in any case the kind of symptom it would be better to be vague about, not define, not name, for fear the naming made it worse, less likely to evaporate out of existence. And sometimes Bernard would wake shivering, from a restless sleep, dreaming of punishments.

'Well,' he said in the new year, a couple of days after term had started, 'I've certainly been and gone and upset Nerina, of all people. And over such a trivial thing.'
'Now what have you done?'
'I told her God didn't exist and she took offence.'
'But she must allow you your opinion.'
'On the contrary. You must remember Nerina's background. The ideological war is as real to her as any war with guns and tanks. If your idea is contrary to my idea your idea must be eliminated, especially if it starts getting a territorial foothold, and might just possibly catch on.'
'Excuses, excuses, the girl's a fool.'
'Don't *say* that, Ellen. Don't even think it!' He looked round anxiously, as if for bugging devices. 'Now listen, Ellen, we've unhinged her from her original faith. We shouldn't have done it. Mention Allah, mention the Prophet, she laughs. It's dangerous. She worships the Devil, Ellen, and that's the truth of it. To say aloud that God doesn't exist is to thereby negate the Devil. What's more, you see, Jed's group is on the point of bringing Satan into corporeal existence. She blames me because it's taking so long. I know she does.'
'Have you said anything about it to Jed?'
'I know what he'll say. He'll say it's all part of continual assessment: the whole point of the course is mass hysteria. The control group will be perfectly sane.'
Married to a madman, thought Ellen. If I don't look at it, it will go away.
'Perhaps I'd better say something to Jed.'
'Don't, don't. Nerina might find out.'
'I should just let them get on with it,' said Ellen lightly, 'so long as they don't start sacrificing goats. On the other hand perhaps they should. Then the Animal Rights Activists can campaign against them, and let you off the hook.'
'You're not taking this seriously, Ellen.'
'No.'
He thought a little. He blinked. His mind clicked back into

another, less agitated gear. 'I mentioned to Jed that Nerina had a crush on him, and I'm afraid it got back to her.'

'You and Jed sit in the senior common room discussing the emotions of students?'

'Sometimes they are relevant, Ellen. The staff is *in loco parentis*. Some of our students are very young. We were discussing the probability of Nerina's essays being all her own work: or whether someone's fronting her. They really are remarkable. She's sent them up to a London publisher who is actually going to bring them out – *Multiculturalism and Pluralism in the New Europe*. Do you think she's sold her soul to the Devil?'

'Is Jed's relationship to Nerina perhaps *very* close?'

'It is perfectly proper, Ellen. Of course there is sometimes an erotic element between teacher and pupil. How can there not be? The point is, Nerina apparently took offence.'

'You mean you told Jed and Jed told Nerina and Nerina told you and blah, blah, blah. Children's playground stuff.'

'I suppose in a way a man remains a child until he has his own.' He wanted a baby. Ellen didn't.

'Prune has nearly had lots of babies. It hasn't grown Jed up, so far as I can see. She has high blood pressure. She's in hospital. Did he bother to mention it?'

'No. Perhaps you should visit her? You have lots of time.'

Bernard thought Ellen should take a proper job. Ellen didn't.

'What a good idea! Perhaps it's the black magic group has put her blood pressure up? Perhaps they mean poor Prune to die in labour so Nerina can marry Jed?'

She shouldn't have said it. He started looking into corners for the bugging device, though he said he was searching for a stray cigarette, left over from the days when he smoked.

'Ellen, don't joke. They've put a curse on me now, for betraying Nerina. I can feel it.'

'Oh dear,' said Ellen. 'I wish I'd stayed on at college. It seems much more exciting these days than it used to be. Perhaps you should start smoking again? It's been all trouble since you stopped.'

That night a bird hurled itself against the window pane and woke them both up. After that a bird – the same one or another – fell through the chimney into the grate and then fluttered and banged in terror around the room. Ellen caught it in a towel and put it out and went back to sleep. In the morning Bernard was pale and his hand trembled too much even to lift his coffee cup, let alone butter his toast.

'You look as you did when you wanted to be a priest,' said Ellen, irritated. 'It was only a bird.'

'Birds don't fly about at night,' said Bernard, 'in the middle of winter.'

'Owls do,' said Ellen.

'How do you know it was an owl?' he asked.

'It had big eyes,' she said, which seemed to satisfy him, though she hadn't noticed its eyes, merely the trembling flutter of the feathers through the thin towel as she caught it. She hadn't liked it. Perhaps her towels were too thin? Perhaps she should buy new?

Bernard reversed straight out of the new garage into the road and hit a passing van. Car and van were written off though no one was hurt. But Bernard fainted so she took him into casualty.

'If I speak to Nerina,' said Bernard, whose blood pressure was so low there was talk of admitting him for a day or so, 'she might lift the curse. On the other hand it might make matters worse.'

'For God's sake,' said Ellen, 'you put your foot on the accelerator not the brake. You were tired. The bird kept you awake.'

Bernard was admitted for tests. Ellen went to find Nerina. She found her sitting on a bench beneath a stark tree in the college grounds, in a snowy landscape. She was alone. She was wrapped in soft brown wool. A snowflake or so glistened in her black hair. She sat as if on a throne: her dark eyes glowed. Her face remained impassive, but her expression was equable.

'How nice to see you, Ellen,' said Nerina. 'How is your husband?'

'In hospital.'

'Well,' said Nerina, 'I understand he isn't really your husband. You did not go through a religious ceremony with him.'

'Who told you that?'

'Your husband did.'

'I see.'

'So there is no protection for him in you. And now he has betrayed us.'

'How did he betray you?'

'I don't think it's proper for me to tell you,' said Nerina. 'Besides not being a proper wife to Bernard, you are also an adulteress. In some countries in the world you would be stoned to death. But you helped me out with my grades so I'll overlook that.'

Ellen thought it safer not to go further into these particular matters. 'Well,' Ellen said, 'I am very fond of my husband, in spite of my western ways, and I know he has a great respect for you, Nerina; and is thrilled about your publishing contract, and any betrayal of confidence has been totally inadvertent. I know he'd want me to say that to you.'

'In my culture,' said Nerina, 'we take love seriously. And if you had indeed repented and reformed – which Jed says you have – why did you have Christmas dinner in a revealing dress?'

'Because it was cheap and I liked it,' said Ellen. 'Honestly, that was all.'

'I suppose that might be true,' said Nerina. 'My mother says that though you were always very pleasant and she liked you, you never paid your share of the office coffee. And she was sorry you had so little belief. She thought it would do you good to be taught belief.'

'I expect I'll come round to it in good time,' said Ellen.

'I daresay you will,' said Nerina, waving cheerfully to the group of smiling students, brightly wrapped in woolly hats and scarves, who now approached her. 'We're going to build a snowman. What fun! You don't have anything of Bernard's on you, I suppose?'

'No,' said Ellen. 'I don't.'

'Well,' said Nerina, 'we can do without. Your husband looms quite large in many of our minds. Some students had to do an extra year because of the staff work-to-rule. Their exam papers weren't marked. Many suffered because of your husband's principles.'

Brenda telephoned a couple of hours later to say she was well, considering, and how was Apricot? She hadn't heard from her for some time.

'Considering what?' asked Ellen.

'Considering I'm eight and a half months pregnant and haven't heard from you for a couple of weeks. Not even a "how are you?"'

'I'm sorry,' said Ellen. 'Well, I'm fine. I just had a man round here declaring eternal love. I looked out the kitchen window and there he was, standing at the back gate with a bunch of red roses in his hand.'

'How nice for you,' said Brenda. 'How's Bernard?'

'In hospital, but nothing serious.'

'That's really very convenient then,' said Brenda.

'It is, isn't it.'

'Who is he?'

'He is the Vice Chancellor of the University of Bridport,' said Ellen.

There was a short silence.

'Are you sure? It seems a little out of character.'

'I'm sure. He's quite plump and I suppose quite elderly, but he has a wonderful mind. Apparently I met him at a conference on the economics of multiculturalism. I was taking the minutes of the meeting. I can't remember him but he remembers me.'

'It all sounds most improbable.'

'It is improbable for those on the ground that an aircraft should crash on to them. In fact the chances are a million to one against it. But there the aircraft is, its fuselage sticking up out of your house. His name is Julian.'

Hugo's further interview with
Eleanor Darcy

Q: It's good of you to see me this evening. I'm very sorry about the disturbance at the restaurant and that we had to cut the interview short. I understand from Valerie – I've been seeing quite a lot of Valerie, as I think she's indicated – that you were visiting your husband today. You must be tired. I imagine such prison visits are very trying?

A: No. Sometimes they can be quite heartening. Julian has lost a good deal of weight. He works out with dumbbells in the prison gym. A non-academic life suits him. Nowadays when his eyes light up for love of me, they are somehow clearer and brighter than they used to be; the lighting up is the more flattering. Julian used to be a good-looking man somehow clouded, dispersed, by layers of fat and the radiation of pure thought; now he is simply a cadaverous, eagly, extraordinarily randy man. We managed a cell on our own for over an hour.

Q: How on earth did you manage that?

A: Some of the prison officers are friendly. He has converted quite a few to Utopianism. Many thought it a cruel injustice that Julian should have to go to prison at all.

Q: I am reminded of Chernechersky, that most fierce and feared of Russian revolutionaries, who was put in prison and then converted the guards to Communism. They simply opened the prison gates and let him walk out.

A: If a thing can happen once it can happen again. I suppose you could describe Julian as that most fierce and feared of monetary theorists. To every age, its terrorist.

Q: Valerie has asked me if you could answer a few questions on her behalf. She is getting on well with *Lover at the Gate*, but sometimes the clues you provide are, well, enigmatic. Of course my piece will be very different from Valerie's: I wouldn't want you to think there was duplication: that we were taking up your time unnecessarily.

> *Hugo was beginning to feel oppressed by his surroundings. The shiny black sofa, the shabby furniture, the dull suburban road the other side of a forlorn garden, seemed some kind of irony. He did not believe Eleanor Darcy lived here. She merely pretended to; he felt the minute he left she and Brenda packed up themselves and the children and took off to more exotic surroundings. Yet was not this how most of the world lived, and thought themselves lucky to do so? – once survival was accomplished the struggle for ordinariness began.*

A: You mean Valerie wants to know more about the role of children in Darcy's Utopia? I thought she would.

Q: Well, you did speak of selection. Her liberal antennae were alerted.

A: Tell her all babies will be automatically aborted unless good reason can be shown why they should be allowed to proceed to term.

Q: Isn't that a little drastic?

A: Yes. Even in Darcy's Utopia it will take quite some getting used to. The decision to 'choose', or not to 'choose' will be taken away from the parents and left to an ad-hoc committee of neighbours. Are these two (or this one) not so much capable of loving a baby, as of being worthy of a baby's love? If the verdict

133

is that they are not, there can be no baby. Down the plughole with it, this little glob of potential life, this putative devourer of the world's resources! The root of delinquency, the alienation, the violent and despairing habits of today's young, has very little to do with the fact that their parents failed to love them – most adults look round quite desperately for something, anything to coo over, however erratically – but that their parents failed to be worthy of their love. Babies are born with a sense of fairness, justice, morality, and a great capacity for kindness and forbearance, and it is sheer disappointment in the character and nature of parent and world that changes this eager infant into a murderous teenager. Some survive, of course: time heals a few wounds, wounds a few heels. The teenager gets older, encounters some nicer, more controlled, more kindly people than he or she ever found at home – most people behave worst in their own homes – and with any luck comes to understand, yes, there is an aspiration or so floating around out there, and, if he, she, hasn't seen too many horror movies, been too beaten up in body and mind, regains a little faith in a world at least potentially redeemable. He, she, grows up into a mortgage-paying, law-abiding adult who at least wants to give his, her, own children a better chance. And may or may not have the resolution, the constancy, so to do. Not to love, which is easy, but to be in truth, in fact, in deed, lovable. I hear the divorced parent saying, 'Oh, the kids are all right. They know I love them,' but it isn't true. The kids are not all right. You may love the kids, but you are not worthy of their love. You look after yourself, not them. You have betrayed them, and they hate you for it.

Q: Well, that is a matter of opinion. And this notion of an ad-hoc committee of neighbours, with power of life and death, is surely very eccentric.

A: What are juries but ad-hoc committees of neighbours? Juries saw no problem deciding whom they were to despatch from this world: let similar bodies decide who is to come into it.

Q: It seems to me that the citizens of Darcy's Utopia are going to be kept very busy.

A: Indeed. Idleness, in this nation of no work, will not be encouraged. There will be no 'training in leisure'. Darcians will be hard at work, repairing the past, safeguarding the future; they will have no need of theme parks. Darcy's Utopia has a Mission Statement, as does any corporate enterprise in the business world. 'We are working towards a secular, unicultural, multiracial society.' When citizens are called upon to make up their minds, pass laws or make regulations – their decisions will be infused with the light cast by this statement, and so by and large will work towards this end. It may be hard to take a step in the right direction, but it will be still harder to take a step in the wrong. We have a time scale, too. We give ourselves two hundred years to achieve it. If it doesn't work, we rethink.

Q: Secular? But isn't religion a civilizing force? Aren't many of our social problems due to the decline of religion?

A: Now look. Nice orderly home-and-family-loving people are the ones who believe in God and even still go to church. They are *nice* people: they believe that everything ought to be fair, that is to say that virtue is rewarded and villainy punished. Since they can't see it happening on earth they invent a heaven in which it does. And a kind of consensus develops amongst right-minded people in your neighbourhood, that if you keep to certain rules and rituals then by God, by magic, you'll get to heaven, you won't even have to die. Eat the wafer, chant the lyric, bow to Mecca: please God and he'll be kind. But these people are not nice, orderly, home-and-family-loving *because* they believe in God. The temperament comes first. Acknowledging God is effect, not cause. And institutionalize the religion, any religion, and you're in trouble. Nice people become guilty people, cruel people, unhappy people, trapped in belief structures their temperaments don't agree with, taught peculiar beliefs in school, threatened by hell and afflicted by superstition. And what terrible damage they do, have done through the centuries, from the Inquisitor General to Stalin, to your young neighbour in the IRA who believes in the Catholic God and uses that to justify his murdering you in your bed, to the Mullah who whips up the faithful to civil strife in the name of Allah, to the Moonie who steals your children's money and affections.

People like rules: it is not good for them to have them. The individual must come to his, her, own decision as to where morality lies. Do what you like in your own home, worship whatever God you please, but shut up about it in public. In Darcy's Utopia church services of various denominations will exist, and blind eyes will no doubt be turned. Common sense will prevail. But the jury of neighbours who decide upon your fertility might not look too kindly upon you if they think you are going to bring up your children as Jehovah's Witnesses or Servants of Baal, or use the terror of hell as a way of controlling them: or beat the soles of their feet if they get the Koran wrong.

Q: Won't terrible injustices ensue?

A: Chance and luck will be a factor in Darcy's Utopia, as elsewhere. But good luck attends the happy. Darcians will try to be happy, to avoid self-righteousness. The self-righteous seldom smile.

Q: Would you describe yourself as happy?

A: I'm getting there. I don't have children, which makes it easier. To have these hostages to fortune wipes the smile from many a woman's face. Consider Brenda. In Darcy's Utopia parents will have some reassurance in the fact that at least the neighbours thought they were fit to rear children: some of the responsibility for failure, should failure there be, will rest with the community. But I like to think the neighbours, the ten just persons, men and women both, who have seen you in the shops, who have watched you cross a road, who understand your body language, will make the right decision.

Q: Could we get back to this uniculture of yours? Don't you mean monoculture?

A: No. Monoculture assumes the domination of the single majority culture: that 'they' will be subsumed into 'us'. That the eaters of curry must learn to love fish and chips, that husbands of four must become husbands of one, that young blacks must drive cars in the fashion of elderly whites: that the custom and laws of the majority will prevail. In a uniculture this is not the case. A uniculture is a matter for rational decision: we will be prepared to make value judgements. Better a culture in which men have one wife and women need not shroud themselves in black, we'll say. Or perhaps we won't. Better one in which marriages are arranged than left to love. Let us all sing the Darcian Anthem every morning at ten a.m. Let men wear skirts, not women trousers. Let us all change our names four times in our lives. Let us take our education in our middle not our opening years. Or whatever is decided. And if it doesn't work, we'll change it. And if you don't like it, you can live somewhere else. And we might even divide Darcy's Utopia into four and have a different Mission Statement in each, and citizens can move to the one they prefer: or work to change the one they're in, if they prefer. Oh yes, Darcy's Utopia will be all freedom and hard work, and all alive and energetic with a perpetual sense of achievement. Who will need religion when heaven is here on earth?

Q: This unicultural society of yours. Isn't it going to be rather dull? What about the richness, the diversity of the multicultural society in which all decent non-racist folk take such pleasure?

A: Goodness, how you do sometimes remind me of Bernard! How all-pervasive is the orthodoxy of right-thinking people. I have never heard a member of an ethnic minority obliged to dwell within the barbarous framework of a powerful, prosperous, white, allegedly Christian culture talk about the richness of the multicultural society. That is left for members of the host community to do, as it busies itself ghettoizing the minority; and as it ghettoizes it mumbles, and if you listen carefully you can just discern beneath the self-righteousness, the self-congratulation, the following: 'Okay, okay, so you were having a hard time in your own country. You poor things! Come over here and join us by all means – but not too many of you, so we'll vet you as you come in; and not make getting in pleasant or easy; and just please stick to your own districts, and keep your own religion and dance away to tambourines, or bow to the East, or whatever you like to do to remind you of home – or home as it used to be a hundred years ago but certainly isn't now – and aren't we clever, and kind, and good, the way we give you your roots back?, and with any luck your children will grow up well-behaved and pleasant; ours certainly aren't; because your children come of a society which, being somewhere else and a long time ago, is probably better than ours. And speak your own language, please: we'll even teach it to you in our schools to prove how understanding we are, just so long as you do our dirty work for less wages than our own kind are prepared to accept: just so long as you keep yourselves to yourselves, and don't let your children marry ours, because what we're all terrified of, so terrified the word's gone out of the vocabulary. Let me whisper, can you hear? MISCEGENATION. The mixture of races! The future, in other words.'

In Darcy's Utopia no one is frightened of the future. We welcome it. Because this is the world's future, and we must hurry towards it with open and welcoming arms. There will be no black, no white, no yellow; no Asiatic, no Caucasian; we will all, individually, be multiracial, multicultural; and then indeed there will be a wonderful diversity, and God's will done upon earth. So don't come to me, Mr Hugo Vansitart, with your 'rich diversity of language and culture'. The richness and diversity will be when your grandchildren, your great grandchildren, are of mixed race, mixed ancestry: look at each other with fondness and love out of eyes which slant every which way and who compare the shade of their skins with interest, not envy: because the paler the skin no longer means the longer-lived, the more prosperous, the more educated, the more capable of reaching the fullness of human potential. And when that has happened, why, we might be able to invent a God as good, as moral, as human beings. That is quite enough for today.

Q: Could I just ask, before I go? You have on occasion referred to someone called Nerina –

A: Is your tape switched off? Good. Nerina remains off the record. Things are stirred up enough as they are, don't you think? Nerina was someone – is someone – whom Bernard tried to help. He shook religion out of her mind, as it were, and into the vacuum rushed something rather disagreeable. Nerina is a very pretty, very bright girl; of Muslim background, though no one in the family actually ever went to a mosque – well, only her brother. You know how fanatical the young can be. Unfortunately and unwittingly Bernard angered her. And that is why Julian is in prison. And why I sit here, husbandless, dependent upon social security supplemented by such pitiful amounts of money as I can wring out of the national press, and Bernard genuflects once more, fled back to his baptismal church, terrified by the very notion of living outside it. All this, you might say, was Nerina's fault – if only it was not clear to me that Nerina was the symptom, not the disease: the pustule, not the pox: that to this end, without need of her intervention, all would still have come. It is a terrible thing to laugh a person out of faith.

Q: A woman's faith, too?

A: As I said, the greater includes the lesser.

Q: When you say that I think you're laughing at me.

A: Now why should I do a thing like that? You are the most serious person in the world, Hugo, with your very neat suit, your very quiet tie, your hotel laundered shirt. I can tell from its whiteness, its crispness. Let me feel! Yes. You have to be careful of hotel cleaners: things come back very white, but don't last long. Perhaps Valerie would wash them for you? Sometimes they have little bottles of stuff called Softwash on hotel shelves, which the guests take with them on leaving. Shall we go to the pub and have a drink?

Valerie is shocked

What Eleanor Darcy has to say is of course monstrous, fascist. Babies, aborted compulsorily in the womb! What about the woman's right to choose, forget the baby's right to life? Though Eleanor Darcy denies the very concept of 'right'. 'It would be nice if only' is her replacement of the term, and I can see the point in that.

Babies selected to live by friends and neighbours! Who'd ever agree to that? What government would even dare? It is true, of course, that women would be spared the agony of choice. I think about my friend Erin, as I often do. She has a Down's syndrome baby. We all knew it would be disastrous; we foretold that her husband would walk out, that her other children would suffer: we saw she was the only one of the family unit who couldn't bear not to see the fruit of her womb, however sour, ripen, drop and live. And that's how it turned out: the child, now twelve, is badly retarded, Erin is no more than its nurse; she manages without a husband, her other children are spiteful and embarrassed. Erin talks about the joy the mindless child brings her – well, so it may, but her love for it has been most destructive for others. Left to us, friends and family, we would have said no, Erin, sorry, not for you. This baby you insist on having keeps other babies out, ones which won't cause this distress to you and yours. Just not this one; Erin, try again. All women have as many babies as they can manage: four, three, two, one, none at all: as many as they can afford – physically, emotionally, practically. I managed two. A woman spends years saying no, not this one, stay out of my bed: I'll wait, a better man will come along: and with the better man a better baby. Let's hope, here's hoping he comes along! The lover at the gate is the father at the gate. Where is he? I'll wait, yes I'll wait, for a baby I can feed better, love better, provide running water for, give a father to, who stays around and bounces babies on his knee. To this end she stays a virgin, or practises abstinence, or contraception, or if things get further in spite of her best endeavours – for both men and her own desires are importunate – terminates. If she didn't, she'd have babies annually from puberty until death by childbirth around the age of thirty or so. How it must have been for our Stone Age grandmothers – swell, oh, oh, pop, look, a little one – oh, it's dead – oh, I'm dying, dying; dead! And even now we get it wrong; how often, for all our knowledge, we get it wrong. Choose a husband who leaves, a father who doesn't provide; the genes don't match, the conjunction goes wrong – the wrong baby at the wrong time; oh, bad luck! My neighbours, my friends, why did you not save me from this?

It wouldn't all be negative. My other friend Edie gave birth to a baby with one leg. It showed up in the scan – one child in three, they say, is now born with some imperfection or other, mostly minor, sometimes major, and whether that's due to pollution, or insecticides, or growth hormones, or radon gas, or nuclear power plants, take your choice, take your pick: and whatever the cause, the mothers stay healthy enough, are sufficiently medicated one way or another to bring babies to term – and we all said to Edie, what's a missing leg? Keep this baby, look after this baby, you have a great husband, the other kids aren't the kind to care, and we were right. It was okay. This child has a metal prosthesis and kicks hell out of the others at football. Of course he'd be happier if he had two legs, so would she, so would everyone, but he'd rather live with one leg than not live at all. We *did* know. We are born into a group, not just into a family, not just to an individual woman. Let the group decide. Ten good neighbours and true.

It isn't the perfect way; it remains horrible, but the lesser of many evils. In Darcy's Utopia it has to be. All babies terminated unless validated. What happens otherwise in our two-hundred-year, five-hundred-year plan? Can we wait for prosperity and education to keep mankind in check; so the humble villager, the wretched dweller in the shantytown doesn't choose the traditional, unthinking, long-term option of a dozen children, the decision which in the long term destroys both them and theirs? We have lost that race: we must face it. It is all paradox, this business of procreation!

141

Every way we look we see a barrier and on the wall is written 'No! Immoral! Unkind! Fascist!' Everything but the free flow of natural selection is disagreeable to so much as contemplate, but the planet sinks beneath the weight of us, stinks because of the shit of us; if we don't do something we all go down together, gasping for air, for heaven's blessing. Governments do what they can. Time and time again they fail. Let neighbours, simple neighbours, try and do better. Meeting their quota, their too-small-for-comfort quota, always with generosity, understanding and compassion, understanding as a group what the individual woman knows by instinct, that this child, by existing, keeps that other child out.

Hugo says I am so persuasive in convincing myself on this subject he begins to wonder who it is who speaks through Eleanor Darcy, is it God or the Devil? This is quite an advance on his initial assumption that poor Julian Darcy, the Rasputin of Bridport, economic theorist and prisoner of his nation's conscience, victim of its guilt, indolence and fear, is the motivating force behind Darcy's Utopia. But how about the side benefits! How religiously, if only in order to obviate neighbourly interference, the Darcian woman would observe contraceptive precautions! If she wanted a baby, what a good neighbour she would be, if only to keep in well with them: how she would feed her neighbours' cats, take in her neighbours' mail, refrain from drunken disturbance! My Sophie, for example – if she were in Darcy's Utopia and in a couple of years were to become a teenage primigravida, which is perfectly on the cards – I reckon the neighbours would know better than Lou or me if she was fit to be a mother or not. As it is, it's the family who takes responsibility for denying the baby existence, though permitting its death rather than allowing its life. 'Family physicians' enjoy the most extraordinary regard in our society: somewhere in our joint head we need to see them as knowing, honest, trustworthy, benign and caring folk – the truth of the matter being that they are as forgetful, spiteful and drunk as the next person – and as likely to grow old, lecherous and incompetent as anyone else. Your family doctor may know one end of a thyroid gland from another– with any luck – but no especial wisdom is granted him because he sits in a surgery seeing one coughing person after another all day; peering into ears and wombs and hearing tales of insomnia and worms. I have been indecently assaulted by many a wise old family physician in my time: the passion for mammary examination – which has saved almost no lives at all over the past few years, it now appears – has been fomented and encouraged by male doctors. I wish Hugo would come back. My thoughts are growing wild. He somehow nails me, pins me, centres me in one spot like a butterfly spread for inspection, wonderful, beautiful; he steadies me. This time he did not want to make love to me when he dropped the tapes off, and in truth I was a little tired. It would be nice to have some conversation as well as sex – dinner out somewhere, say. But his editor had to see him.

If Eleanor Darcy can manage a private room in a prison, perhaps she manages one in the local pub as well? But this is paranoia; of the kind her poor Bernard suffered from. The breathing lake, into which suspicion drops, like a stone, the ripples spreading! I trust Hugo, of course I do. My body is his, his is mine: one flesh. What was it Eleanor Darcy said? Love is the evidence you need which proves the benign nature of the universe. Love lets you know you are alive. Fate weaves its heady patterns all around; good luck attends you, nobody fools you: Hugo does not repair with Eleanor to the back room of the pub. Of course not.

Babies by licence only! There'd be abuses, there always are abuses: those with money would do what they wanted. Except that money, in Darcy's Utopia, will count for nothing: just as it counts for nothing in Moscow today: where pockets are stuffed with roubles but there is nothing to buy. In Darcy's Utopia money will be as meaningless as coconuts in a country where they fall from the trees: it will cease to be a corrupting cause. Would my neighbours have let Lou and me have Sophie and Ben? Of course they would. I am a good citizen, a nice person; I am just at the moment in the grip of a sexual passion, in the throes of love; I am alive: I who have been so nearly dead for decades, which is why I am currently neglecting them, just a little.

The phone goes. It's Ben. How did he know I was here?
'Mum,' he says. 'Dad said to call you if we wanted anything. He's out at a concert. Sophie and me haven't got a babysitter. There's just us. Sophie's got a pain –'

Sophie always has pains. It's her age. I tell Ben to tell Sophie to put a hotwater bottle on it. How dare Lou leave them on their own? He either has to give up music, or organize live-in help of some kind. Where is Kirsty Bull? She can share his bed for all I care. Bath from ten forty-five to eleven; teeth for five timed minutes, lights out by eleven fifteen. Love from eleven twenty to forty on Tuesdays and Fridays should there be no concerts on either of those nights: otherwise do without. I am sure the world is full of women who would appreciate a pleasant, hard-working man with regular habits, and would be happy to babysit Sophie and Ben.

What do the children expect of me? I brought them into the world. Isn't that enough? In another ten years they can come and visit me to their hearts' content and I won't object. Unless Ben remains a computer freak – he has his father's appreciation of the mathematics, the square lines, the patterning out of existence; unless Sophie fails to lose a little of her egoism – or unless Hugo objects to their visits. I'm sure I don't want his puny little creatures visiting me. I want his life to have begun the moment he met me, as he wants mine to have begun, simultaneously. Together, we exist. Separately, we are nothing.

Brenda finds Ellen in a state of enchantment

Brenda knocked on Ellen's door, nervous of what might happen next, anxious to know in detail what her friend Ellen had been unable to voice on the phone. Ellen opened the door wearing household gloves, her underwear and a wrap.

'The kitchen sink is blocked,' she said. 'I'm trying to clear it with the plunger.'

'Has he gone?'

'Who?'

'The Vice Chancellor,' said Brenda. 'I forget – is it the Chancellor who does all the work in universities, or is it the Vice Chancellor?' She knew about polytechnics, not universities.

'The Vice Chancellor,' said Ellen, returning to the sink.

Brenda followed, and gratefully sat down at the kitchen table. Her pregnancy rendered her unexpectedly top-heavy: no matter how she tried to balance back on her heels, she kept feeling that she was about to topple forward. Ellen made no comment on Brenda's state. Usually she at least went through the motions of expressing concern, and of sharing some of the apprehension and excitement of the pregnancy. But today, Brenda could see, the talk was to be all of Ellen. She was sorry for herself, but happy for her friend, whose life in the last few years, while Brenda's went forward into the tumult of marriage and babies, had become predictable, unambitious and, to Brenda's mind, surprisingly dull: as if Ellen's peculiarly bright and individual life flame was losing its incandescence: that the sheer everydayness of married life to the difficult Bernard – Brenda, Belinda and Liese all agreed that Bernard was 'difficult', with his passions, his principles, his politics and policies – and though they marvelled at the ease with which Ellen, as they put it, handled him, had somehow expected something more dramatic, more marvellous, for their friend, than that she should, as they felt she did, stand round kitchen sinks all day, taking a little job here, a little job there, failing to make any impression on the world at all. When they asked her what she was doing with her life, she would reply 'thinking', which seemed a singularly flaky answer.

Now as Ellen stood at the sink, working the rubber plunger in, out, in, out, listening and watching in the dirty water for the signs of vacuum working, of pressure releasing, the shoulder of her blue housecoat fell down and Brenda was startled by the white luminosity of her flesh.

'The Vice Chancellor,' said Ellen, 'is the chief executive officer of the university. The Chancellor is merely its figurehead. A position of great dignity, of course, but you only really have to work once a year, when you spend a week or so conferring degrees. The Vice Chancellor is the one who really counts. Bridport is a small, efficient, research-orientated, cost-effective university in the new mode, which specializes in the philosophical and economic sciences, and its Vice Chancellor works extremely hard and has little time for personal life.'

'Did he tell you all that?'

'Yes. He said he felt it was appropriate to present his credentials at the beginning of the courtship. He said he hoped I didn't find him hopelessly old-fashioned.'

'And did you?'

'I thought he was rather sweet.'

'You said he was old and fat.'

'Yes but his *mind*, Brenda. A mind makes up for such a lot.'

'Bernard has a mind, Ellen.'

'Eleanor. Julian Darcy called me Eleanor. First I had to put up with Apricot because of my crazy parents, then Ellen when Bernard was trying to punish me and make me share his guilt – now at last I have been invested with some kind of romance, of unearthliness. You know Julian is a member of one of the government's think-tanks?'

'I don't keep up with these things.'

'You should. He's a very busy man. When he's not running the university, or sorting out the government, he writes books on monetarism and the economics of multiculturalism. He was looking out photographs for his publishers when he came across one

of himself at last year's conference on the economics of multiculturalism, and there I was in the background, my hair a halo around
my head in a shaft of sunlight, and he faced at last what he had
tried to avoid for so long – his love for me.'
Brenda wondered if perhaps Ellen were fantasizing, or teasing,
and thought on the whole not. There was such a smell of sex in
the air she wanted to open the window. She had thought at first
perhaps it was the blocked drains, but no. Ellen gave up the
plunger, took a towel, laid it on the floor, opened the cupboard
beneath the sink and, with wrench and bucket at the ready, lay
flat on her back on the towel, manoeuvred her arms inside the
cupboard and unscrewed the joint beneath the sink where the
soakaway met the drain. Brenda, female as she was, eight months
pregnant as she was, felt an urge to join her friend upon the floor,
kiss her, embrace her. It was perhaps as well – for Ellen would
not, as she realized later, have reacted at all favourably towards
such an advance – that the joint was quickly loosened and a whole
flood of filthy water poured down into the bucket, as was expected,
overfilled the bucket, as had not been expected, splashed and then
poured over the prostrate Ellen. The water was deep brown, bitty,
scummy and smelt dreadful. Ellen stood up. 'Extraordinary,' she
remarked as she went to the shower, but quite calmly in the
circumstances. 'The sink wasn't all that full, was it, Brenda?'
'I hadn't thought so,' said Brenda, following, perching on the end
of the bath, 'but I suppose it must have been.'

She was glad when Ellen at last covered up her nakedness, her
luminosity, with jeans and sweater, and they went back to the
kitchen to mop up the floor. The room smelt even more sweet and
sickly than before. Brenda couldn't make out what had been in
the water.
'When he said courtship,' said Brenda, 'what exactly did he mean?'
'He wants to marry me.'
Brenda pointed out that Ellen was married already.
'So's he,' said Ellen. 'He has two grown-up children, and a wife.
She's very elegant and charming, he says – her name's Georgina.
She has to do all the social side of things. Vice Chancellor's wives
have to entertain a lot. It's rather like being first lady at the White
House.'
'Isn't she doing it well enough, or something? What's his com-

plaint?' Brenda felt quite snarky. She had always remarked upon and lamented how little consideration wives were granted in adulterous relationships. They took on the role of the mother on a family outing – the nuisance and the spoilsport, the one who says 'don't go too near the edge', 'those apples aren't ripe', 'shouldn't we get home before the fog sets in?'

'His present wife does it too well, if anything,' said Ellen. 'He says the magic has gone out of the relationship. He asks what is life without love?'

'And what did you reply? I hope that life in his case was his commitment to the university, his students, his governments, his publishers, his wife, his children. Of all the men in the world this Julian Darcy seems to have a remarkable amount to give up for love.'

'That's what's so wonderful about it,' said Ellen. 'And it's strange, Bernard's always been so good in bed – once we got going – but now all that with Bernard seems somehow too facile. Julian really had quite some difficulty, and yet spiritually, emotionally, sexually – Brenda, with Julian just now I was transported. It's the only way I can describe it. Transported.'

Brenda felt a twinge or two in her belly. She hoped the strains of the morning were not going to induce labour early. Ellen was nutty; so much was evident. There was a condition called paraphrenia, of which she had heard – in which a person was recognizably insane in one area only, seldom certifiable, but just a terrible nuisance to family, friends and neighbours. Perhaps Ellen was a paraphrenic?

The door opened and Bernard came in.

'Darling!' said Ellen. 'How wonderful! I rang the hospital and they said they didn't think you'd be home until tomorrow. I was coming in this afternoon to see you, during visiting hours.'

'Visiting hours are all day,' said Bernard. 'There's a terrible smell in here. What is it?'

'I've spent all morning unblocking the sink,' said Ellen. 'Haven't I, Brenda?'

'Yes,' said Brenda.

'Anyway,' said Ellen, 'they let you out, that's the main thing. They were just being over-careful. Well, I'm glad they were. I rang the college to say you wouldn't be in.'

'They're running the college on such a mean and cost-effective margin,' said Bernard, 'there'll be no sick cover arranged for me whatsoever. I'd better try and get in this afternoon.'

'They can't arrange sick cover for reasons other than meanness,' observed Ellen, making, as Brenda was glad to see, a cup of tea for her husband. He looked quite pale and shaken but perhaps, Brenda thought, no more than usual. Bernard always had the air of a man to whom a disaster had happened, or was about to happen. 'They can't arrange it because teaching staff decline to notify the office as to their whereabouts, let alone their projected absences, their sabbaticals, their leave-takings, legitimate or otherwise as they may be.'

'Whose side are you on?' asked Bernard sharply. 'All of a sudden you're talking like management,' and then he seemed to forget that, and gave an account of his breakfast at the hospital; it had come three hours after the ward had been woken, and consisted of a soup plate at the bottom of which some grey fat-free milk swilled, into which a long tube of a kind of cornflakes was to be poured. He had read the tube. The flakes contained one third of the day's vitamin, mineral and carbohydrate requirements for an adult. There was a slice of thin white bread, already curling, so long it was since it had left the loaf, spread with a kind of non-fat oil, and a cup of warm decaffeinated coffee with a packet of low-protein milk powder to go with it.

'Poor darling,' murmured Ellen, preparing toast, butter and marmalade. 'Poor darling!'

Brenda felt quite weak. Was she meant to endorse her friend's hypocrisy? She supposed, yes, she was.

After breakfast, Bernard had been told he was in good health; he was told to go home but had to wait for the consultant's round before his departure could be officially sanctioned. The consultant was delayed, unusually, by an emergency, so Bernard had to sit like an idiot beside his bed, waiting for another couple of hours, fully dressed, while the work of the ward went on around him. He'd wanted to call home but had no change, and his phone card, when he tried it, had no credits left upon it, though he could have sworn it was all but new. The consultant when he arrived was scathing to the ward staff; saying there was no need whatsoever for Bernard to have been admitted: he had merely taken up a badly needed bed. Bernard had made his own way home. He missed the bus by a hair's breadth and had trod in some dog shit but had stopped in a public toilet to remove it. He had been accosted by two rather aggressive homosexuals –

'Gays,' said Ellen.

'Homosexuals,' said Bernard –

but had managed to avoid them.

'Bernard,' said Ellen. 'Such a chapter of accidents! I know what you're thinking: that all this is proof that there is indeed a curse upon you. But I think you imagine it. I don't expect you got much sleep last night. That's a perfectly normal hospital breakfast: consultants are always saying things like that to ward staff: many of those phone cards are faulty: you are always missing buses because you've got your back turned checking the timetable when they do arrive.'

'The dog shit was real enough.'

'No doubt it was. But the dog population of this town is phenomenal. You probably mistook the concern of two perfectly ordinary people in the gentleman's toilet – you look dreadfully pale – for sexual overtures. Anyway, here you are, safe and sound.'

'Why do you try and avoid it?' said Bernard. 'I have had a curse put upon me by Nerina. Look what's happening to poor Jed's wife. There's no doubt about it at all.'

'Well,' said Ellen, 'this morning I feel singularly blessed, so there you are! I am surprised at you, Bernard. You're such a rationalist, and here you are talking about curses. I expect you're still a little shocked after the accident, and somehow the feeling-tone of your childhood has returned. All that heavy, doomy religion. Punishment round every corner.'

'I expect that's what it is,' said Bernard, cheering up. 'God, I'm glad to be home.'

Brenda made the generalized motions to leave that the wife's friend is expected to make on the return of the husband. Ellen said she'd run her to the bus stop only their car was a write-off. Brenda said she thought perhaps she'd call Peter and he could run her to the hospital. She thought labour might have started.

And so indeed it had. Brenda's baby was simply and safely delivered, happy and healthy and not noticeably premature. Whatever had been going on in the Parkin household had at least not affected Brenda, or her baby.

A taped telephone interview between
Valerie and Eleanor

A: Punishment, you ask? Perhaps it's because I've never been a mother that thoughts of 'punishment' do not spring at once to mind. What kind of punishment will be meted out to evil-doers in Darcy's Utopia? Good heavens, it will simply be exile from the place. To know that 'punishment' entails being kept away can only make a place more desirable to those who live there.

Q: But where will these exiles go?

A: To any of the other traditional societies which will no doubt abound: to places where they lock murderers in death row for years while debating whether or not to kill them, or child molesters with violent gangsters who love little children, or imprison maintenance defaulters who cannot bear to finance their ex-wife's boyfriend, while letting others off who simply abandon all responsibility for their children: where the horrors of TV are the reward for good behaviour, and large sums of money for the sin of usury. Let defaulters be sent out to live for a while in the grimy, exhausted, baffling society we take for granted: where we must travel in underground tunnels to get to our place of normally quite unnecessary employment (unnecessary for the group other than to keep the wheels turning; necessary for the individual to provide the money which must be made but brings so little pleasure), to be consumed therein, like as not, by flash fires; let our troublemakers-in-exile go but for a breath of fresh air and camaraderie on a boat upon the river – to find the rules of navigation so irrational, so clouded by the custom and practice of the past that even to do something so human, so natural, is to endanger life itself – they will soon reflect on the errors of their ways. The wheels of industry outside Darcy's Utopia turn to make products no one wants or needs, from nuclear warheads to teabag squeezers. What is wrong with fingers when it comes to tea bags? Let them hop about a bit in the heat of the moment, it will do them no harm, and under those turning wheels the human spirit, the human love of doing nothing for quite a lot of the time, except tinkering a bit here, fixing a bit there, lulls in activity which alternate with periods of hard and concentrated work, is crushed. I hope *Aura* pays your telephone bills at the Holiday Inn?

Q: Yes. You were saying?

A: I was saying I wasn't sure that it was morally sound thus to ask *Aura* to support you in your love nest. I think the *Independent* should foot at least some of the bills. If you were living in Darcy's Utopia your punishment would be being required to slip out to Birmingham, say, for a day or two, to wander around the concrete walkways that intertwine above its tangled motorways, and breathe in the fumes, observe the struggling sun. You certainly wouldn't do anything to threaten your stay in Darcy's Utopia again – or at the very least you would keep your telephone calls short.

Q: You mean there are to be no cars in Darcy's Utopia?

A: There will be a few cars, many bicycles, and recycling stations on every street corner. There will be a free restaurant in every square – and tree-lined squares will abound which will refresh the ozone layer – where such local people as love cooking will compete in the culinary arts.

Q: Hang on a bit. Who's doing the cooking? Whoever it is isn't doing it for wages, because there aren't any wages.

A: The cooks are working out their Community Unit. How does that grab you, Valerie? No more income tax, merely a Community Unit charge. We will not be taxed out of existence, will not watch the noughts wiped out on our bank statements, as happens wherever as a group we try to make things fair, but into existence. We will not pay our taxes in money – what will be the point, for

152

money now pours in a ceaseless stream from the high street cashpoints? Yes, Valerie, that is what it does.

Q: Not just on Sundays, as your husband advised the Treasury in those heady days of the Bridport Scandal?

A: He did not go far enough. Every day of the week. It is how we make the transition from the money economy to Darcy's Utopia. And nothing will taste better than food cooked by the community cooks – the healthier, the cleverer, the more energetic you are, the more work will be required of you. As things are, twenty-five per cent of us work to support the seventy-five per cent who do not. I don't think we will see much drop in production – merely in anxiety. And of course if work is unpleasant you will cross off your Community Units really quickly, and be free to do as you like.

Q: I still think people only work for money.

A: Do you? No. You work because you like to do it. Mrs Khalid worked to get out of the house, for company. Her husband, the lawyer, I daresay worked from a sense of commitment. Nerina worked to earn the attention of Jed. Her black magic circle worked to raise the Devil, and I'm sure without thought of monetary reward. You may say 'you are talking about professional people, self-conscious people, the clever and the intelligent' – and yes, I am, but we have machines to do work, and people whose intense pleasure it is to make these machines. Any man who will only work for money let him not work at all. I don't mind keeping him. It seems a small price to pay to live in Utopia. As it is, now that money buys so little, now the thrill of owning a car better than your neighbour's, a better designed pair of jeans, begins to wear off, people work not for money but for the status money brings. Valerie? Are you still there?

Q: I was just moving the phone to my other hand.

A: You did call me. I didn't call you. Where were we? Competition in the culinary arts. Yes, Brenda is a terrible cook, but a very good mother. She will expend her Community Units in childcare, not the communal cooking pot. Cooked food can of course be taken away to eat within the family unit, or eaten on the spot with friends. There will be little loneliness in Darcy's Utopia. Solitude for those who seek it, company for those who need it. The old and the young will mix freely: the young won't hate the old any more because the old will be more than just a reminder that the flesh is mortal and youth and life itself a passing thing, because the old will no longer be miserable; they will not feel their uselessness: they will be full of tales not of the good old days, but of the bad old days before Utopia, and so they will be loved and not abhorred. There will be no granny beatings in Darcy's Utopia.

Q: But if there were, if I can return to this subject of punishment, because I don't quite share your trust in human nature, would simple exile really be sufficient punishment?

A: You worry about exile. Perhaps you feel exiled yourself? Unable, because of your behaviour, to return home; obliged to live forever in the Holiday Inn. How are you getting on with my life story? How far have you got? Has Julian turned up on the scene?

Q: Yes. He has. How long was it after his declaration of love that you left Bernard? I realize you don't like these direct questions, and use them as a starting ground for your preoccupations, but perhaps subjects such as exile are really more suitable for discussion with Hugo. The readers of *Aura* are more accustomed to thinking about matters of the heart: they like to know about *you*. Do you believe in short, sharp shocks for offenders, in abortion, in fidelity and so forth? What life has taught you, in fact? Personally I find Darcy's Utopia fascinating, but my readers aren't at ease with politics.

A: More's the pity. Let them become so. Let each and every one of them consider the nature and purpose of punishment. Do we imprison other people to satisfy our desire for vengeance, to deter others, or to reform the wrongdoer, by making prison so horrible he never does it again? We know this latter seldom works but we go on trying it as a solution. There will be no prisons in Darcy's Utopia. I advise you to have none in this society of yours you seem so proud of. Close them! Simply open the doors and let everyone out, into the streets of your horrid societies, littered already with the homeless, the lost, the indigent, those who have had the misfortune to be three days without washing – after that clothes and body smell so there is little chance of either employment or rehabilitation: they will be back out on the streets anyway as soon as their sentence is up. Why wait? Why hang about? If any prisoners are by common consent truly and irrationally violent let them be shut up in secure hospitals, but kindly dealt with in the most pleasant circumstances possible. Ugliness in the external world is the cause of much internal ugliness. Deglamorize crime, say I: define the criminal as insane, and he may be less anxious to be a criminal. The heavier the sentences for rape, the more rape there is. Hadn't you noticed?

Q: You have that the wrong way round. Surely?

A. No, I have not. A man rapes a woman because he wants to do something very nasty to her, pay her whole sex out for not managing to save him from distress, for not being worthy of his love – and the nastier the community tells him it is, the more likely he is to do it. Of course it is a horrible thing for a man to do, but nothing is gained, practically, by underlining this fact – except I suppose it comforts women to feel the judiciary begins to take their woes seriously. Eight years slopping out! Ten years! Twelve! But it doesn't stop rape. On the contrary. There will be very little rape in Darcy's Utopia: generation by generation it will fade away, as only women fit to be loved by their children are allowed to bear them. And since if you want money you have only to stand outside a cash disposal unit to receive it, on any day of the week, so there will be little point in crime. That is enough for today.

Q: Don't go. Let me get this straight. You are seriously relying on the distress of exile to deter the wrongdoer?

A: It used to be considered so. The newspapers of my childhood were full of the sufferings of exiled kings. To be sent from the kingdom, never allowed to return, was considered a fate worse than death. And we have so very many exiles these days – dissidents, political refugees – people who have escaped or been sent away from oppressive regimes, never to be allowed to return, and yet we fail to acknowledge their distress. The Iranian taxi driver in New York weeps for the land of his childhood, the friends he once knew: the family he once had: he has had to start his life again; he will never be a whole person, and he knows it. But he does not have the word for it: the word that defines it, explains it, and in the explaining makes it just a little better, as when a doctor diagnoses a pain. Exile. It is what the wife feels when her husband locks her out of his life: the husband likewise. That is why changing the locks on the door of the marital home is so powerful and horrifying a symbol. The erring partner is sent into exile, both real and emotional.

Q: I'm sure Lou wouldn't change the locks.

A: I wasn't speaking personally. Good heavens! Here comes Brenda with the coffee. We drink decaffeinated: she insists. I seem to remember the Holiday Inn coffee as being rich, powerful stuff. Don't drink too much of it: it's bad for the nerves.

Q: Thank you for the warning, Mrs Darcy.

A: Do call me Eleanor. Ta-ra.

Q: Ta-ra.

Valerie misses home

Make no doubt about the pull of habit: the anxiety that ensues if any regular, familiar, pattern of event is disrupted, let alone stilled, however disagreeable the pattern of events might be. The first few mornings in Hugo's company – usually a flurry of sexual activity, followed by a pleasant languor – prevented me from feeling any sense of early morning loss. As the flurries became a little more familiar, a little less accompanied by the shock of the new, indeed in general rather less, thoughts of home began to obtrude. I missed, of all things, *breakfast*. I missed Lou's petulance, Sophie's agitated search for missing garments, Ben's repeated refusal to feed the cat with canned meat but only with tinned salmon: his apparent motive laudable – if he was a vegetarian, of the kind who eats fish, so should the cat be – his real motive to irritate his father, who was daily irritated.

I missed the hassle, the subdued indignation of a woman who, her husband insisting on a 'sit-down breakfast for the family' and not one taken merely on the wing, on the grounds that a family that eats together stays together, has on that account to spend twenty minutes every morning getting up and down from her chair, fetching fresh coffee, making more toast, answering the phone, removing the cat from the table, irritating that same husband every time she does so, because he likes peace while he eats. *Must* have peace, he, the creative artist, having barely recovered from last night's concert, already tense about the next. Why of all times of day should I miss this particular dreadful hour? Had there been some real achievement here, after all, in the ritual sopping up of breakfast aggro in the interests of happy family life? Which seems so often, in spite of all theory and effort, to be the maternal and not the paternal role? When I had finished *Lover at the Gate* I could perhaps persuade the editor of *Aura* to run a piece on the problem;

I didn't want to write it myself – I just wanted to know; to be told, for once, what everything was all about, not to be the one who did the telling.

The pages of *Lover at the Gate* mounted steadily beside my printer. As the pile grew higher, so it seemed to me, little flickers of interest in the outside world returned. I both longed to finish it, yet dreaded the finishing. What then? When Eleanor had let me go, if Eleanor let me go, what then?

Bernard and Ellen part

A month or so later Prune's baby was stillborn – one of those apparently perfect babies who turn out to have failed to develop a brain – and Bernard said, 'Nerina's group ill-wished it.' Ellen said, 'That's absurd. It was conceived with a genetic defect: its handicap predated the insult to Nerina.' Bernard said, 'Well, perhaps black magic groups can predate curses. How do you know they can't?' and Ellen replied, 'You should have been Witchfinder General. You'd have picked out and burned a thousand witches,' and Bernard was upset and insulted, feeling she was seeing him as reactionary when everyone knew he was a radical, a feminist, a reconstructed man, liberal in outlook, tolerant in behaviour, his heart and mind firmly in the right place. Ellen and Bernard were not getting on too well. The phone had gone a couple of times lately and a man, with a gravelly, upper echelon civil service note to his voice, rather than the serviceable tones of the locality and the polytechnic, had asked for Eleanor, and Ellen had taken the call on the extension.

'Who was that?' Bernard asked, too proud to listen in to the call.

'He's a man offering me a job up at the university,' said Ellen. 'You know I had my name down at the agency for temping work. I think I'll take it.'

'Why does he call you Eleanor?'

'I put Eleanor on the form. I thought I might get paid more as Eleanor than as Ellen.'

They needed the money. The Inland Revenue had discovered a mistake in their accounting: they were demanding six hundred and fifty pounds from Bernard forthwith, which he did not have. He had bought No. 93 from the landlord at a good price, but now dry rot had appeared in the porch, and if not seen to soon would damage the fabric of the house. Wendy's ghost made a dramatic appearance again, knocking Ellen's contraceptive pills off the mantelpiece: drifting around the bedroom in a kind of orange glow. Ellen was prepared to call in a priest to exorcize it but Bernard said drearily it was all too late, too late. Bernard's white shirts had somehow got in with a pair of Ellen's red socks and were now a pinkish grey. He hated to be so sloppily dressed. All misfortunes were blamed upon Nerina. Nerina would sit in class staring at him, Bernard said, her steady brown eyes, half-reproachful, half-triumphant, plotting further troubles for him, big and little stabs of revenge. He slept too much, not too little: he was too desolate, too anxious for lovemaking. The curse of depression lay upon him: Ellen suggested lithium, which does so much to calm the manic-depressive temperament, but Bernard said lithium was no defence against Nerina. Nerina had it in for him.

'Bernard,' said Ellen, 'are you sure you didn't make a pass at her? If you ask me, only excessive guilt would make you quite so fanciful. Though it's better to have this Nerina blamed for your pink shirts rather than me. If she didn't exist I would have to invent her.'

'Of course I didn't make a pass at Nerina,' said Bernard. 'That might be the trouble. Jed did. Jed's the kind to bed his best friend's wife if he thought he'd get away with it. Jed has just got a senior lectureship and won a five-hundred-pound premium bond, and poor Prune's baby is dead.'

Julian Darcy did not believe in curses. Julian would just have looked startled, even indignant, had Ellen seemed for one moment to give any credence to the powers of black magic. Black magic was for the credulous, the ignorant, the uneducated. Julian moved amongst the powerful of the land: the thought behind the Conference: the mind behind the Act. Julian had a benign and cultivated air. Julian took a sip of claret here, a glass of Perrier there: Julian made a trip to 10 Downing Street: Julian went up to a shoot in Scotland: Julian and Georgina gave a dinner party and who was guest of honour but the Chancellor of the Exchequer and his wife. After dinner, Ellen asked, when the guests had gone, when the house was quiet, when the mind was stilled, what then? No, Julian and Georgina had long since given up sex. They were friends, good friends, no more.

Julian's conversation, when not about the beauty of Eleanor's body, the freshness of Eleanor's mind, was about recession and government intercession, exchange rates, the International Monetary Fund, and occasionally what minister was sleeping with what actress, and who had behaved shoddily pre-privatization and which member of the Stock Exchange was going shortly to be nailed for malpractice. Julian didn't worry about whether dry rot in the porch had been caused by a leaky gutter or a curse: he would simply curse the cheque that had it eradicated forthwith. Eleanor knew: now she worked in the Vice Chancellor's office she made out his personal cheques. Julian was not business-like about his own finances: he would hand her tattered files stuffed with letters, bills and uncashed cheques, which he had found at the bottoms of drawers. She would divide them as best she could between university and personal, and hand over to Miss Richards in the faculty office whatever seemed relevant, and Julian would murmur into her ear, 'Brilliant, brilliant: I am so *bad* at this kind of thing!', and Eleanor would say, 'You are a person on the grand scale, not a detail man at all,' or some such thing, and he would seem to be relieved, as if a lifetime's self-doubt had been lifted. She enjoyed making him happy. It was so easy. Georgina was perfect, he would say; he had to be as much on show if he got up and went to the bathroom in the middle of the night as he would receiving guests. He liked to shamble sometimes, he confessed. To belch, to burp, to fart. Georgina wouldn't let him. Ellen purred over his imperfections; his belly, his broken tooth, the hairs in his nose. 'I love you for what you aren't,' she'd say, 'as much as for what you are.'

Julian's wife Georgina came to call upon Julian at work one morning: strode in, tall and elegant, in pale, impeccable clothes. She was as coldly charming to Eleanor as no doubt she was to everyone of lower status – which, as Ellen confided in Bernard, must be almost the entire world – and would have gone straight through to see her husband but Eleanor said, 'One moment, please, Mrs Darcy, I'll just see if he's free,' so Georgina Darcy had to stand there until Eleanor said, 'Professor Darcy can see you now. You may go through,' which pleased Eleanor as much as Georgina Darcy's cool nod had displeased her.

Bernard said, 'Why do you always have to work so late?' and Ellen said, 'Because there's so much to do,' and so there was. Bernard said, 'At least he's not the kind to make passes at a secretary: not a secretary without a qualification to her name: beats me why he employed you.' 'Beats me,' said Ellen, and Julian did, sometimes. She liked that.

He took her up to Bridport Lodge, the Vice Chancellor's residence, a country house of elegant Georgian proportions, when Georgina was away visiting friends in Scotland – naturally she had friends in Scotland: that kind of person did, said Liese. Leonard went shooting grouse sometimes. He sold Rolls-Royces now. Liese confided he wasn't the man she'd married. She was glad her father was dead: Leonard was a mass murderer of little birds. 'I expect he has to do it for the contacts,' said Ellen, but it didn't comfort Liese. Ellen, Brenda and Belinda were a little pleased to see this cloud pass over their friend's life. While Georgina was away, Eleanor fingered through the garments in Georgina's walk-in wardrobe: it was full of good tweed skirts and cashmere sweaters. Eleanor picked through Georgina's jewel case, which was neatly packed with pearls and stud earrings – and then Eleanor would spend the evening sporting on the antique brass bed between Georgina's linen sheets. She thought perhaps Ellen would have behaved differently. But linen sheets! Of course, there were staff to iron them, paid for by the university. The staff were always about. Julian was too grand to notice their presence, or else it served his purpose that they should be present, witness to his and Eleanor's passion. Sometimes Eleanor had the feeling that Julian was devious, more devious than she allowed. Vice Chancellors, she supposed, often were.

'Are you out of your mind?' Brenda asked Eleanor. She came up to the university office one morning, pushing her loaded pram up the hill. 'Can't you even keep it quiet? The whole town knows. The whole polytechnic knows. Everyone in the world knows except Bernard and Georgina, and eventually someone will break ranks and tell them too.'
'Knows what?' asked Eleanor. 'What am I doing wrong?'

Brenda called Belinda and Belinda drove all the way to Bridport to see Eleanor. She came in a little Deux Chevaux. She and her husband had joined a religious group and now gave most of their money away to its leader. Her baby came too, in a carrycot on the back seat.

'You don't even seem to understand that what you're doing is peculiar, Ellen. People have extramarital affairs in a hole-in-the-corner way. Not like this. You are throwing everything away. And Vice Chancellors of universities, especially with political connections, do not normally risk careers and marriage for the sake of someone like you.'

'Then perhaps he's mad,' said Eleanor. 'And I don't see I'm throwing anything away. I'm having a really nice time, and I'd rather have a lover than a baby any day. If you ask me, it's only women who can't find lovers, who only have husbands, who have to make do with babies.'

Belinda's baby dickered and fretted in her mother's arms.

'Well,' said Belinda, 'that puts me in my place,' and Eleanor had to apologize. She did not wish to hurt her friend unnecessarily. But Belinda pulled out a very full breast and offered it to the baby. She had put on weight again.

'Tell you what,' Eleanor said, 'I'll speak to Bernard if that makes you feel any better.'

She did. She said to Bernard they'd agreed always to be honest with each other, and anyway he hadn't married her properly, only at a civil ceremony which he hadn't really acknowledged at the time, and out of pity, not love, and now she had found someone she really loved, who really loved her, whose interests coincided with hers, and so forth, and since they had no children she was free to follow the desires and devices of her own heart, surely, and so forth and so on, and what it amounted to, she was seeing and sleeping with another man, and it didn't mean she and Bernard would have to split up, she needed time to discover if this was what she really wanted.

Bernard wept. She had hoped he would hit her, but all he did was sit there with tears running out of his eyes and snot running out of his nose. Julian would at least have reached for his handkerchief

– and there would have been one to hand, crisp, white and laundered. Eleanor found Bernard a tissue and gave it to him.

'For God's sake,' she said, 'this kind of thing happens in marriages all the time.'

Then he asked her what he could do to make the marriage better, asked how had he failed her; he would do anything, anything, to keep her; and the more he grovelled the more she despised him: and yet she was surprised. She had not expected this. The old Bernard would not have behaved so: the moral high ground would automatically have been his. He was in some way denatured, and by no doing of hers. Was this what depression did to men?

'Don't leave me,' he said. 'Whatever you do, don't leave me. They want you to leave me; it's part of my punishment. I'm cursed, can't you see it? Are you completely blind? First they destroy your car, then your wife leaves you: next you lose your friends and your job. You'll see!'

Eleanor couldn't bear it. She went and slept in the spare room. Bernard brought her a cup of tea in the morning and gazed at her with wet, exhausted eyes; he hadn't slept: of course he hadn't slept.

'You're insane,' Eleanor said. 'You'll have to see a doctor.'

Eleanor didn't even drink the tea he brought. She said she'd rather have coffee, knowing there was none in the house. It was a long time since she'd bothered to go shopping. The more Bernard suffered the more she wished to hurt him. She supposed that was human nature. She decided not to think about it too much.

Eleanor took a short-cut through the polytechnic grounds to get to her office and the bracing nearness of Julian. It had been snowing in the night, but now the morning was clear and crisp. The early sun dazzled. The students had remade their snowman. She left the swept path the better to inspect it, treading as delicately as she could through the snow in her little new laced boots with their thin soles and impracticably high heels – Julian had opened accounts for her at all the city's better stores, and occasionally Eleanor would use them, but only occasionally, and always in Julian's interests: he loved to see her in the boots and nothing else. The snowman was wearing a scarf of the kind Bernard wore, and the kind Julian would never wear – a fuzzy blue scarf in prickly wool with patches of pale grey struggling through the weave. Julian wore silk scarves, soft against the face. Black stones stood for Bernard's eyes, and little grey pebbles for tears trailed down his cheeks. And a stick just casually pierced where his heart would be.

The sun was beginning to warm the snow: a thaw had begun. The whole shape of the snowman was becoming indecisive even as she watched: its edges were sloppy and imprecise. She stepped forward and pulled the stick out of the heart, and a whole side of the snowman collapsed, and now only an untidy half of Bernard remained. Then the head toppled forward and fell. She was conscious that her boots were wet: her toes were becoming cold and uncomfortable. Her boots were not intended for such adverse weather conditions. All around the thaw was noisy in her ears. Snow fell and slopped in lumps from branches overhead. Bernard melted, formless, and was gone.

Eleanor called Brenda as soon as she got in to her office and had taken off her boots. She had put the electric fire on and stretched out her toes towards it, to warm them.
'Brenda,' she said, 'you may be right about my being out of my mind. I do have very peculiar feelings of disassociation from time to time. I seem to be on some kind of automatic pilot which is none of my setting. Every moral weakness I ever had is somehow getting magnified to absurd proportions.'
'It's interesting you should say that,' said Brenda. 'Personally I blame Jed. You know I had this affair with him –
'I didn't,' said Eleanor.
'It was nothing special. I worried because I didn't like sex with Pete. I thought if I tried it with Jed it might be different.'
'Was it?'
'No. It's just me. Apparently if you do too much sport when a girl you never become – well – properly sensual.'
'I'll never have that problem,' said Eleanor.
'I noticed,' said Brenda.
'What is this to do with the magnification of my moral weakness?'
'Jed is trying to set standards of positive religious tolerance throughout the college. The new policy is that from the Moonies to the Muslims by way of the Jesus freaks all Gods are equal, and

if they want to worship the Devil that's okay too. Mind you, the Academic Board only okayed it by one vote. A group of students have set up a black magic group and they've got a drawing of you up there and they go over it with a magnifying glass and that's why you're the way you are. A fornicating adulterous zombie. Night of the Sexy Dead.'

'You're joking.'

'Yes I am. But they are experimenting in black magic in Jed's media communications course and he is having an affair with one of the students, and that's always trouble.'

'Nerina?'

'Yes. The Brat Nerina. It makes me feel furious, I can tell you. Not to mention tall and gawky and ugly. Pete and Bernard are the controls, Nerina says; they being the least pervious to suggestion, by virtue of their education and integrity. Or else because Jed's got it in for Pete and Bernard.'

'Why should he?'

'Because Pete's my husband and Bernard's your husband, idiot. Don't think I don't know about you and Jed. Mr Kiss-and-Tell himself. Of course it may be unconscious on Jed's part.'

'How's Peter?'

'Pete's just fine. So am I. We're impervious to the flesh. But you and Bernard are susceptible because you're at it all the time.'

'Who says so?'

'Jed.'

'Brenda, susceptible to what? Black magic?'

'Of course not, idiot. Suggestion.'

Eleanor thought there was not much future in the conversation and put the phone down. She opened the press file and searched for and found the photograph taken at the conference; herself near the head of the table, her head bent over her notes, and it was true that the light shone through from the great arched quasi-ecclesiastical window behind her and gave her hair a bright outline, but scarcely a halo. Julian Darcy sat at the head of the table, as chairman, with the potentially ferocious, fleshy, rather pudgy amiability that characterizes men of power in their middle age. He was, on the face of it, not the kind of man to excite sexual passion in anyone other than his wife, and that only by force of habit and custom. She took a magnifying glass from the desk drawer, left there by her predecessor – Julian had had to let go a junior clerical assistant to make way for Eleanor – to examine the rather strange patterns made by the light from the window. What she had taken as a composition of trees and clouds in the window she could now interpret as an alarmingly goatish face; slit eyes, hair, horns and all. The winter sun shone through the magnifying glass and focused on to the glossy paper. A small circle began to smoke, to crinkle, to hole, to burn, to curl – she blew the flame out as soon as she had worked out what was happening, that this was fire – and though she remained, as if trapped forever writing minutes, both the field in the window and Julian Darcy had ceased to exist.

She put the photograph back in the file and swept away the little pile of embers with her hand. Julian liked her hands dirty. Georgina was always so clean. She called Belinda.
'Do you believe in the Devil?' she asked.
'Of course I don't,' said Belinda. 'I believe in the one, the eternal, the wholesomeness of light and all that junk. Frank believes in it, that's to say, and it's easier for me to take it all on board than fight it, what with the baby and all.'
'If you'd stop breastfeeding,' said Eleanor, 'you might get a little intellectual rigour back, not to mention your figure, and be more help.'
'You don't need help,' said Belinda. 'It's Bernard needs help. You're a real pig to him, Apricot. And to me. You know I've always had a weight problem.'
'Sow,' said Eleanor, 'and my name's Eleanor,' and put the phone down. Liese was out. She rang Ken, but his line gave a high-pitched buzz. He had not paid the bill. This was what came, she thought, of not not-believing in your own mother's ghost. One thing led to another. Astrology today is witchcraft tomorrow. Give the occult an inch and it took an ell. Sections of Mafeking Street were prone to subsidence: if things fell off the mantelpiece it was because the earth moved.

Julian came in and said, 'You haven't got your boots on. Or your stockings. If you put your feet too close to the fire you'll get chilblains,' and he went down on his knees and took her toes in his mouth. She felt puzzled rather than excited: it occurred to her that when with Julian she usually felt more puzzled than excited. His mouth worked up her legs.

'I don't think any of this is quite right,' she said. 'There's more going on here than meets the eye. I think I'd better give up the job,' and she looked up and Georgina was standing watching. Julian hadn't locked the door. Julian never locked doors: it was beneath him so to do.

Georgina was wearing a prickly wool skirt in a dreary blue with grey patches which reminded Eleanor very much of Bernard's scarf, which she had last seen lying in a murky pool of melted snow. But her green cashmere sweater was so admirable Eleanor thought she'd look better in it than Georgina, whose bust was rather small. Negligible, as Julian would put it.

Georgina said, 'Well, I knew something was going on. I didn't know it would be so disgusting. I am leaving now. I am filing for divorce.' And she left.

Julian said, 'Do you think you could organize the various graduation ceremonies, Eleanor?', and Eleanor said, 'I don't see why not.' And Julian said, 'The senate won't like it, but I will. How empowered love makes one feel.' Julian spoke a lot of 'one' when others would say 'I': it was something to do with his class and age. Just to hear him speak made Eleanor's spine tingle: they resumed their lovemaking. It can only be a marriage of true minds, thought Eleanor: forget his paunch, the hairs in his nose, the softness of the upper arms. Outside in the antechamber to his office, faculty heads waited unduly long for their appointments, even by Vice Chancellor's standards. 'He's busy,' said Miss Richards, the faculty secretary. They looked at each other but no one said anything. What could they say?

Eleanor went home to tell Bernard that events had precipitated her decision and she was going to leave him and live with Julian forthwith, and Bernard, with unexpected calmness, said that Julian would be expected to resign and Eleanor said no, if any man was irreplaceable in his work, in his field, that man was Julian Darcy. What was more, by virtue of his contract, he could only be dismissed from office by reason of insanity or depravity and to love a woman other than his wife was neither insane nor depraved. Bernard said, 'You've worked all this out,' and Eleanor said 'Yes.' Bernard said alas, his own contract of employment was not so secure; it contained a 'failure to carry out duties to the satisfaction of the college' clause. What was more, he said, he had that very day been asked to resign: the director had sent for him. For a long time, it appeared, management had been assembling a dossier of complaints against Bernard: accusations came from friends and foe alike – allegations of academic negligence, imprudent memos, and, now, it seemed, and totally unfounded, of misconduct with female students. What it really meant, said Bernard, was that they had him pigeon-holed as a political agitator. The truth of the matter was irrelevant. They simply wanted him out. His face no longer fitted. They just didn't like him. And now, as he had predicted, he was a man without a car, a job, or a wife. Of course he was fighting it: he would go on teaching till they forcibly removed him, but what would he do for money? The union ought to support him, fight his case, but they too had deserted him. And he had lost his scarf, the blue one with the grey squares he was so fond of.

'I'll go and find it,' said Eleanor, 'but it will be the last thing I do for you.'

'You won't get rid of me so easily,' he said. 'I am your conscience. I am the real you. There is a little of me left to fight Nerina.'

'Bernard,' said Eleanor, having one more try, 'a man's misfortune lies not in the events that happen to him, but in his reaction to those events. Why can't you just rejoice in the fact that I'm leaving you? Then it could seem to be a blessing, not a curse.'

But the pebble tears began to run down his cheeks, and she packed the nice new clothes he hadn't noticed, and left. What else could she do?

She went by the polytechnic grounds and picked up Bernard's scarf. No one else had bothered. It was wet. She would dry it out in Georgina's airing cupboard and post it back.

Transcript of a Hugo/Eleanor tape

Q: Yes, but come along, surely a perfect society isn't possible?

A: How do you know? Why shouldn't we have heaven on earth? You really make me tired, sometimes. You're so full of ifs and buts, and looking for flaws, no wonder nothing ever happens: we all just drift on in the way we always have, bowing under legislation which builds on old legislation, precedent which builds on existing precedent: saying because this didn't work then it won't work now. But 'then' isn't 'now'. In Darcy's Utopia everyone will understand that the lessons of history are nonexistent. No doubt history will be taught but in classes, remember, made up solely of children who wish to be in them, and teachers who enjoy imparting information and rejoice in the excitement of new ideas, who have a sense of the flow of mankind's history: how we have progressed out of primitivism, barbarity, into self-knowledge and empathy with others; how in the spite of our natures we have achieved at least an attempt at civilization.

In Darcy's Utopia nostalgia will be out of fashion. We will look back into the past with horror, not with envy and delight – we will stop our romantic nonsense about the rural tranquillity of once upon a time, which is, if you ask me, nothing but the projected fantasy of old and miserable men who, looking back into their own childhoods, see paradise. But it is a false paradise, falsely remembered. Wishful thinking clouds our memory. Times were better then, we think. We assume that what is true for us individually is true for society too. But it isn't. The antithesis is true. One by one we grow old and decline, but our societies increase in vigour, grow richer in wisdom, stronger in empathy, as we hand our knowledge down, generation from generation. Our own individual fate clouds our vision: we stumble and fall, exhausted, but pass the baton on, runners all in this great race of ours. We should not get too depressed about it. I, Eleanor Darcy, have no children: children are the great cop-out, the primrose path to non-thought, to destruction. Leave it all to them, the fecund say, that's all we have to think about. Wave after pointless wave, generation after generation, looking backwards, saying better then. Mine is the pebbly, difficult, problematic path, thorny with impossible ideas, genderless; here you get spat upon, jeered at, derided, but it is the only path which leads forward to heaven upon earth.

And why should we not have it? I tell you, if you look back, you will get burned, like Lot's wife, to a pillar of salt; Lot's wife, nostalgic for the past. In Darcy's Utopia it will be very bad form to hark back; collecting antiques for the domestic home will be *outré*. A museum will be the only place for the artefacts of past ages, and let them be as gloomy and dismal as can be. In Darcy's Utopia it will be accepted that museums will be very boring places indeed. If you want to subdue the children you only have to take them on a visit to a museum, and they will behave at once, for fear of being taken there again.

> *Room service had brought breakfast, and the mail. Valerie sat up in bed, Hugo still asleep beside her, and read the transcript. What bliss, she thought, what paradise, thus to live. Someone else to cook and clean, and bring the food: to be a man's lover, not his mother/wife. She would live in the present. She would avoid for ever the trap of nostalgia. She could see that the pleasure of this moment could, so easily, turn into pain, simply because it no longer existed. How was that to be avoided?*

Q: But won't that make for a heartless, soulless place? Surely we need the resonance of the past in order to enrich the present?

A: There you go again! Well, it's understandable. Set foot outside your door, outside your little patch of safety, and lo, chaos waits; disease, poverty, madness, hurt, ebbs and flows all around: you're knee deep in it. If you don't get mugged your conscience gets pricked: the beggar at the door offends, the homeless in the alley hurts; drunkards sleep in every alley, the mad stand on the motorway and shake their fists. Those that have not reproach you: those that have, braying about profit and self-interest, offend you. You cannot believe that the past was worse than this. Rather, you don't *want* to believe it was. Wars lay waste a generation, they say: fear of war has wasted one of ours.

And how we made them feel it, our young, with our talk of nuclear winter and Armageddon! The revenge of the old upon the young, to deprive them thus of all hope of the future. Look at them now: how they appal you! Hollow-eyed, white-faced, black-clothed, they walk like zombies round the streets, puffing in or shooting up the dreary stuff, which makes the present real, enables them to smile, and lift a languid hand in salutation to their friends. They vomit if they can, they sick it all up: and if their digestions in spite of all abuse stay sound, they drop their litter instead: walk ankle deep in discarded Coke cans, beer tins, fast food packs, dust and rubbish of every kind, not to mention the excreta of rats and dogs, and they don't care one bit. It even seems to cheer them up a trifle. Looking at all this, you are assailed by guilt and confusion, and you think, what's happened can only be this: that once there was a golden age, and everything ever since has been a falling away from that. Well, it shows a niceness of nature. You believe there's something good somewhere: if only by process of polarity: that is to say, your profound belief in the existence of opposites; that if there is bad, there is also good.

Q: Isn't there?

A: As it happens, yes. But it lies in front, not behind. We move towards the golden age, not away from it: it is inscribed in gold upon the gates which open into Darcy's Utopia.

Q: You see it as a walled city, then?

A: I'm not quite sure. It stays vague. There are shining towers, golden spires. Or is that some memory I have of Toronto? I suspect as a place it may be rather boring to the eye, being ecologically sound. A lot of people will be doing a lot of painting pictures and making music, so the standard won't be very high. But we'll make up in quantity for what we lose in quality. And of course affairs of the heart will keep most of us very busily occupied, and make up for a lot.

Q: I take it that, in the manner of Utopias, the streets will be clear of litter?

A: Singapore changed from the dirtiest city in the world to the cleanest, by dint of one month in which the police shot on sight anyone dropping litter.

Q: And that will happen in Darcy's Utopia?

A: I was joking, Mr Vansitart. I am teasing you. No, there are no firearms in the place. No one can point a stick of metal at anyone else and kill them from a distance, that goes without saying. Since it will be a recycling society, rather than a consuming society, there will be very little litter available for the dropping: and being a pleasant enough place, no particular desire to spoil it: and profit no longer being the object of the manufacturing process, Coke won't have to come in cans: it will flow free from taps. There will be Coke points everywhere. Money will flow freely from the cash points next to them, in the transitionary period while we move from a money economy to a Community Unit economy. If you remember, our taxation comes in the form of a sliding scale of units – the young, strong, able, good and bright are awarded the most, the weak, ill, inadequate and feeble the least. Natural justice demands it. To each according to the ability, from each according to the need. The aim ceases to be to acquire money, but to expend Community Units. Those who are left with least at the end of their lives win the game! Unpleasant work gets rid of more units than does pleasant; cigarette smoking will actually gain you more units: the consumption of luxuries likewise. Necessities will be available in plenty in the shops – shopkeepers will be honoured; to keep shop will be a high status occupation, eating up Community Units by the hour! A coveted job. But we're getting bogged down in detail, Mr Vansitart. Don't you think it's time for a drink? (Calls) Brenda, you don't mind, do you? We're going for a drink.

*Valerie looked down at Hugo's sleeping body,
and the thought came to her, a little hard nugget
in a meringue which otherwise melted on the
tongue, that this was the wrong body, Lou's was
the right body. She spat the little hard nugget
out of her mind efficiently, and rapidly, and her
body dissolved back into rapture, but the pleasure
of the moment stayed spoiled.*

Eleanor entertains

Eleanor brought habits of economy with her from her life as Ellen Parkin: she brought them into Georgina Darcy's bed, changing the sheets from user-unfriendly linen to easy-care Terylene: she brought them to Georgina Darcy's table, eating with Habitat cutlery not Darcy family silver, on the grounds that the latter wasted staff time in the cleaning. Julian would be offered Cheddar not Stilton at the end of dinner. Stale bread was used up, not thrown to the ducks on the moat that half ringed Bridport Lodge. The face that stared out from Georgina's bathroom mirror, marble-set, made do with a smear of Oil of Ulay, not, as had Georgina's, layer after layer of creams and unguents, one for the eye zone, one for the lip line, others for cheeks and chin. Eleanor was not too proud to use up what Georgina left, in this respect as in all others, but once the pots were empty chucked them out and did not replace them.

And Julian Darcy didn't mind one bit. Eleanor's presence in the bed outweighed the cheapness of the sheets, her company at the table was more reassuring than his family's silver: the Cheddar, she assured him, was healthier than Stilton (by which he knew she meant cheaper) and he said he did not care about the state of her complexion, he had more important things to think about.

Eleanor told four of the six staff at the lodge that they were redundant to her needs, and so they were. These were Mrs Kneely, Mrs Foster, Edward the under gardener and Joan Baxter who came in to do the laundry. These four members of staff were the ones most visibly distressed and startled by Eleanor's sudden appearance in their midst; the ones who tittle-tattled in the town. who admitted to signing a letter of condolence and support, drawn up by Joan Baxter and posted off to Georgina before Eleanor could intercept it; who somehow or other never managed to make the marital bed, either because of the new sheets or the behaviour of those who now slept in it. It was a better bed, however.

'It seems that only married Vice Chancellors get their beds made properly,' observed Julian. 'When they live in sin they don't.' It was Eleanor's custom to make a bed by straightening a sheet and flinging a duvet. Julian was accustomed to blankets, in the old-fashioned style, tucked and tidied. But who, as Eleanor enquired, could make love properly under tucked blankets? It was absurd.

Julian received letters from his children: Julia, twenty-five, and Piers, aged twenty-two. Both said they would never see their father again, he had treated their mother so disgracefully, and would never accept a penny from him.
Julian said, 'My children have treated me disgracefully; they have brought humiliation upon me. Julia dropped out of a promising academic career to be a nurse. Piers never gets up before two in the afternoon. Why do they think I want to see them again? I don't.'

Brenda brought news that the black magic group had been disbanded, and Nerina was to be married in a Muslim ceremony to her brother's best friend, and no longer went to college. Brenda's husband Pete had, at Brenda's insistence, made representation to the academic authorities about the sacrificing of a goat on college property. The RSPCA had been called in. There had been a terrible scandal. The media communications course had been re-evaluated. Hadn't Eleanor read about it?
'I'm kind of cut off here at the university,' said Eleanor. 'I can never work out which is the real world and which isn't. But I'm very happy with Julian. That's all I need to know.'
'Don't you even think about Bernard?'
'I can't say I do,' said Eleanor. 'Out of sight, out of mind.'
Brenda said she felt rather the same about her baby. She'd left baby and pushchair behind in the supermarket queue and gone home without them, quite forgetting, but she'd had the baby under a year and Eleanor had been married for fifteen years.
'That was Ellen,' said Eleanor. 'I have been re-born. Risen guilt

free as Eleanor from the ashes of the past. Do you think Nerina is continuing her black magic from home?'

Brenda said, from the sound of it, it was perfectly possible. Bernard was still in a bad way: clinically depressed, many reckoned.

'Won't Nerina get into trouble for not being a virgin?' asked Eleanor.

Brenda said she thought there were spells to see to that kind of thing; failing that, cosmetic surgery could put it right. There were local doctors who specialized in it. What did Eleanor *do* all day?

'I keep very busy,' said Eleanor. 'Julian is giving me a crash course in monetary theory: we mean to write a book together. And there is a local trouble here we have to sort out.'

Eleanor wrote to the emoluments committee declaring that she had reduced the running costs of Bridport Lodge by forty-two per cent, producing figures to prove it, and when it came to difficult and embarrassing votes at Convocation, Senate and Academic Board level, as to whether or not Professor Darcy could be seen to be in his right mind, it was this document that swung the feeling of the various meetings in his favour. Men fall in love: it was their right to do so. To be open about these matters was clearly in the mood of new university thinking, thrusting and energetic, and the various governing bodies did what they could to adjust themselves gracefully. Even when Eleanor enrolled as an undergraduate to do a degree course in economics they did not flinch. And so eventually Professor Darcy's stock rose, not fell, at the University of Bridport, thanks to his wife leaving him and him taking in, to share his bed and board, and publicity, a young woman half his age, already married to another.

As for Georgina, she went to live with her daughter, and said she wouldn't take a penny from Julian. Nor did she try to sue him for possession of the matrimonial home – although, as Eleanor pointed out, the house went with Julian's job, so she wouldn't have stood much of a chance anyway. She showed little interest in reclaiming her clothes, jewellery, or personal effects. Georgina made it generally known that anyway she'd had it up to here with university life in general and Julian in particular: no one was to make a fuss. The first response antagonized the academic community, who felt as a result more kindly disposed towards Eleanor than they otherwise would: the second eased Julian of guilt.

One morning, as Eleanor and Julian sat at the polished mahogany breakfast table, sipping coffee, and spreading toast made with white sliced bread and Marks & Spencer marmalade, and looking out over the Dorset hills, to the glimpse of sea beyond, Eleanor wearing an Edwardian silk wrap from Oxfam and Julian in a dressing gown inherited from his father – both his parents, perhaps fortunately, for they were the most respectable folk and divorce unknown in the family, were deceased – Julian said, 'Eleanor, what preparations have you made for the graduation ceremonies?' and Eleanor said, 'Why, are they very special?' And Julian said, 'Well, actually yes, they are the high spot in the annual university calendar. There are graduation dinners – we hold them here – garden parties in the grounds, teas likewise, concert suppers, around two hundred at each, I suppose; honour graduands to be fêted and so on. Georgina spent quite a lot of time and energy doing it.'
'I think the university office should do it,' said Eleanor.
'Well, no,' said Julian, quite firmly, and she saw for the first time the glint in his eye which unnerved governments and faculty boards. 'I think it is your job. You could get in outside caterers,' he added, and from an untidy drawer drew an untidy file, in spite of which untidiness he laid his hand unerringly upon the card he sought: 'Highlife Caterers – Academic Functions a Speciality.'
Eleanor said, 'Caterers are a wicked waste of money. I'll do it myself.'

Word got round college and university that Ellen Parkin was going to do the Graduation Week catering single-handed and many predicted her downfall. There would be poached egg on toast for tea, they said, instead of salmon canapés with caviar; Irish stew for dinner instead of filet mignon: bread and butter pudding for dessert and sweet sherry all round. There was glee at the prospect. Julian Darcy would realize his mistake and Eleanor would be out on her ear and plain Ellen again, and serve her right. A man who got rid of one woman would get rid of another. And would Bernard take her back? No one knew. No one had seen Bernard lately: his name no longer appeared on the college's staff list. They assumed they'd know if he was dead, but no one much cared.

Bernard was in fact quite often seen by Eleanor and Julian. He would stand on the gravel drive in front of Bridport Lodge in the very early morning, unshaven and unkempt, staring up at their bedroom window. When he knew he had been seen he would slink away.

'If only we had dogs,' said Julian, 'we could set them on him. Would you like a dog, Eleanor?'

Eleanor said no, she was not a doggie sort of person. Julian said he was glad: Georgina Darcy had been. Georgina was spoken of, when at all, in the past tense. Bernard, in some respect still unfinished business, was at least accorded an existence in the present.

Liese and Leonard came to dine with Julian and Eleanor. Liese had abandoned her principles and now wore a fur coat, and Leonard made up in funny stories anything he lacked in a capacity for abstract thought.

Eleanor went out to the pantry to bring in the trifle the maid had left before going off duty. Liese followed her.

'Eleanor,' said Liese, 'don't you care any more what's going on in Mafeking Street?'

'No,' said Eleanor.

'Bernard's had to move out of No. 93. The mortgage company have repossessed it. And he's moved in with your father Ken and his girlfriend Gillian.'

'Gillian? Ken was living with Gillian's mother.'

'She's moved out.'

'No wonder I have amnesia,' said Eleanor, and dropped the glass bowl of trifle. It broke. She and Liese scooped what was eatable into a plastic bowl, rearranged it, and served it. Eleanor was the only one who cut her mouth on a sliver of glass. The sight and taste of her own blood falling on to whipped cream recalled the memory of snow, and the snowman which represented Bernard. The next morning she called him, at Ken's. The bill, she was glad to note, had been paid.

'Bernard,' she said, 'is No. 93 up for sale?'

'It has been for three months,' he said. 'Now the mortgage company own it. It wouldn't sell because it was haunted.'

'Only a tiny bit haunted,' said Ellen. 'Only by my mother.'

'It got worse after you left,' he said. 'The estate agents said when people came to look over it they'd see things on the stairs, and smell dry rot, though the surveyors couldn't find any. How are you? Why do you keep sending these divorce petitions through the post? You know I'm a Catholic.'

Eleanor said she'd better come over and see him, and her father, and her father's new girlfriend.

'She's not new,' said Bernard. 'It's been going on for years. She's much too good for him.'

Ken's fingers had become arthritic and he could no longer play the banjo. Gillian had a back problem and a cataract in one eye, surprising in one so young, but Bernard said the depletion of the ozone layer and the consequent increase in ultraviolet light was causing an epidemic of cataracts. It was not a cheerful household.

Bernard said along with everything else the curse of invisibility had been put on him. He existed but did not exist. People looked through him in the street, in shops. He might as well be a little old lady for all the notice anyone took of him.

'Bernard,' said Eleanor, 'you are very visible to me and Julian when you stand outside our window. I wish you wouldn't. It does no one any good.'

'It does me some good,' said Bernard, and smiled. He had shaved. He was looking a little less pale and thin. Gillian was a good cook, he said, considering her one eye. She was better than Eleanor had ever been.

'I never set out to be a good cook,' said Eleanor.

Ken said, 'The trouble with you, Apricot, is that you take after your mother. Unstable.'

Eleanor said to Ken, 'The trouble with me is that I like men twice my age, the same way you like girls half your age.'

Gillian said, 'It's tea time!', and sat them all down to scones, cream and jam, and chocolate cake served on rather dirty plates and tea from a grimy teapot. It seemed her one eye enabled her to cook, though not to pick up Ken's scattered tissues from the floor, or tidy away Bernard's many combs. But perhaps she didn't see it as her business so to do. The combs were all matted: Bernard seemed to be losing his hair. Gillian was a stolid girl, with a pasty face and thick lips. She had pale blue, rather prominent eyes, one very cloudy.

'You're going bald,' said Eleanor to Bernard.

'It's that curse,' said Gillian. 'That black magic group they set up at the college. They've really got it in for poor Bernard. They mean him to lose everything. You were only part of it. It's not official now but it still goes on.'

Ken said all women were the same, they were all gullible; if Rhoda hadn't spent all his savings on a quack faith healer he wouldn't be in this state now.

Eleanor held her tongue and ate some more chocolate cake.

Bernard said, 'Ellen doesn't believe in black magic any more than the Marxist dialectic, any more than she did Catholicism. Ellen won't let anyone believe in anything, except her. Ellen is the new religion.'

Eleanor said, 'They weren't really trying to raise the Devil, according to Jed. They were trying to create an optimum environment for an experiment in mass suggestion.'

Bernard said, 'Jed was trying to create an optimum environment to seduce girl students. Yet he flourishes like the bay green tree.'

Eleanor said, 'His baby died,' and Bernard said, 'That's flourishing,' and Gillian said she'd make him wash his mouth out with soapy water and Ken said so far as he could see there wasn't any soap: there hadn't been for weeks.

Bernard said, 'I say what I want. That group of Jed's ruined me and what's more it raised the Devil. I saw him. He was floating outside my window, on the second floor. It is not something I care to remember.'

Gillian said, 'Have some more chocolate cake. I'm sorry I was nasty. It was only a dream, Bernard. He's been in a bad way, Ellen.'

Bernard said, 'Dreams are something you wake up from. This was not a dream. It was real. I didn't wake up from it. He was real. The Devil is real. He has a mouth with flabby black lips and slit eyes like a goat: they glow like a dog's eyes do in the dark but it wasn't dark, it was still light. His breath smelt sickly sweet, like dry rot. His skin was scaly and hairy. His edges were a bit blurred but he was real. He was floating, not standing: the ground was too far beneath him for him to be standing, unless he was totally out of proportion, which I suppose is possible. Then he faded away. It wasn't that I woke up but that he faded out. Except of course he's still there. Just because you can't see him doesn't mean he isn't there.'

'I wish you wouldn't, Bernard,' said Gillian. 'You upset yourself. He came home and gibbered for weeks, Ellen, and never went into college again. Now we're all on benefits.'

'Just as well,' said Ken. 'He was making a fool of himself; he should have resigned before he was fired. They gave him every opportunity, but you know our Bernard.'

They were very cosy together. Eleanor felt excluded.

Eleanor said, 'So you won't be standing outside our window any more, Bernard?'

Bernard said, 'Oh yes I shall. I have nothing else to do. No car to drive, no job to go to, no hair to comb, no friends, no visibility; I reserve the right to stand beneath my wife's window and fart while she makes a fool of herself having sex with a buggering old fascist.'

After a little while Eleanor said, 'Ex-wife's window, if you'd only sign the divorce papers. It might make you feel better.'

'Wife,' said Bernard. 'Catholics do not believe in divorce.'

'So you're back in the faith,' said Eleanor, coolly and politely. 'After all that! I couldn't believe it.'

'Yes,' said Bernard. 'It's safer. I keep my nose to the ground, think what I'm told, obey the rules, and go to Mass on Sundays. I have been punished for the sin of intellectual arrogance; God has demonstrated to me that the ecstasy of pure thought is reserved for heaven, not for earth; it is for angels, not for man. No, virtue lies in obedience; I will never teach again: it is a sin to interfere with the simple belief structures of innocent students –'

'Let alone their bodies,' said Ken, who as he grew older seemed to grow simpler. 'Heh, heh, heh!'

'And if I stick to all this,' said Bernard, ignoring him, 'my belief is that at least I won't see the Devil in the flesh again, and that's just about the height of my ambition. I've learned my lesson.'

'Superstition,' said Eleanor, 'will get you nowhere. Shall we change the subject? How's poor Prune?'

Gillian said, 'Who's Prune?'

Eleanor said, 'Poor Prune is Jed's wife. We all used to be quite close: not any longer. Jed had an affair with Nerina, but Nerina never liked anyone mentioning it. Now more than ever, I expect, since she's married.'

Bernard clutched his stomach and said he had a bad pain, as if a needle was being driven into it. Ken said he wasn't taking Bernard up to the hospital yet again, Bernard needn't think he was. Gillian wept – equally out of both eyes, Eleanor was interested to see.

Eleanor said, 'Well, I must be off. Have you ever thought of taking up catering, Gillian? The chocolate cake was wonderful!' Gillian said tearfully she couldn't say she had. Eleanor said perhaps now Gillian was part of the family she'd like to help her out in a little something she'd said she'd do up at the university, and Gillian said okay, anything to get away from this dreary lot. What she couldn't stand was ill health, especially if it was mental.

Valerie sits up in bed and listens to tape

Q: Will there be political censorship in Darcy's Utopia?

A: Of course not. Why should there be? If anyone can think of any better way to organize things, let them say so: if they can get ten people to agree with them, let them put it to our parliament of popular folk (leavened, if you remember, with a few obvious and self-declared baddies) and everything will be done to accommodate them. It will be government by consensus, not confrontation: government not by power seekers, for where will be the advantages of power since not money, but diversion, and the pleasurable exercise of skill will be the reward of work? Government not by robber barons, for what can they rob that will be of value to them that others cannot have by simply stretching out the hand? But by those who like to see things running smoothly, and who will be able to dis-invest themselves of a block of Community Units on the day they resign – the exact amount subject to popular vote. There will be no censors and, as we know, very few policemen, though sufficient well-meaning and officious folk, no doubt, to organize the short-term or long-term exile of those people others simply cannot stand.

Q: You mean to be unlikeable will be a crime?

A: Put it like that if you must. 'Unlikeable' in the sense of 'antisocial'. There will be no obligation to chatter and smile, if that's what you mean; though I hope many will feel like doing so.

Q: How large is Darcy's Utopia? It seems, if you'll forgive me saying so, an airy-fairy kind of place. A city of dreams, with glittering spires and no reality.

A: I suspect initially about two million people. Any larger unit will be hard to organize: we depend so greatly in our existing societies upon the accumulated traditions of the past, on the habits of custom and practice, built up to our disadvantage through history, to regulate ourselves and our behaviour. And in Darcy's Utopia we have to start again, rethink everything, from how and why we brush our teeth to how and why we bury our dead; we must do this in the light of our new knowledge of our inner world, and our new technological control over the outer one, and we must do it by consensus. Any smaller unit and the rest of the world will say oh, it only works because it's so small, it has no relevance here.

Q: I see. The rest of the world is watching, is going to follow suit?

A: Of course. We start small, and little by little the boundaries of Darcy's Utopia will expand. Our only problem in the end will be there'll be nowhere to send the exiles to, but I don't suppose we have to worry about that for a while.

Q: Supposing it doesn't work?

A: Supposing, supposing. It may not work. But nothing else is going to be working, not for long. Look around. The poor and the dispossessed, forget the lover, are at the gate. The third world spills over into the first, the second. Your guilt will not let you be happy or at peace. The oceans warm up: the very air gets hard to breathe. So let the community of nations try it: let Europe set aside the land: let two million with a common language and a common will there congregate. Let Europe feed, house and clothe them for five years, while they get their high-technology, low-consuming, recycling act together. Europe feeds, houses and clothes its refugees: let them do it to some purpose: let us find our blueprint for the future, our multiracial, unicultural, secular society: let us locate it in the real world.

Q: Why Europe?

A: Who else is ready for the shock of the new? And because Darcy's Utopia is built upon the resonances, if you'll forgive me being so pompous, of the Greco-Judeo-Christian tradition: that life should be of meaning here on earth, not just bungled through any old how in the expectation of life hereafter.

Q: There is no life hereafter?

A: I'm not saying that, another motto of Darcy's Utopia being 'let's have our cake and eat it too'. But you're distracting me from practicalities. The State of Israel was created by international consensus: why not Darcy's Utopia?

Q: An unfortunate analogy. Look what happened there!

A: We don't know yet what happened there. And as I have told you, you must refrain from believing you will learn lessons from history. Nothing now is exactly the same as anything then. Apart from anything else Darcy's Utopia will be surrounded by friends, not enemies. The only thing to assault it will be a flood of ideas, suggestions, recommendations; which will be difficult to fight off, because the hope of the world goes with them, and there is a terrific energy in that, you may be sure.

Q: There will be no tourists?

A: There will be no tourists. Frankly, there won't be much to see, there being no history to Darcy's Utopia – no roots, and none sought. But there will be celebrations, feast days. Did I tell you how, when I was first with Julian Darcy, before he became known as Rasputin and myself as the Bride of Rasputin, I organized and catered for all the Graduation Week ceremonies at the University of Bridport? It all worked wonderfully well. Friends and relatives turned up to help. The sun shone. There were strawberries and cream, and champagne at the garden parties. We had guests to stay at the lodge – a couple of other Vice Chancellors plus wives – and they were easy with me, not condemning at all. I had expected some hostility, since they were accustomed to Georgina, not myself, at the table, but none was apparent. Mind you, Julian was then one of the most important and influential men in the Joint University Convocation. That might have had something to do with it. He had the ear of the government, of the Secretary of State himself; no one wanted to believe his judgement could be suspect. The myth was that Julian knew what he was doing. The smooth running of Graduation Week seemed to prove it. If the sun shines, and there is champagne, strawberries and cream for tea, who can doubt it? Later, of course, when Julian was being prosecuted for evasion and misuse of public funds, the champagne, strawberries and cream were held against him. It was seen as gross extravagance at a time when he knew, or should have known, that the university was in acute financial difficulties. It was alleged, quite wrongly, that I had thirty pairs of shoes in my wardrobe. Some photographer got in and took pictures of them. 'Luxury and extravagance at Bridport' went the caption. When husbands fall from power, the number of shoes in the wife's wardrobe are always a source of marvel, shock and abhorrence. In actual fact most of the shoes were Georgina's – too good to throw away, too big and boring for me to wear. She had really big horsy feet.

Q: There was always an undercurrent of feeling at the time of the trial that your husband had been framed. That some people were out to get him. Can you comment on that?

A: Of course they were. Everyone was out to get him. The government took on Julian's proposals for a radical rethinking of fiscal policy, but compromised at the last moment with the traditionalists: the nation got the worst of all worlds, instead of the best. Inflation took off, but not the hyper-inflation Julian and I were seeking. The myth that was Julian crumpled: the rumbling discontent in the university over the question of Georgina and myself could no longer be held down: the Board of Governors discovered flaws in the accountancy system and declared the university bankrupt. Criminal proceedings against Julian followed. You might almost think, if you were superstitious, that the curse which fell upon Bernard fell upon Julian too. That is enough for today. Thank you.

Brenda's letter to Hugo

Dear Mr Vansitart,

I don't get a chance to get a word in edgeways when you and Apricot are talking. She's still just Apricot to Belinda and Liese and me. We've seen her through her Ellen years and her Eleanor years, though sometimes, I don't mind telling you, our patience has worn a little thin, and her recent experiences haven't seemed to calm her down one bit.

> *Jack the bellboy had brought the letter, addressed to Hugo, up to Room 301. Hugo wasn't there. Jack offered to take the envelope down to room service and steam it open. Valerie accepted the offer, recognizing a woman's hand.*

She is now talking of buying a new car, a BMW, and the man from the garage calls her Alison – always a sign that she's about to be off. I'll be sorry when she goes. I know I'm just the one in Apricot's life who brings in the coffee and takes the clothes to the cleaners – but all the same she brings a kind of light with her, and what she has to say is interesting: there's a lot in it, though it's sometimes hard to tell when she's joking and when she isn't.

I'm writing because I want to put my point of view. I take this business of Utopia seriously, and I want you to do the same. Not Darcy's Utopia; that's Apricot's crazy vision: but let's say Brenda's Utopia, a kind of toned-down version of Apricot's. I want a world fit for my kids to grow up in. Look, I want a world fit for *me* to grow up in. I don't want us to go back to anything, I want us to go forward to something. I want to believe that my daily life has a purpose which is more than just me. I used to be a real peacenik during the crazy time when we all thought we'd be pulverized by nuclear war, that the future was just rubble. I'd stand around in the town square with banners, with a lot of chalk marks on the ground for bodies, scaring everyone; saying if we don't do something we'll all be dead. And that really kept me going, believing I was right and everyone else was wrong. In fact the more wrong I could make them be, the more right I'd be. Those days, in retrospect, were dead easy. It was dead easy. Then Gorbachev came along and swept the ground from under our feet: and it began to look as if we had a future after all, but if so, what was it going to be? And we hadn't got a thing worked out, not a thing. Down here in the outer suburbs we just sort of stand about, dazed, trying to make a living, and having babies (if you're me) because it's the only positive single thing we can think of to do, and even that's suspect because the world can't stand the weight of its population any more. Who can you work for who isn't corrupt? Where can you go to get out of a climate of lies and hypocrisy? I want to rebuild the world, and I'm stumped as to how to do it: but at least Apricot is trying. When you write your articles don't laugh her out of court completely.

And a word of warning – though I suspect it's too late – people who have anything to do with Apricot do seem to keep getting into emotional muddles: she's a love-and-muddle carrier, the way some people are typhoid carriers. I'm inoculated from it, by virtue of general running exhaustion, I daresay, and the effort of trying to make ends meet can de-sex a girl fast. I do worry sometimes about Pete. Now he's a mini-cab driver, he meets so many new people, women out shopping with money to spare and a whole lot of them are going to be better-looking and more lively and better conversationalists than me. And we do, the three of us, sit down to supper in the evening. Though perhaps Pete is safer on the road than he ever was at the poly. That place was a *hot*bed. I was relieved when Pete was made redundant; the shock waves from the closure of the media communications department just kept on coming. Jed was the only one who seemed to survive. I'm just saying beware: keep your hands on the steering wheel, your eyes on the road. The fever goes

when Apricot departs, and you can be left in an awful mess.
That's all for now.
With best wishes,

Brenda Steele

> *Valerie had some trouble finding matches to burn
> Brenda's letter; she went down to the hotel bar
> for the first time, ordered a drink and purloined
> a cigarette lighter; returned to 301, used the
> bathroom basin as a grate, and put the ashes
> down the WC.*

Julian overdoes it

It was shortly after Graduation Week that Julian turned to Eleanor and said, 'That went very well, my dear. Surprisingly well, in fact. Do you think we should be married as soon as my divorce comes through?'

Eleanor said, 'I think that would be a very good idea indeed, Julian.'

'You're not,' he said, 'by any chance actually married to your Bernard? I take it you tied no formal knot?'

'Good heavens, no,' said Eleanor. 'He was a Catholic and I wasn't. Marriage was out of the question.'

'More fool Bernard,' said Julian. 'You are everything a man could want, even a man such as me. How wonderful it is when a clever, competent and organizing head sits upon a body as young and supple and glamorous as yours.'

They went through a quiet marriage ceremony when Julian's divorce came through. Eleanor said she wanted no big splash; she saw it just as the tying up of loose ends.

'You didn't ask me,' said Brenda, 'and I'm not surprised, considering, just a little hurt. So you've actually done it. Little Apricot Smith has turned into Eleanor Darcy and has the ear of the most powerful man in the kingdom and can murmur into it whatever she likes, any time, albeit bigamously.'

'Well,' said Eleanor, 'at some times of day and all times of night.'

'And Julian is in good moral, physical and mental health?'

'Absolutely,' said Eleanor. She was arranging flowers in a crystal bowl. She had a real gift for it. Sun streamed in through open windows. Soon it would be time for the coming year's Graduation Week ceremonies. This time round she would not ask her friends to help out. There had been some comment on the standard of waitressing. A one-eyed girl behind the teapot was not, she had come to realize, what proud parents wished to see. They wanted the occasion unblemished by thoughts of the real world, from which their children were this very day escaping.

Eleanor was not speaking the exact truth to Brenda. Julian's heart kept missing a beat. He was doing too much. The campus doctor told him it was stress: the condition was usual enough, not damaging to the heart, but a sign perhaps that he should slow down a little.

'Of course, you've got a young wife,' he said, jokingly. 'I've known that carry off many a man in his prime.'

Julian reported the conversation to Eleanor.

'What a very old-fashioned doctor,' she said. 'Perhaps the campus doctor of a young thrusting university should have a young thrusting attitude to life, and be rather better informed. Research shows the more sex you have, the healthier you are.'

Julian startled her by asking to see chapter and verse of the research. Every now and then she forgot and thought she was still married to Bernard. She found some published research which at least said that sexually active men were twenty per cent less prone to heart attack than the sexually inactive. Julian said twenty per cent wasn't very reassuring. To avoid temptation he would sleep in a spare room for a day or two.

'It's not that I don't want you,' he said to Eleanor, 'it's that I daren't. And I have a convocation in the morning; a faculty lunch, and golf with John Hersey of the polytechnic in the afternoon. We have to get a few things settled in the trans-binary field. And of course Downing Street next Wednesday, and an article on the Europeanization of the pound sterling still to be written.'

'Julian,' said Eleanor, 'it occurs to me that things other than our sharing a bed make your heart miss a beat.'

But Julian found that hard to believe. If the heart misbehaves, the principle of Ockham's razor suggests that affairs of the heart can only be to blame.

While Julian was at his convocation, Eleanor most civilly received a journalist from the *Daily Mail*. Normally, when the time for the three-monthly Downing Street meetings approached, no matter how they clustered, journalists would be kept from the door.

'In matters of economic science,' Julian would say, 'the layman knows nothing, assumes much and fears more. All the press ever does is compound that ignorance, folly and fear; deliberately it fosters mistrust of change. Therefore, Eleanor, when faced with the ladies, gentlemen and guttersnipes of the media, let it be our policy to remain silent. Besides which, I've had murmurings in my ear in high places, and I can tell you this, mum is very much the word at the moment.'

In the high places of both government and academia, it seemed, messages came in the form of words in ears, little snippets fed out over dinner, or over the telephone from which the minds of those at the top of the pyramid of power could be construed by those further down. Eleanor would lie in bed watching Julian pull on his socks, with their thin little snappy red suspenders, and marvel at his villainous urbanity. He made her smile. She loved him. His mind rather than his haunches, which were, granted, a little flabby, turned her on. She always got up later than he did. She loved to watch and listen, and he loved his audience. He would go down to the kitchen and put on the coffee and toast: she would follow. The staff were not required to start work until 9.55 in the morning, thus allowing the happy couple their privacy. It meant the staff seldom finished until eleven at night, for every detail of the spontaneous breakfast must be prepared in advance, from time-setting the microwave for .25 of a minute at fifty per cent power to soften the butter; to grinding the coffee beans at the last possible moment to avoid any loss of flavour. Julian would be in his office by ten, relaxed, happy, accustomed to adoration, expecting more, and unworried by the necessity of making decisions, inasmuch as he knew they would be the right ones.

But now Julian's heart had missed a beat, and he mistook the reason, and Eleanor was encouraged, and said to Freddie Howard of the *Daily Mail*, 'Yes, by all means. I should be happy to be interviewed. If you believe that the home life of the Vice Chancellor of Bridport might be of interest to your readers, on your head be it. You'll find us very dull, I'm afraid.'

Freddie Howard arrived at twelve in the morning. Eleanor wore black leggings and a silky top, which showed both legs and top to advantage. At that time she assumed a long-legged, supple, Jane Fonda look; hair plentiful and curly about the head. The spirit of Georgina still hovered about the house, as the spirit of first wives is wont to do, leaving some indefinable reproach behind, lurking in eggcups or under saucepan lids, and Eleanor took care to resemble her predecessor as little as possible the better to outwit her, exuding a young energy rather than a cool elegance. She offered him champagne and asked Mrs Dowkin to bring in 'some of the caviar snacks, you know, the kind I love. I'm sure you will too.' She ate at least a dozen of the piled biscuits when they arrived, her little even white teeth greedy – he ate two, one to try and the next to reaffirm he didn't like true caviar at all: he preferred the lumpfish kind. He was a fleshy, saturnine man in his early forties, normally sent out on heartbreak stories. He was known to be good with women; they'd tell him anything.

'I'm only a wife,' Eleanor said, 'and of course I'm not trained in economics. But economics is only a matter of common sense, isn't it? I like to think I give Julian confidence – that's the main thing.' Freddie asked what she thought Julian's advice to the PM would be, in this time of crisis.

'Is there a crisis?' asked Eleanor, calling for more champagne. 'Down here at Bridport we don't notice much. Yes, I believe the academic staff are on a work-to-rule, something about wages and inflation: but they're never contented, are they? And they have such long holidays! Why can't they do two jobs, if they're short of money?'

'Let them eat cake,' murmured Freddie.

'I never understood why poor Marie Antoinette got such stick for saying that,' said Eleanor. 'It seems a perfectly good suggestion to me, though cake's not very good for you. Eggs, sugar, butter and so forth. Bread's healthier, I agree. Of course,' added Eleanor, 'Julian's salary is inflation linked, so inflation doesn't affect us particularly. He got a hundred and twenty thousand pounds last year and a hundred and fifty this. Everyone should be really careful about their contracts, these days. I think if there's a message he'd want to give everyone it would be this: "Watch your contract!"'

'Now unemployment is surging up again, the workforce may find that difficult,' observed Freddie, writing busily.

'Of course,' she said, 'Julian's view is that money itself is the problem with the economy. Most people would be far better off with none at all.'

'Do you have a pet name for him?' asked Freddie.

'I call him Rasputin,' said Eleanor.

The photographer arrived, late and dusty, as press photographers normally do. He looked Eleanor up and down and said, 'This is better. I thought it would have to be a desk-shot. Typical Vice Chancellor stuff. The best background you ever get in academia is an ivy wall.'

He posed her sitting perilously on the stone balcony, with the hills behind, and the breeze playing through her curly hair, head thrown back and long legs to advantage. 'Oops!' she kept crying as he kept snapping. 'Nearly fell that time!' Freddie went on pouring more champagne, and she went on pouring it over the wall but Freddie didn't notice that. 'Natural light!' the photographer rejoiced. 'Natural light and no ivy, no books. You've made my day.'

When Julian came home from playing golf he found Eleanor in tears. She said she'd let a journalist in – he'd pressured her and she'd somehow been manoeuvred into it – and she just knew he was going to make everything up; and a photographer had come along and snapped her as she sat on the wall playing ball with Mr Dowkin's son.

'Playing ball?' enquired Julian. 'Playing ball – ?'

'I do sometimes,' she said. 'You wouldn't know, Julian. You're always in your office or running the world. And my legs were showing, I just know they were.'

'Eleanor,' said Julian, 'this doesn't sound like you.'

'It's because I'm so tired and miserable,' she said. 'If you're not in my bed I can't sleep. My judgement is all to pieces. I need you as much as you need me. How was golf?'

'Bad,' he said. 'My heart was all over the place. The word from above is that trans-binary adjustments across the PCFC and UFC are out. They keep changing the goal posts. Now I doubt we'll be able to asset-strip the polytechnic, even if they lie down and ask us to.'

'I've never heard you put it quite like that before,' said Eleanor, drying her tears, bored with those, as so was he. 'You've talked about dual funding, incorporation, merger, maximization of resources, trans-binary unification across the field, but not asset-stripping. These things should never be put so crudely. This is academia, not the business world. If you don't mind me saying so, I think not sleeping with me affects your judgement as much as it does mine.'

'Eleanor,' he said, 'I think you're right about everything.'

He returned to her bed forthwith and by the morning both his spirits and his judgement had returned. His heart still missed beats but he didn't care. Eleanor handed him the *Daily Mail*, in silence. He studied it carefully. Eleanor was on the front page. ' "Let them eat cake," says leggy young bride of the new Rasputin.'

'You take a good photo,' he said. 'Rasputin? Do they mean me?' He read on. 'The upshot of this absurd piece,' said Julian, eventually, 'is that while the government dithers and listens to the outrageous advice of a maniac economic advisor, of dubious sexual morals, who lives in an ivory tower on champagne and caviar, the nation collapses further and further into economic crisis.'

'A really vicious unfounded attack,' said Eleanor.

'They've even got my salary wrong. Thirty-five thousand pounds too low; and inflation has been evening out at fifteen, not twenty-two per cent. They can't even do their sums.'

'There's the proof they made the whole thing up,' said Eleanor. 'Julian, I'd die if you thought I'd been indiscreet.'

'My darling,' said Julian, 'whatever you do is okay by me. Just don't leave my bed again or unfortunate things happen.'

'Of course I won't,' she said. They embraced. Mrs Dowkin came in and asked Eleanor rather pointedly if she wanted more jars of caviar bought in. She was not above making trouble. Georgina, the real wife, the true Mrs Darcy, had she allowed herself to be photographed in the first place, which was doubtful, would have stood beside the family hearth, or by the big Chinese vase filled with flowers from the garden, not perched on a wall, all legs and hair. Julian looked at Eleanor rather shrewdly, she thought, but said nothing.

'Get in some more,' said Eleanor calmly, 'but not too much. And some fish paste. We only had the caviar because the fish paste had run out. It was an unfortunate kind of day.'

'Well,' said Julian, putting down the *Mail*, taking up the *Independent*, 'at least now we have nothing to lose,' and went off to staff-management meetings to calm the uproar and assure the union delegates that the *Mail* article had been an unfair and unprovoked attack on himself and the government, based on lies, untruth, malice but, worst of all, ignorance.

Journalists thereafter gathered in considerable numbers outside Bridport Lodge, as well as outside 11 Downing Street, where the government's economic think-tank was accustomed to assemble. Julian Darcy was henceforth known as Rasputin Darcy: Eleanor as Rasputin's Bride. Everyone loved it. The academic staff settled for a twelve per cent rise, which in view of current inflation was seen as a considerable victory for management but did not cool tempers.

Valeries speaks to Belinda

Now Hugo and I had been having a small ongoing indifference of opinion. He wanted to read *Lover at the Gate* – I'd said no, not until I'd finished it, polished it, was happy with it. The real reason was rather different – firstly, the piece seemed intensely private: secondly, he might decide I'd got everything wrong. And of course it was a severely fictionalized piece of work – it had to be; Eleanor provided so few clues, and in such a roundabout way. Yet I believed, I *believed*, I had got her right, and I didn't want Hugo puncturing the balloon of my belief.

At least I knew that Hugo was so honourable that he wasn't going to read the manuscript against my wishes. He was a better person than I was; he didn't steam open other people's mail and then burn it. Valerie-with-Lou would never have done such a thing. Valerie-with-Hugo seemed capable of anything. I wondered why I didn't worry about our steadily mounting hotel bill. Was I not the kind of person who worried about such things? Lou had put a stop on our joint account – when you look into the finances of a marriage it is astonishing how little a trusting wife can claim as her own, should that marriage disintegrate (another piece for *Aura*? I might even write it myself) but even this did not perturb me. If I thought about it, it seemed unlikely that Hugo could pay it. Stef had used his and her bank account to pay off the mortgage on their house, and there was nothing in it at all. And he had told me his Amex card had been withdrawn after some mix-up with his last payment.

We remained suspended, Hugo and myself, here in the Holiday Inn, bound in servitude to Eleanor Darcy by virtue of the words we fed into our computers. Neither of us wanted to break the spell. Neither of us wanted to be reclaimed by the real world.

The fact was that I was becoming more and more institutionalized in the Holiday Inn. The outside world seemed noisy, and dangerous, and difficult to decipher. Inside everything was safe and cosy. In 'Hotel Services – A Guide' was everything necessary to sustain a peaceful and comfortable life, from Church Services (dial 5 for Concierge) to Ironing Board (dial 3 for Housekeeper). I had to get a colleague to go down to St Katherine's House and check the marriage and divorce records. And yes, I was right, there was no record of a divorce between Ellen and Bernard Parkin, and Eleanor Parkin and Julian Darcy had certainly gone through a marriage ceremony. Also, Bernard Parkin had recently married Gillian Gott in a religious ceremony. Both were bigamists! I was tempted to call one of the gutter newspapers and raise the money to pay the hotel bill, but refrained. A large sum for me, a small agreeable snippet of news for them, could disrupt lives most unpleasantly – though I could see that Julian Darcy, in prison, might have found it welcome information. Also, it's always useful in the media world to have something secret up your sleeve. You never know.

The operator put through a call from Belinda Edgar, who wanted to see me. She was a friend of Apricot's; she'd heard I was writing a book about her. She thought she might be of help.
'So long as you come here,' I found myself saying, 'and I don't have to go out, that's fine by me.'
She said she would. She asked if she'd be able to see what I'd written and, although I was nervous, I said yes she could. She sounded a bright, positive, friendly person, and so she turned out to be. An initial impression given by a voice on the telephone is usually the right one.

She came – pale-skinned, small-eyed, rounded, exuberant – and skimmed through the manuscript. She worked, she said, part-time as a publisher's reader. She lived a pleasant life: she and her husband had two small children and, unlike Brenda, she had help in the house. It's a sorry fact that a woman's fortune so often depends upon the man she marries.
'Well,' said Belinda, when she finished reading – I tried to appear indifferent, not to pace up and down – 'you've got a lot of it right. I hadn't realized that Apricot's marriage to Julian was bigamous. Poor Julian: I went to visit him in prison once, but I don't think

he was pleased to see me. He remembered me as one of the waitresses the year we helped Apricot out when she catered for Graduation Week. He couldn't think why he was being visited by a waitress. He always was a terrible snob. Liese got asked to dinner because Leonard shoots grouse with the best people, even though it's only because they want a cheap car, but Frank and me never qualified. Too arty. Even in an open prison he manages to be hopelessly urbane. They all hate him. But he was right about a-monetarism. There's quite a group of us believe in it, you know. The only way to move society out of its present predicament, the dead end of the surplus society, is to devalue money itself.'

'You must talk to my friend Hugo Vansitart about that,' I said. 'I'd very much appreciate your views on the supernatural. Was there, in your opinion, any sort of curse on Bernard?'

'You mean other than just being married to Apricot?'

'Well, yes.'

'Of course not,' said Belinda. 'The media communications course set off a kind of mass hysteria, that's all.'

'Brenda seems to think there was. Is.'

'Oh, Brenda!' said Belinda. 'She's got four children under seven. You can't expect sense from her. It was all simple cause and effect; Apricot left Bernard and he went to pieces. He was already halfway there. The economy went to pieces when the cash dispensers started pouring out money; but on Sundays only, thus spoiling the whole idea. It had already more or less collapsed. Of course there was resistance. No one was properly prepared. People panicked. They saw the differential going between rich and poor: they didn't understand what was happening. They can understand Communism and they can understand Capitalism, but that's all. That the West should try and adopt the Soviet non-money economy, just as the Soviets try to take Capitalism on board, blew their minds. People like polarities – Apricot's always saying that. Had Julian and Apricot simply wanted to switch them, that would have worked; people would have accepted it. But in the end the courage to see it through wasn't there.'

'In other words, the Devil got into the works and spoiled everything,' I said.

'So long as you're talking metaphorically,' said Belinda. 'So long as you don't get any idea into your head that there's some power out there talking through Eleanor Darcy's mouth, at any rate one which knows what it's talking about.'

'Well,' I said comfortingly, 'Hugo is dealing with the political and economic background. I'm more concerned with the human angle.' I had the feeling she didn't like me very much. But the mistress is always an offence to the married woman. 'You feel I've got her more or less correct?'

'You've got Apricot's life the way she would have wanted it to be, let's say that. Well, thank you. I've made up my mind. I've thought for a long time I might write something about Apricot, now I'm pretty sure I will. You do the gospel according to St Valerie, I'll do the gospel according to St Belinda.'

And I realized I hadn't been milking her for information, she had been milking me, and I, like a fool, had let her read my manuscript. And I also thought, serve me right. Since holing up in this Holiday Inn I hadn't been a nice person at all. I'm sure when I lived at home I was a *better* person all round.

As soon as my hand had stopped trembling I set to work again. There is nothing like work for putting an end to unhealthy introspection.

Eleanor goes to visit Jed and Prune

Eleanor went to visit Jed and Prune. She found poor Prune in tears, but that didn't surprise her. Prune had miscarried another baby, at three months. It was clear to Eleanor that she intended creeping about her kitchen for the rest of her life, trying to bind her errant husband to her by having babies she was not fit to have.

'Oh, Ellen,' said Prune, 'you're so famous now I hardly know what to say to you.'

'You never did,' said Eleanor, brutally. Poor Prune always made her feel brutal. 'And to be Rasputin's wife hardly counts as fame.'

'I don't know why you don't just do a nude centrefold and have done with it,' said Prune. 'Aren't you going to ask me about me? Don't you care? I'm so unhappy. I am a failure. Three miscarriages and a stillbirth.'

She was peeling onions and seemed in no hurry to stop.

'If you didn't keep rubbing your eyes, and pressing more and more onion juice into your eyeballs,' said Eleanor, 'I expect you would soon feel better. What are you making? Stew?'

'Steak and onion pie,' said Prune. 'Jed loves steak and onion pie.'

'Love my pie, love me,' said Eleanor. 'You've got a hope. Why don't you just give him frozen curry? How is Jed?'

'Working in his study,' said Prune. 'Poor Jed. He works so hard. He longs for a son and I can't give him one. And if I gave him frozen curry I'd feel even more useless. One day he'll leave me and it will all be my fault. Then what will I do?'

'Begin your life,' said Eleanor. 'You'd better begin soon or it'll all be gone.'

'You've changed,' said Prune, through onion tears. 'You're hard and cynical. I'm glad I'm not like you. Besides,' she added, 'what can I do? I never got my degree; I'm not trained for anything; I can't do anything. I get asthma if I try. All I do is cry all the time, or gasp for breath, so who would ever employ me? What kind of CV have I got?'

'Spent life trying to have babies,' said Eleanor, 'and failing,' and went on up to see Jed.

'Are you staying to lunch?' Prune called after her. She had long straight hair and wore flat wide shoes. 'Do stay to lunch. I'm sorry if I was rude. I'm upset, that's all. Jed would love you to stay to lunch. We never see anyone.'

Eleanor went up the red-carpeted suburban stairs and knocked at the door on the left, where a little white plaque with a rim of roses said 'Study'. Inside, in a leather chair, sat Jed, at ease and happy, smoking a pipe, reading galley proofs. He had a pleasant, lined face and a jaw which protruded, as a goat's does, and slightly rheumy eyes, though Eleanor remembered them as bright, bright, bright. Books lined the walls; papers lay on the floor: on ledges stood mandalas, icons, pentacles. A book jacket rough lay on the table – 'The Story of the Pentacle: a Study in Self-oppression'. Incense burned and mixed with the pipe smoke: the room was warm, scented, foggy.

'I know why you've come,' said Jed. 'You've come looking for the villain of the piece. Well, you're looking in the wrong place. How healthy you seem. The high life suits you.'

'It suits everyone,' said Eleanor.

He rose to his feet. His jacket was brown and tweedy, and had orangy leather patches on its sleeves at the elbow. He smelt of pipe tobacco and wet dogs; a Labrador lay by the hearth. Jed was taller than she was by some four inches. She laid her head on his shoulder; she could not do that with Julian. He wore sandals and no socks. He would never wear red sock suspenders. His feet would look strange in the shiny, elegant, pointed shoes which Julian wore. Jed and Julian were two bookends. Other men took their place in between.

'Yes, you are a villain,' said Eleanor. 'You seduced your best friend's wife.'

'You seduced me,' he said. 'You were bored.'

'And Brenda?'

'She asked me to. She was inquisitive.'

'And Nerina?'

'She wanted a little excitement before she settled down. It was not my idea.'

'She was a student. You were her teacher.'

'Quite so. I taught her and her friends what they wanted to know. All anyone really wants to know about is sex. Information is second best.'

He undid the buttons of her blouse. She stayed where she was, for once indecisive.

'Same shape,' he said, 'same size. I have good tactile memory.'

'And poor Prune. What about poor Prune?'

'Sex is the great energizer,' he said. 'I wish poor Prune could understand that. She only gets pregnant so we can't have sex: she's liable to miscarriage, you know. I see it as an act of vengeance. It is not a happy marriage. But I can't just ditch her, can I? Where would she go? What would she do? Poor Prune. She loves me.'

'Poor Prune,' said Eleanor. 'Was she always poor Prune?'

'When I married her,' said Jed, 'she was a lovely, lively Prunella. Her name was a joke; her life was a joke: that was why I married her. Marriage is a fearful institution. What it does to people! Take off your clothes, Ellen. Poor Prune won't come in. She's hurt her ankle. She can't get up the stairs. She won't mind. She just wants me to be happy. She thinks if I'm happy I won't leave her. She thinks it's unhappiness breaks up homes.'

'But it isn't,' said Eleanor, 'it's sheer surplus of energy.'

She took off her jacket, belt, her scarf, her jeans, her blouse. She wore a red bra, red pants and red suspenders to keep up her black stockings.

'That is nice,' said Jed. 'Prune wears washed cotton, whitish grey. It's so sensible. It stretches. And you wear red and black and end up with a poor withered old stick of a Vice Chancellor. It doesn't bear thinking about.'

'He is not so,' said Eleanor, refastening her bra as fast as Jed undid it. 'He's a fine man and I'm proud of him. In fact I love him.'

'Nerina's curse strikes again,' said Jed. 'How's he keeping?'

'A little heart palpitation,' said Eleanor.

'I should watch that,' said Jed. 'How's Bernard? I heard he was back in the faith. I heard he had a bad back. I heard all kinds of things and none of them good.'

'Don't you see him at all?'

'He's a loser,' said Jed. 'I don't.'

Eleanor put her jeans on.

'What a pity,' said Jed. 'I seem to have said the wrong thing. Suspenders under jeans. Prune would never do a thing like that.'

'You've kept in remarkably good health,' said Eleanor, putting on her blouse. 'Considering.'

'I have my punishment,' said Jed. 'I have poor Prune. I'm sorry you're leaving. Can't I persuade you to stay?'

'Not with Prune downstairs making lunch,' said Eleanor. 'I really shouldn't.'

'That's what I mean,' said Jed. 'As you see, I'm no villain. Just another victim. Personally, I blame Philip Horrocks, Head of Faculty. He panicked and disbanded my mass hysteria group overnight. They'd used the college library to try to castrate a goat. I would have stopped it had I known. There was blood splashed over the walls – it got away, mid-slice. Tender-hearted vegetarians, most of our students. No idea how to deal with animals. Have they, Rufus?' He stirred the dog with his sandalled toe. Rufus sighed. 'You won't change your mind, Ellen? No? Pity. Academia lost a very promising student in Nerina: that's my main quarrel with Horrocks. One more little balls-up: one more contribution to the drop-out rate. Another young person turns their back on education. Yes, I blame Horrocks. Why don't you go and see Nerina? She and I are still in touch, of course.'

'She scares me.'

'Nothing scares you, Ellen.'

'I don't like Julian's heart jumping about. Where will it end?'

'Go and ask Nerina. She's quite safe, at the moment. She's de-energized. Married, covered in black, with a nose mask and pregnant. Her mother lives with them.'

'Is it your baby?'

He looked helpless, but flattered.

'How would I know?' He shook his head sagely, sat back in his armchair and attended to his pipe. He was not the man he was, but hadn't noticed.

'Once they'd castrated the goat, what would they have done?' asked Eleanor.

'God knows what their fantasy was. Boiled its balls for dinner and served them up to Satan. They'd left me way behind.'

'Lunchtime, darling,' called poor Prune from down below.

Nerina had set up house with Sharif above a betting shop and next to a fish-and-chip takeaway, as if to underline her determination to be ordinary. Eleanor felt Nerina had somewhat overdone it and was not reassured. The door was opened by a young man in his mid twenties, dark-eyed, olive-skinned, hook-nosed, broad of shoulder; in general handsome in mien and appearance. He was both smooth and fierce. Lucky Nerina, thought Eleanor, and lowered her eyes from the brilliance of his countenance, as she could see she was expected to do.

'Well?' He wore a white shirt, open-necked, and dark trousers. He had a heavy gold bracelet on his wrist and rings on his fingers. He was tall. His feet were long: his shoes were clean, but not pointed, as Julian's were. She felt dissatisfied with Julian and with herself for not having been dissatisfied with him in the past.

'I came to call on Nerina's mother,' said Eleanor. And she explained how she and Mrs Khalid had worked together at the poly: she wished to renew an old acquaintance.

Sharif yelled over his shoulder, 'Ma-in-law!' and Mrs Khalid came clatter-clatter downstairs wearing a sari and solid black walking shoes.

'Oh, it's Ellen! Ellen can come in. She's okay,' she told Sharif, and Sharif moved aside, though he seemed doubtful as to whether it was wise. Eleanor walked in, brushing past him, conscious of the mere breath of the air that stood between her flesh and his: the hairs on her arms stood up to make the distance less. But he had no interest in her. She was beneath him – it showed in his expression: naked-faced, naked-armed, green-eyed and indecorous female that she was.

The room was small and cosy, stuffed with sofas and chairs and little tables, and the telephone was a prostrate Mickey Mouse with his legs in the air, yellow-booted. Mrs Khalid served tea and sticky cakes and asked about Ellen's life. She herself was no longer working, Mrs Khalid said. Her son-in-law Sharif didn't want her to. Nerina was pregnant and needed her at home. Sharif, satisfied as to the tenor of their conversation, left the room. Presently Nerina came down, in black robes and nose shield, and with only her eyes showing. Her face was plumper than before: her figure could scarcely be observed. She took off her mask and her skin had a clear and rather attractive pallor. Then Nerina smiled, and Eleanor wondered why she had told Jed she was scared. Who could be scared of this sweet, bright, pretty girl? 'Don't ask,' Nerina said. 'Just don't ask! But I'll tell you – yes, fancy dress is worth it.'

'But supposing,' said Eleanor, 'he brings in another three wives?'

Mrs Khalid laughed a little curtly.

'He couldn't afford it,' she said. 'He can only just afford us. Look at it like this,' said Nerina,' 'a quarter of my husband is worth one of any other man.' Her hands came out from beneath the black robes and they were long-fingered and red-nailed. They moved with a kind of nervous energy. 'Look,' she said to Eleanor, 'I tried it out there in the western world. I really did. I just got myself and everyone into trouble. I like it like this. Doing nothing, just being. Honour the Prophet and keep his laws: nothing to it. It gets quite boring, but presently you just slow down to keep pace with life.'

'She's having twins,' said Mrs Khalid. 'That slows anyone down.'

'Congratulations,' said Eleanor.

'You don't want babies yourself?' enquired Nerina politely.

'My husband already has grown-up children,' replied Eleanor, even more politely. 'We have decided not to have more.'

Mrs Khalid went out to boil water for another pot of tea.

'I was always surprised that worked,' said Nerina. 'You and Julian Darcy. Not just worked but stuck. I thought it was going to be quite a problem. Part of the curse on Bernard, of course, was losing you. He was to have a faithless wife, but that involved two other people, you and Mr X. We used a photograph of you at a meeting: it was Jed's idea of a joke to pick the Vice Chancellor. If you can get two people on paper you circle them and dance around a bit and whip up the vibes and you can get them into bed together pretty quick, which we did. We didn't mean it to last, but then the college made a stink and we couldn't get back into the library. We were banned, because of one stupid, smelly goat. Anyway you can't put spells on guiltless people. They don't work. So I thought you probably all deserved whatever was happening. Then it had all got tacky and I wanted out.'

'What was Bernard guilty of?'

'He and Jed tossed up as to who would have me, and I found out, too late. Jed won, as you know.'

'Oh.' She felt like crying. Bernard! 'Too late for what?' she asked.

207

'For my virginity, stupid,' said Nerina, and her black robe heaved as her babies kicked and churned.

'Nerina,' said Eleanor, 'Julian's heart isn't too good.'
'Nothing to do with me,' said Nerina. 'I expect you just wear him out. I expect that's his punishment for leaving his wife.'
'But,' said Eleanor, 'you just said it was all your doing –'
'Always twisting and turning,' said Nerina, crossly, 'looking for someone to blame. Why choose me? Why not blame yourself?'
Mrs Khalid came back with a teapot and some shortbread.
'And I don't want any of anything mentioned in front of Sharif. If Sharif found out he'd kill me.'
'Twins are always premature,' observed Mrs Khalid. 'Just as well.'

Sharif came back and walked around the room to make sure nothing untoward was happening, high cheekbones glistening, bony hand through dark hair in anxiety. Nerina replaced her mask. Sharif clearly felt better. He nodded his approval. He almost smiled. He loved her. She was his most precious object. He wanted no part of her harmed. He went out again. The black bundle that was Nerina glowed with self-congratulation. Ellen thought of Bernard, thought of Prune, thought of Jed, thought of herself, transmuted from Ellen to a goat-inflicted fantasy that was Eleanor. Eleanor laughed and said, 'Twins! Twins with orangy yellow elbows!'
Nerina stopped being a cosy black bundle and turned into a thin black wraith, by virtue, Eleanor thought, of standing straight, still and offended. Her metal nose mask caught the light from a dancing-girl lamp.
Mrs Khalid said, rather sharply, 'I don't think much of your idea of damage containment, Ellen.'
Nerina relaxed and said, 'That's okay, Mum. I don't think it was anything too bad. I'll go and lie down a bit. They aren't half kicking about inside.' And she smiled at Eleanor. Mrs Khalid relaxed too.

Mrs Khalid said as Eleanor went, 'Lovely to see you again, dear. Such a pity Nerina didn't stay on at college. But you know what love is.'

'I do,' said Eleanor.

Mrs Khalid's nails were worn to the quick. When she'd been working they'd been long and polished. Eleanor had admired them.

'I hope everything goes well for you,' said Mrs Khalid at the front door. 'I really do. As for me, I just try and keep Nerina happy.'

She shut the door, and it seemed to Eleanor that everything was safe and cosy inside, and noisy and dangerous outside. On the wide pavement in front of her, people of all shapes and sizes and ages crossed and criss-crossed, frenetic in their activity, like ants; yet dull in expression, apathetic of mien. No one was beautiful. Most were in some way distorted or deformed. It was not a good area. A vent at her feet gusted steam from the processes of frying fish in what smelt like everlasting oil, and whirled discarded wrapping paper about her ankles. What was everyone doing? They seemed to understand their own purposes but perhaps they didn't, any more than she did. A mini-whirlwind lifted a polystyrene dish – large chips, large fish – and it hit her midriff. It didn't hurt but she was quite afraid.

Valerie laughs thrice

Had my relationship with Hugo been like any other in the world, and not so very special, I might have thought he was what the columns of *Aura* refer to as 'cooling off'. He arrived at the hotel room which was our home apparently exhausted and just a little offhand. Instead of instant lovemaking he sat in the armchair and asked me to ring room service for coffee. There are no coffee-making facilities in the Holiday Inn; if you want any you have to ask them to bring it up, and however hard the staff try to look disinterested, professional and enigmatic, I have no doubt but they return to the kitchens and have the most animated conversations about myself and Hugo. Especially since Stef, on leaving, apparently shouted at the unfortunate girls in reception, 'There are a pair of adulterers living it up in Room 301, and like as not paying only the single rate. I suggest you look into it!' Or so the bellboy, trying to be helpful, told me. He is a pleasant lad, Jack, who brings up and takes down the many faxes that travelled between myself and *Aura*, Hugo and the *Independent*.

Hugo then took out a packet of cigarettes and smoked one. The entire third floor was designated as a non-smoking area. They ask at reception when you book in. 'You haven't started smoking again!' I said in surprise.
'The first one for six years,' he said. 'The strain of all this is getting to me.'

Now this disappointed me. Naturally I wanted to be a source of happiness to him, not strain. Sensing my reaction, he put out his free hand and stroked mine. I didn't remind him about the third floor being a smoke-free zone. Stef, I have no doubt, would have done exactly that. It's all too easy to fall into a maternal role in any relationship – being either the good mother, or the bad mother

– and it doesn't do. (I write for *Aura* – I read *Aura*. I know these things. I have no choice.)

I told Hugo about Belinda's visit, but not about Brenda's letter; the burning of which now seemed to me a rather pointless exercise in deceit. Hugo's actual presence dampened the smouldering mixture of anxiety and jealousy which I was learning to live with. Soon, I supposed, I would be so used to it I would hardly notice my changed state. Valerie-with-Lou and Valerie-with-Hugo would feel the same, though they were not. But just to have him sitting there, long-legged, loose-limbed, the two of us engaged in a common purpose, enfolded in a cloud of intimacy that now seemed as real out of bed as in it, gave me great pleasure.

Then he said, 'I have something I ought to tell you, though Eleanor Darcy asked me not to.' I felt myself shiver with apprehension, fear of what he was going to say, but it turned out to be nothing. 'She even makes me turn the tape off and insists I treat it as off the record. She has revelations. All this stuff about Darcy's Utopia is dictated to her, she claims, by a kind of shining cloud.'
I laughed. I couldn't help it.
'Like God appearing to Moses in a burning bush, or the Archangel Gabriel to Mohammed as a shining pillar?' I asked. 'If nothing else, Eleanor Darcy has delusions of grandeur.'
But Hugo did not laugh.
'I was walking to the pub with her,' he said, 'and there was definitely a kind of light dancing round her head. I was dazzled.'
And I remembered how I keep writing about the luminosity of her flesh and I felt another kind of shiver, this one starting in the back of the neck and travelling downwards so that Hugo seemed to feel it too: his hand pressed more firmly on mine to quieten it.
'Well,' I said, as lightly as I could, 'we're all dazzled by Eleanor. But does the light come from God or the Devil? The Church is still arguing about St Joan's voices and St Teresa's visions. Whether they'd beatify you or burn you alive you never could be sure. Anyway,' I added after a little, because he'd wanted my attention not my comments, my agreement not my doubt, and it was obvious on his face, 'all this Utopia stuff, as you put it, is for you to deal with. I don't know why she keeps going on about it to

me. Me, I'm just human interest, women's magazine. You're the big time.'

'I'll have none of that professional rivalry from you,' he said, relaxing. 'Leave that to Stef. I'm really proud of the way you sent Stef packing. She causes trouble wherever she goes. She's used to being the one in control. She's the arch-manipulator of all time. I should never have married her.'

And we talked about other things than Eleanor Darcy and our coffee came up; and the waiter raised his eyebrows at Hugo's cigarette, which I was glad to see he didn't stub out but continued to smoke, defiantly. I like a man who is not frightened by waiters. And presently when Hugo and I found ourselves in bed, for once a little later than sooner, he said to me – 'Together we remake the universe, you and I,' and I knew what he meant. He'd had a vasectomy: I'd had my tubes tied: there was no way we could make children. But infusing our love was that sense of a further, deeper purpose than our pleasure alone, which comes so naturally when we're young and fertile, and is not noticed till it's gone. I wondered where it came from. It seemed hardly ours by right: it seemed like something given, but who was there to give it?

Later, I asked him where the shining cloud was located that spoke to Eleanor Darcy and he actually said, why, down the end of Brenda's garden; the other side of the fence, in a little copse just this side of the railway embankment. And I laughed again but, remembering the uneasy vividness of the afternoon she and I had tried to talk in the garden and the tape had failed to record, felt less like laughing.

'She calls it Darcy's Utopia, surely,' I said, 'because it was all part and parcel of Julian Darcy's mad scheme to reshape the economy.'

'I'm not so sure,' said Hugo. 'A great many of Darcy's ideas came from Eleanor. He was obviously very much under her thumb. And the ideas are not as mad as you might suppose.'

And Hugo, I knew, though he couldn't bring himself quite to say so, was beginning to feel Eleanor's ideas came from the Supreme Being, the Prime Mover: that they were more than notions – they were instructions.

'You know what she told me?' said Hugo. 'She told me we should not see ourselves as God's children, but as God's parents. We are not the created, but the creators. What we have to do is be worthy of the love offered us by our creation.'

And I laughed for the third time, and said, 'Well, I'd have more trouble than the Apostles ever did cleaning up Jesus's act, let alone the Companions with Mohammed, in trying to present Eleanor Darcy to the readers of *Aura* as saint and/or messenger.'

And I kept to myself the notion that God must work in an exceedingly mysterious way, in choosing so flawed and cracked a vessel as myself to record Eleanor Darcy's life, obliging me to write it while myself trapped in a state of most acute sin – if we were to look at it traditionally, which I had no intention of doing, or through Lou's beady eyes, or Stef's manic ones, or the puzzled eyes of the five children Hugo's and my love for each other affected – so mysterious indeed as to make you think we were much more likely to be talking about the Devil than of God. But I didn't say that to Hugo. I wanted him there beside me on the king-size Holiday Inn bed and that was that.

A disturbance in the economy

Julian was to spend Wednesday at 11 Downing Street, in conference with the fiscal advisers to the Treasury. At two in the morning he stirred Eleanor awake.

'These ceaseless problems with the economy,' he said, 'are because we've never had the nerve to do things properly. We've talked about cheap money,' he said, 'but we've never made it really cheap. We devalue the pound but only on paper. We use it to make people poor, not rich.'

'Of course,' said Eleanor, 'to make the poor rich is to make the rich poor. That's why we never do it properly.'

His fingers strayed over her breast. She thought of Sharif the beautiful. She wasn't surprised Mrs Khalid had encouraged her daughter's marriage. Now they were all bound together: like Rhoda to Wendy to Ken to herself to Bernard, and round again to one-eyed Gillian, for Ken would lose Gillian to Bernard; it was inevitable. And through Jed, through the joining of flesh, to Nerina, and all others before or since: except some seem to count, and some not to count, as did, or did not, death. Some deaths affect you: others don't, for no reason that you can see. A close friend dies and not a feeling in you stirs: an acquaintance passes on: you weep and wail. As with death, so with sexual partners. Some count, some don't. Jed counted and she hadn't known it. If you knew it, would you do it? Most certainly you would. The connections are there to be made. They are foretold, inevitable. That's why the pleasure goes with them: what you do is the fulfilment of fate's will.

'Think of me,' said Julian, 'think of me, not whatever you're thinking of.'

'I am thinking of you,' she said.

'What did you just say then?' he asked.

'To make the poor rich is to make the rich poor,' she repeated. 'That's why we never do it properly.'

'The creative approach to economics!' he murmured, not without disparagement, into the dark. 'But you're right. Now if we were to make money *really* cheap – the Treasury just might do it. They have to do something. Shortages are endemic. It's almost as bad in London now as it ever was in Moscow: if you want petrol you have to buy it out of someone else's tank.'

'That's because the tanker men are on strike.'

'No, it's not,' he said gloomily. 'They were provoked into striking in order to mask the true situation, to give us time to think our way out of this one. We have no option but to jolt the economy. Electric shock it out of depression!'

'You could always stand on street corners and give money away,' she said. 'Why not?'

'It might do it,' he said. 'It just might do it. The old Keynesian way of work creation without the distorting effects of actually doing the work.'

He rolled over and went to sleep. She did not mind one bit. She dreamt of Sharif, which she seemed to be able to do to order. He beat her for her wickedness, and made her shroud herself in black robes as punishment, and she and Nerina shared a bed and he came to both of them while Mrs Khalid listened in the room next door. She had no choice. The house was small, the walls were thin: no wonder she bit her nails.

When Eleanor woke, luxurious and sated, Julian was pulling on his socks and suspenders. He was bright-eyed and elated.

'It's the answer,' he said. 'The answer! And thank God it's one of those days when I could convince anyone of anything!'

And so it seemed it was: the meeting went on for only four hours of an anticipated six. The media, domestic and international, hovered outside the door both at Downing Street and Bridport Lodge. Eleanor was much photographed in mesh tights, but remained loyal, though, she felt, in some way coy.

'If anyone can find a way,' she found herself saying, unable to stop it, 'my husband will. He's a genius. He's quite nervy, but that always goes with brilliance. He was hospitalized for depression when he was twenty-one. He had a course of ECG, which cured him. Just like Tom Eagleton: remember? McGovern's running mate. Wasn't that unfair, that whole business of being unfit for office because of a nervous breakdown? But it was all part of some smear campaign, wasn't it?'

The think-tank emerged beaming from its meeting. A statement would be made on Monday. On Sunday morning at ten o'clock, without warning, the cash dispensers of the high street banks up and down the nation began to spew out notes. An hour of fives, an hour of tens, an hour of twenties. Then an hour's pause. Then the cycle began again: neat packages of new notes slid gracefully, unasked, from under their tactful slots, on and on and on.

At first, as the press later reported – the home press subdued and embarrassed, the international press quite hysterical with glee – the public were nervous and suspicious: they kept their distance: then quickly the police arrived, suspecting a malfunction, to guard this enigmatic money supply from looters. As it so happened it was a wet and windy day: in many parts of the country the wind that so often whistles along the high streets whistled to good effect, and whipped wet notes over shops and into alleys and gardens and under the noses of the drunk, the wretched and the homeless, who on the whole disregarded them, understanding well enough that money was not the solution to their problems; what they needed was not to smell and to find someone to like them enough to be prepared to take them in. Word came from on high and the police went back to their headquarters: and, nervously, those who needed the notes to pay electricity and gas bills and mortgages began to gather them up and took them home to their children to count, and were thus relieved of anxiety, and smiled over the meal, and forgot to blame whoever was usually to blame, and made love to wives or husbands, as well as inclination or vigour would allow, and said to their children, okay, if you don't want to go to school, don't go: and to themselves, the job I do is pointless, useless; what is more I hate doing it and stayed in bed, and only those who thought, the job I do is valuable, others need me, depend upon me; I like doing it, went, and the traffic moved freely, because there was half the usual volume, and the petrol tanker men went back to work because, as their leader said that Monday morning, 'Everything's upside down; the government's gone insane; we'd better not add to it.'

On Monday noon the machines stopped exuding money.
'The fools,' said Julian Darcy. 'The fools. If they lose their nerve now, they've had it! Compromise, compromise! It will be the end of us!'
The move had been made on the strength of a majority of one, he told Eleanor. He had been eloquent in support of the action; others had supported it in theory but wanted time to think about it. An amendment had been moved but lost, to first educate the public, issue instructions; dole out money to the deserving poor, not undeserving: which, as Julian had pointed out, was no different than an increase in benefits: this faction had been defeated. Julian had argued for surprise, for the shock tactics which would jolt the economy out of depression, and he had won the day.

The fury of the country was very great indeed: though whether because it had happened or because it had stopped happening those who stood in the crowds in the public squares did not seem quite to know. The Prime Minister resigned: the EEC put in a stop-gap government of bureaucrats: martial law was briefly imposed: a new currency introduced, conforming to EEC standard. Although, as a few dissidents observed, the three hundred million pounds' worth of notes which the corner banks had distributed had scarcely affected inflation rates at all. But it was not a popular thing to say. Public pride had been offended. To believe a nation could do without money! Somebody's fault: Rasputin's fault: Rasputin of Bridport, the genius who had nervous breakdowns, moved his young mistress into his wife's bed, dined on champagne and caviar while firing his staff.
'They'll blame me,' said Julian. 'I know they will. A prophet is always dishonoured in his own country. I'll be the fall guy. Why did you say that about my having shock treatment when I was twenty-one?'
'Because it was true.'
'You don't love me, you never have. My troubles began when I first encountered you, when I came to your gate –'

'The lover at the gate,' said Eleanor, 'comes for more than he knows.'

'I should never have left Georgina,' said Julian. 'This is my punishment. In my own house I am not believed.'

'In your own house you are believed,' said Eleanor. 'And it was a good time while it lasted.'

The police came in the early hours and took Julian away, giving him not even time to put on his socks and shoes. They made him wear his slippers. They had trumped up, it seemed, charges of tax evasion, corruption and waste of public funds. Eleanor followed him to the police cars in the drive. There were four of them, all flashing their lights in the dawn.

'It goes against the grain to apologize,' Julian said, 'but I shouldn't have said the hard things I did. I was upset. I love you very much. I don't regret a minute of it. Two years' perfect happiness is more than many a man has in his lifetime. But now the nation is humiliated in the eyes of the world and it seems I must pay the price for it. I wonder how many years I'll get? Will I be allowed pen and paper?'

'Goodbye, my dear,' said Eleanor. 'I'll see you are. The nation mustn't lose a genius. I'll wait for you.'

And she smiled and waved encouragingly, though she knew she lied. There was no need for him to be more unhappy than he had to be.

Eleanor, pursued by the press, went first to stay with Jed and poor Prune, but Prune, who seemed to have regained her will and spirits, and was considering adoption, asked her to leave within the week. 'It's not just the media forever at the door,' she said, 'or you and Jed droning on about free money economics at the dinner table, or the way you sneer at my stews, it's never knowing what you and Jed are up to. If Jed kept himself to himself more I'd get pregnant. He just wastes his energies.'

'That's hardly scientific,' said Eleanor.

'I don't care what it is,' said Prune. 'You just leave me and Jed alone. Go and live with your husband.'

'I can't. He's in prison,' said Eleanor.

'Where you put him,' said Prune, 'with your mad ideas. I mean your real husband, your proper husband, the one and only. You married poor Bernard to get away from home, but that's your bed; you chose it, you lie in it.'

It seemed not a bad idea to Eleanor, who felt an unusual need for friends and family, but Gillian said she'd rather Eleanor didn't come to stay, one way and another. Why didn't she just go on swanning around up at Bridport Lodge? But Eleanor said she couldn't: Georgina had returned with a battery of lawyers: the university was being merged into the polytechnic: the place hardly existed any more. It had no future role as the arbiter of national economic policy.

'Oh dear,' said Gillian, 'you've come such a long way and ended up with nothing! At least Bernard and I have each other. He's got quite a little business going selling fancy cars.'

'He doesn't know one end of an engine from another,' said Eleanor.

'He doesn't have to,' said Gillian. 'He was born honest and people know it. That's all that counts.'

But Gillian did let her round to see Ken. Last time she'd seen him he'd been wrapped in blankets because the gas bill had not been paid and the central heating had been cut off. But he'd been quick off the mark on Loony Sunday, as the media now referred to it, and all the bills were paid. The house glowed with heat and light. It had even been dusted. He was uninterested in Eleanor's predicament, or the events which had led up to it. A jazz band, circa 1925, was in performance on the television. He did not turn the volume down.

'I lost Gillian to your Bernard,' he said, loudly and cheerfully. 'Can't say I mind much. She goes on looking after me. Tell you what, I tottered round to No. 93 the other day. It's been sold at last. Loony Sunday saw to that. Saw your mother there, bold as brass, bright as day.'

'Rhoda?'

'No, not Rhoda, Wendy. Your mother.'

'Did she speak?'

'How could she? She was dead. She just stood there in a kind of pillar of light.'

'Was she angry with you?'

'Not particularly. Why should she be?'

Eleanor switched off the television.

'Because you made her pregnant, failed to marry her, neglected her, drove her to drink and then married her mother.'

Ken considered. 'It's one way of looking at it,' he said, 'but not the way I do. Personally, I blame Rhoda.'

He turned the television on again, but Eleanor thought he looked a little shaken. She was glad.

Belinda was cool on the telephone and said, 'Frank really had a hard time over that stupid money business. It was beneath his dignity to go round picking up money from the street and now everyone's paid off their mortgage but him. Whatever was Julian thinking? It's distorted everything and Frank's furious. You struggle and struggle and suddenly what's it all about? I don't think it's really sensible for you to come to stay, Ellen.'

Brenda said Eleanor was more than welcome to stay as long as she wanted, but perhaps she should wait until the media attention had cooled down a little, and the trial was over: she wasn't too keen on having the children exposed to the full glare of publicity; she wanted them to live simple lives. Eleanor said she thought it was very likely they would, and took up Liese's offer of her holiday home; a pretty, simple house in the Forest of Dean. Here she sat out Julian's trial. Julian was acquitted of tax evasion but found guilty of misuse of public funds – the hospitality offered at Graduation Week events seen in retrospect as grossly extravagant – and was sentenced to three years' imprisonment. Eleanor, in the healing tranquillity of nature, for the space of a year, kept her silence before returning to civilization and ordinary society, and most generously offering the story of her life to you, the readers of *Aura*.

Of her spiritual journey during that year she remains silent: it must be left to someone other than myself, Valerie Jones, to record and communicate. It is my part to write the gospel only of the early years.

Lou comes to the Holiday Inn

I went down to reception myself to ask them to fax through the last pages of manuscript to *Aura*. The manager asked to have a few words with me: there had been some trouble with Hugo's Amex card: he was sorry to have to trouble me, but could I register my card with him? I said naturally I would, but the truth was I only had Visa and that, I knew, was way above limit. I looked around for Lou, who, although he growls at such times, usually gives good advice, and then thought, but I've left Lou. I've left home. I'm with Hugo. And I found myself thinking, Hugo? Who's Hugo?, which was very strange.

I could hear the fax machine going in the office behind reception and with every page it was as if some blight were being scraped away, some languorous, over-sweet, sickly fungus. It hurt as it lifted: as sudden bright light hurts those long incarcerated in the dark. Of course it did. Bits of tender, soggy skin were tearing off with the mould.

'Could I just sit down?' I said to the manager, and he helped me to an armchair with a rather firm squeeze, which might have been a policeman's touch, or that of a man who knows the woman he touches has been holed up in a room with a man for weeks. How could I tell? Had it been weeks, days? I would have to look at the hotel account to find out. I could see myself in the mirror: bleary, hair uncombed. What was I wearing? One of Hugo's shirts? Quite a nice pink striped one, I was glad to see: and track suit bottoms in mauve velvet. Not me at all. My children! I was a woman with children. Where were they? Who was looking after them?

I was beginning to feel quite distressed by my own confusion: but then the revolving doors, which had never ceased their activity as I sat there, perpetually throwing in and drawing out the well-heeled and the faceless, produced quite suddenly three people with faces: Lou, Sophie, Ben, preceded by another, whom I presently recognized as Kirsty Bull, if only by the size of her legs: she had the kind of flat pudding face which could belong to anyone. She came straight up to me.

'Look,' she said. 'I made them come. They didn't want to. They're all furious. You've been a right bitch. They're helpless without you. Your husband's insane. Everything's done to the metronome, from the washing-up to sex. I can't leave them on their own. They're not fit. So here they are. You organize them.'

And she swept out of the revolving door.

'What a terrible woman,' said Lou. 'Female double-bass players are always like that. I should never have asked her in, but what was I to do? I had a concert and Ben had an exam.'

I had forgotten about Ben's exam.

'What happened?' I asked him.

'I got my grade eight,' he said, 'no thanks to you.'

'Don't you talk to me like that ever again,' I said, thinking fast, and to Sophie before she could open her mouth, 'Or you either. If you've learned your lesson then I'll come home. Pay the bill, Lou.'

And the children looked quite nervous and subdued and Lou just went to the desk and took out his credit card and paid what was owing, without even studying the details of the account, and I felt not guilty but self-righteous. It was a very strange feeling, as if it came from outside me. The words 'a sure touch' came into my head: it seemed a bequest from Eleanor: a compensation for injury more like it. 'She has a sure touch with men.' What a gift! Especially since what to other women might be injury – to fall in love against your will and almost without reason – to me had been both an enlightenment and a joy, inasmuch as it was not an ongoing state of affairs, but had, just like that, and with the finishing of *Lover at the Gate*, come to a full stop.

While Lou was still at the desk Hugo came into the hotel and walked straight past me to the lifts. I called him. He turned to look at me and for quite a while he didn't recognize me. Then he said, 'Oh, it's you, Valerie. You look so different!' I said, 'So do you.' He said, 'Are you going home now?' It was like the embarrassment after a one-night stand, when neither knows quite how to behave. Yet we'd shared so much. He seemed as puzzled as I had been a little earlier.

'I finished *Lover at the Gate*,' I said, to put him at his ease. 'And Lou has paid the bill.'

'Lou?'

'My husband.'

'That's good of him,' said Hugo. 'Some mix-up with my Amex card.'

I introduced him to Lou.

'We've been working together,' said Hugo. 'On a most extraordinary story.'

'So I gather,' said Lou bleakly.

Hugo said, 'It's going to change the face of the world,' and I said, 'It may take more than Eleanor Darcy to do that,' and Hugo handed me a tape and said, 'Listen to that. I had it copied. You can keep it. We'll be in touch, naturally.'

'If you don't come home at once, Valerie, I may not have you,' said Lou and I said, 'I'll come home when I'm good and ready,' which shook him and shook me, and Sophie and Ben watched open-mouthed as their parents spatted. I asked Hugo to give them a pound coin each so they could go and play the fruit machines. Lou said, 'I don't allow the children money just to gamble away,' and I said, 'That's why I didn't ask you, Lou.' And he meditated this, while Hugo found the coins.

Hugo was a tall man with rather stooped shoulders and a lean, intelligent look. I thought I'd probably quite like him if I met him at a party, or was sat next to him at a Media Awards Dinner, but no more. I wondered what he thought of me, now that we could see each other clearly, now that whatever wrinkle it was, whatever upset in the general run-along pattern of events had brushed us up against each other, and held us in place until we could be let go. The marvel was that others had waited for us – for me, at any rate. I was not sure what Stef would do.

'Lou,' I said, 'wouldn't it be really nice if Hugo and his wife came round to supper one day?'

Lou said doubtfully, 'It might.'

Hugo said, 'Well, actually, I think I'm going to change my way of life. I don't think you'll see me on the dinner-party circuit any more.'

Lou said he'd never noticed him there in the first place, but that was just Lou. Some things don't change and I wouldn't want them to.

And I went back to Room 301 to change and presently walked out of the hotel dressed in the same clothes I had come in – the boring little black dress and the sand-coloured wrap. I couldn't think why I'd bought either in the first place.

That night I listened to the tape Hugo gave me as his last gift, the brief record of his final interview with Eleanor Darcy.

Hugo and Eleanor walk down to
the end of the garden

A: Rules? You want rules? You really can't survive without a book of rules? Hasn't the human race progressed at all? Can't you decide, one by one, what's right, what's wrong? Do you have to continue *to believe in groups*? Do you have to believe in the God of your neighbours? Can't you create one of your own? Surely you know enough by now about yourselves, your compulsions, your motivations, your sibling rivalries, your anal retentiveness, your territorial aggressions and so forth? Have your prophets and wise men, your therapists and social philosophers, taught you nothing? Is it so confusing that you just can't begin to solve it at all; can't work hard to build heaven on earth, but prefer to trust in the one after death? I don't believe it. You underrate yourselves. So you'll get no rules from me. I tell you this much, there is no excuse any more, you can't claim ignorance: if you get Darcy's Utopia wrong there's going to be no forgiveness: it'll be too late.

Then Hugo's voice, a commentary:

Eleanor Darcy was trembling. The morning was chill. She had refused to put on a coat. I took her arm but she shook me off. The grass was bright with dew. The sun had reached the edge of the railway embankment. It dazzled.

Q: Can you be more explicit?

A: This is off the record?

Q: Of course. Who exactly is giving this forgiveness? God?

A: Good lord no, man, in whom I incorporate the lesser, woman.

225

God has no concept of fairness. Man must place himself above God. God is not the father: God is the child.

Q: Don't you think that's rather, well, *enigmatic* of you?

A: Be quiet. These things are difficult to get hold of. And I'm in a hurry. Sometimes I get things wrong. How can I not? I'm human. Man exists not to worship, not to glorify, but to comprehend God so that by that comprehension God can grow. How about that? That seems the gist of it. Sometimes there are not even words for the thoughts. Other languages might be easier.

Q: I'm not hot at theology.

A: Pity. Julian was starting up a new faculty of divinity when he got struck off. They said he would have been better advised cutting courses, not adding to them. Theology, they said, wasn't sexy as a subject. Little did they know!

Hugo's voice:

> *I asked if we should turn back, on the pretext that we were cold. The front room, the sofa with red roses, seemed preferable to the dazzle we approached. I was surprised that Brenda's children seemed so ordinary, snotty, peevish. Fed by this source of light, they should be little gods. She did not hear me; she was clearly listening to something other than me; I was glad: my nerve returned.*

Q: No rules about diet, or marriage, or sex? These are the messages which usually get through.

A: Well of course, but they're so obvious we all know them. No beef, no sheep, no pig to be eaten: they are all ecologically unsound. Dairy products in moderation. Chicken, fish, so long as the animals breed and live naturally. Empathy must be found with the animal kingdom. If you must have more protein eat each other.

Q: What did you say?

A: You heard me. But boil well first. Those are the only dietary rules I give you. Your desire to live for ever should make it easy for you to fill in any number of others. Personally I find them boring. Now you have Darcy's Utopia to create there will be some point in longevity. I have already spoken to you at length about marriage and sex. Don't worry too much about HIV infection. Everyone dies. A virus is a small price to pay for sex. You will have to resort to nuclear power while you reduce your population and learn to live simply. You'll just have to put up with the consequences: it's your own fault for letting things get so badly out of control. You lost your way: you lost your vision. No one could look more than five years ahead.

Q: No punishments? No sanctions? No hellfire, no grappling hooks to drag you to the fire, no skinning alive? What are the consequences of the non-forgiveness you speak of?

A: The end of the earth, the end of you, that's all.

Q: No hell? No heaven? Just blanking out?

Hugo's voice: *She turned and looked at me: her being was luminous: I lowered my eyes. She laughed and the laughter was all around me. It was not nice at all.*

A: It depends what you make of Darcy's Utopia. If you find it heaven, lucky old you. Some might simply blank out with boredom, but if that's hell it is a kinder one that any promised you in the past. I hope you see some improvement here. I do. Define yourselves more kindly; do yourselves and me that favour. After all, you're the adults: I'm just the child.

Hugo's voice: *I turned and went back to the house: I couldn't bear it any longer. She went on into the light. Brenda said, 'Oh God, she's at it again. She goes down there, has a kind of fit: I have to drag her back to the house: she mumbles for hours: I don't know what to do about it. I'm glad you're*

227

writing it all down. Someone has to. I haven't time, what with the kids and my husband working all hours.'

Valerie observes the birth of a new religion

Hugo's articles were received with the kind of enthusiasm reserved for pieces with titles such as 'The Concept of Fiscal Negativity – a Long Hard Look', that is to say, muted though respectful. Little by little his by-line dropped out of the columns altogether. I wondered what he was doing, and why, and where, but not for very long or very hard.

Lover at the Gate came out in *Aura* in serial form and won me another prize. 'Best Fiction Biography of the Year', a category devised, apparently, especially to meet the case. But no one interesting sat next to me at the Awards Dinner, and the decision went against publishing the work in book form, to my chagrin.

'In a year's time,' my editor said, 'everyone will have forgotten Eleanor Darcy. Pretty girls are only as interesting as the men they are with.' And Eleanor was no longer with Julian Darcy. When he was released from prison she was not there to meet him; the media observed it, and forgot it. Julian was offered a top appointment with one of the larger banks, and accepted it, which event struck up a short-lived flurry of indignation and hilarity: when Georgina returned to him he was granted in the public mind a kind of forgiveness. But no one, it seemed, thought of Eleanor any more. My editor was right.

The house where I had interviewed Eleanor Darcy had somehow burned an impression of itself onto my eyelids. I'd see it when I closed my eyes: the most ordinary house in the world, except I'd given up thinking of houses, let alone people, as ever being ordinary. Let us just say there were many like it: semidetached, with a little square garden in the front, a rather longer one at the back; a house without pretension – just a place to live and think yourself lucky, as vibrant or dreary as its occupants.

I'd called Brenda from time to time but received no reply. I assumed she'd gone away. I wanted, without reason, to see the house again; and one day, without reason, other than that I was between assignments and both children were staying with Lou's mother and it was eighteen months to the day from my first setting eyes on Hugo Vansitart, I drove over to the house, half remembering the way but having to consult the road map. I parked outside. The one good thing about these long, long, suburban streets is that there is usually somewhere to park. The house was empty, as I had expected. There was a 'For Sale' sign outside. After Loony Sunday and the resultant sudden surge in house sales, as everyone swapped over and moved to be next to jobs and friends, the market had stuck again. I had not expected its desolate look. The side gate which had barred Brenda's children from running out onto the road swung open, off one hinge. Someone had pinned up net curtains in the front windows; an attempt, no doubt, to persuade robbers that the house was in fact occupied when it was not. I went up the side path and through into the back garden where I'd once had so unsatisfactory a tea with Eleanor Darcy. Then I had been besieged by wasps, children, passing trains; I had been assailed by the noise, the chaos, of everyday events. I had longed for order and been given none. I had felt thoroughly *disrupted*. Now there was nothing but silence and I didn't like it. The signalling light up the railway line was stuck at red. I wondered again, as I often had, about the 'dazzling light' out here which Hugo had spoken of. I wondered if Eleanor and Brenda had rigged up some kind of spectral light machine the better to bamboozle him. It is hard, really hard, for the sceptical to give up their scepticism. It is even harder to believe than to love. How cruel Ellen was, in retrospect, to Bernard: not for leaving him, which may indeed in the end have been a kindness, but for mocking faith right out of him.

I walked down the garden towards the low back fence: on the other side of which was a width of wild, nettled ground before the steep gravelled slope of the railway track began. I hopped over the fence – these days I wear jeans and trainers: I have given up little suits and pumps, much to Sophie's disapproval; my daughter likes to keep the differential going. I looked for, but found no wires, no bits of metal, no gauze for ectoplasm, just a kind of – how can

I put it? – absence. A negativity. Wet nettles brushed the back of my hand. The leaves were rusty: there was not much sting left in them. I got back over the fence. The garden, naturally enough, was unworked and untidy, but still retained its trampled, overused, flattened air, as if even a year's rest from small children had not been enough to get the processes of growth properly underway. Nothing, it seemed, had quite recovered from the withdrawal of whatever it was that had been there. What had Eleanor once said? What a fine fellow the Devil is, all fire and sparks and energy, but temporary? You only knew what you'd encountered by the permanent wasteland left behind, all that was left after, in such a rush, he'd sucked up that amazing burst of life. I wished I had not remembered that.

I went next door and knocked. I asked the woman who answered if she had a forwarding address for her erstwhile neighbours. She was stocky, forthright, and middle-aged: her leg was grossly swollen and wrapped in loose bandages. She wore slippers.

'Thank God they've gone,' she said, as if she spent her days waiting for the enquiry. 'At last a little peace and quiet! All those people forever knocking at her door, all thinking they were going to be healed, that nothing would hurt any more. That woman was no healer. I took my leg to her and I'll swear it made it worse. But try telling that to them. They believe what they want to believe.'

'You don't know where she went?'

'She ran off with a BMW salesman, so they say. Just up and left one day. The nice one, the one with the children, left soon after. I did hear she'd moved around the corner into Mafeking Street. I can't think why. It's much the same as here. I don't know what number; I don't go out much. I'm sorry I can't help you more.' She lied. She was not at all sorry, but she was obviously in pain and Eleanor Darcy had failed her, so I forgave her.

I found my way to Mafeking Street, some half a mile distant. I was conscious that had I done my research for *Lover at the Gate* with any integrity I would know the street intimately. But I had not done so. I have relied on my intuition: that is to say I was not going to waste time on facts while Hugo was in my bed and

Eleanor Darcy in my imagination. I was relieved to see that the street was exactly as I had imagined it. I came into it halfway along its length, where it was bisected by Union Street. It was a long road of semidetached houses, two up, two down, most in desultory repair, many lace-curtained, some, although small to begin with, converted into flats. Few of the cars which lined both sides of the street were new: most were clean and better kept than the houses; quite a few the kind that young men like to tinker with, to keep on the road in the face of all odds. I could see a couple of motorbikes; a clutch of bicycles leaning against a fence: a group of children, a couple of black faces amongst them, playing ball in the road, able to do so because this was a street which was a throughway to nowhere: on the corner where I stood was an Asian newsagent – it was empty of customers; closed until evening, no doubt, when the employed would begin to drift home from work. People of no aspiration could live here all their lives, and women married to men without aspiration, and I supposed vice versa, and forget easily enough that there was anything to aspire to.

I stood unsure of what I was looking for. Perhaps I hoped to find Brenda out walking with the children, or to run into Eleanor Darcy herself. Perhaps, I thought, if I knocked on another door someone would help. I had come a long way to go home with no reward. I wondered which way to walk, but both ways seemed equal. I started to go west, but the same sun which shone on deserts and mountains, baked the wide steps of city halls, glazed the air in gracious parks, shone into my eyes in Mafeking Street and dazzled me. So I turned my back on it and went east, and in the shadowed end of the street saw movement, people clustering in groups, and I was both disconcerted and pleased, because there seemed more of them than the houses around could possibly disgorge, and because here at last was a sense of event, of gathering together, of something about to happen. A minibus passed me by, and a coach. I walked towards the source of activity: there were men, women and children here. Why were they not at work, not at school? What was so important that kept them away? They were of all races, all classes: the kempt and the unkempt, the rich and the poor, but mostly those in between. They were devout, I could tell that – something mysterious and important was going on here – but not the black-shawled devout who all over the world mourn and murmur at shrines and pray for forgiveness: a *sous-surrous* of grief and reproach to rise to heaven: no, they were the kind who have library tickets in their wallets and cinema stubs in their pockets, and they are a multitude, stronger than they know.

I saw that they were waiting to go into a house, rather larger than the other ones in the road, and detached, which had been turned into a meeting hall. Outside was a wooden boarding, and on it was painted the words 'The Darcian Chapel (16), Mafeking Street Branch', and underneath that a poster, on which, handwritten, was the inscription 'Today's meeting: 4 p.m. Pastor: Hugo Vansitart. Subject: The Fiscal and the Self.' I stood and stared at it, trying to take this remarkable sight in, and while I stared a Rolls-Royce pulled up, chauffeur driven. The door opened and Hugo stepped out: he wore a grey suit and a crimson cravat. Many in the crowd, I had noticed, wore just such crimson scarves. Hugo did not see me. I was one of many, and glad, at least for the moment, to remain so. He went into the chapel: the crowd followed, jostling, joking, their faces eager with expectation. No sombre religion this.

I stood at the back of the chapel and listened. I wondered if I should make myself known to Hugo, after the service, but thought I would not. I could not afford to have so much life force stirred up in me again. I would not survive it. And perhaps nothing at all would be stirred up in him. I could not face that.

Around me people chanted. They sang some kind of hymn to Utopia: there were no word sheets, but no hesitation in the singing either. It was a variation, from the sound of it, of the old Fabian hymn 'Earth Shall be Fair, and All Men Glad and Wise'. The Darcian Movement had, I supposed, been going for some time, Hugo its founder member, this branch the sixteenth of how many? A religion for the new world, already thriving, unnoticed by those who ought to do the noticing – myself, and my agitated, agitating colleagues.

> Age after age our tragic empires rise,
> Built while we sleep
> And in that sleeping dream . . .

And where was Eleanor Darcy? Was she here in the spirit? Did Hugo truly believe? I thought yes, he probably did. The Rolls-Royce was not necessarily a symbol of ostentation, merely that he needed to travel comfortably in order to preach the better.

Would man but wake from out his haunted sleep
Earth might be fair and all men glad and wise.

Men to incorporate women, of course. The greater to include the lesser. How could you ever tell when Eleanor Darcy was joking, or when she was serious? Babies aborted compulsorily in the womb! If she heard a voice on that one, it came from either the Devil or a God so rational as to be one and the same. I struggled with my scepticism. How wonderful, how easy, to believe. If only I could.

The hymn was finished. Hugo spoke.
'Sisters and brothers,' he said, 'in the beginning was the word, and the word was with God, and was made flesh and dwelt among us, and of her fullness we have all received, and of her grace. And we asked her, what art thou? Prophet? And she replied I am the daughter of music, and the spouse of the wise, and I bring a new light into the world, of the world and for the world, that there shall be no heaven but here on earth – and that if you keep my commandments this heaven, this Utopia, shall be yours.'

No, I thought. I can't. I want to but I can't. I know too much. Eleanor didn't issue commandments. Hugo has put them in. I have done my bit. She can't ask any more of me. I slipped out. I closed the door behind me. I turned to walk to the corner where I had left my car. A movement in the back of the Rolls-Royce caught my eye. The window was open. I looked inside. Leaning back in the far corner was an attractive woman: she was buffing her fingernails. She moved forward, but I could not recognize who it was, though I saw her face clearly, if briefly. I didn't want to appear inquisitive, so I walked on, found the car, and drove home. Afterwards I thought, but that was Eleanor Darcy; or at any rate, I couldn't say it *wasn't* Eleanor Darcy. I puzzled about it, but not very hard, or for very long. I thought she would approve of that.

I could not become uncritical; I could not ever come to worship and adore Eleanor Darcy as Hugo did, but I could sure as hell admire her spirit.

Fay Weldon

Life Force

Into the lives of Marion, Nora, Rosalie and Susan erupts Leslie Beck, an old flame not quite extinguished. Recently widowed, though somewhat weepy Leslie is still a man with the Life Force. To the four friends he is Leslie the Lucky, Leslie of the magnificent dong – his force forever pulls. Old secrets stir, old rivalries are resurrected and scores are settled as the friends are catapulted back into their murky past.

This copulative story of passion, jealousy, fidelity and faithlessness is Weldon at her most provocative.

'Weldon's funniest novel yet'   *Cosmopolitan*

'Weldon sends up all the novels of sex 'n' marriage 'n' kids in NW3 by triumphantly writing one of her own that is witty enough to finish off the breed'   *Mail on Sunday*

'Fay Weldon's *Life Force* is a scathing indictment of rampant seed-shedding and moral vanity. Through the voices of women Beck has seduced, Weldon joyously wields the scalpel, cutting deep into the sexual psyches of both men and women'   *Woman's Journal*

'A breezy book, often very funny and, as can be expected, full of energising satire'   *Times Educational Supplement*

'Weldon at her most wicked'   *Elle*

'Everywhere is the unmistakable zippiness of her narrative style'
                                    Daily Telegraph

'Fay Weldon can tease, tantalise and scandalise better than any other writer today . . . Not recommended for the faint-hearted with something to hide'   *Financial Times*

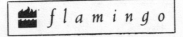

Fay Weldon

The Cloning of Joanna May

Joanna May thought herself unique, indivisible – until one day, to her hideous shock, she discovered herself to be five: though childless she was a mother; though an only child she was surrounded by sisters young enough to be her daughters – Jane, Julie, Gina and Alice, the clones of Joanna May.

How will they withstand the shock of first meeting? And what of the avenging Carl, Joanna's former husband and the clones' creator: will he take revenge for his wife's infidelity and destroy her sisters one by one?

In this astonishing novel, Fay Weldon weaves a web of paradox quite awesome in its cunning. Probing into the strange world of genetic engineering, *The Cloning of Joanna May* raises frightening questions about our identity as individuals – and provides some startling answers. Funny, serious, revolutionary, this is the work of a master storyteller at the height of her powers.

'Another totally original novel by the best woman writer in Britain'
Woman

'The deadly accuracy of Fay Weldon's psychology makes this bizarre tale a compulsive page-turner' *Daily Mail*

'An outrageously funny novel!' *Daily Express*

'A triumph of complex entertainment' *The Times*

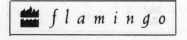

Fay Weldon

Growing Rich

Bernard Bellamy has done a deal. He's sold out to the Devil, in all his forms. In return, he is promised that all his wishes will be granted, all his desires fulfilled. One of them, young Carmen Wedmore, is proving to be quite a challenge.

Carmen lives in the new town of Fenedge, East Anglia, near her former schoolfriends Laura and Annie. The three girls dream of the day they'll escape their dullsville existence. While Annie flies off with a fluttering, blipping heart to the snowcapped peaks and frothy rapids of New Zealand to join the man of her dreams and Laura marries, capably moving the population graph a few notches higher, Carmen stays in Fenedge, under the powerful clasp of Sir Bernard and Driver, the Devil's agent. Disguised as a suave chauffeur, Driver cruises in his plush, shiny, sinister limo, stalking her every move.

But Carmen becomes ever more determined to ride out the temptations laid in her path and not to sell her soul. Will she eventually succumb? Or will the Devil, for once, not have everything his own way?

Fay Weldon's *Growing Rich* is a turbine-driven fantasy of love and revenge, values and morals: a witty and compelling elixir.

'Fast, funny . . . a glorious entertainment for the Nineties'
Woman's Journal

'Breathtaking . . . catches its reader up in a gale of good spirits and devilment that keeps on blowing from beginning to end'   *Observer*

'A typically Weldonesque tale of cleverness, with tongue-in-cheek asides'   *Good Housekeeping*

'Another Fay Weldon classic'   *New Woman*

'As exuberant as ever'   *Daily Telegraph*

'Absolutely hypnotic'   *Irish Press*

 *flamingo*